THE BLOODY TEXANS

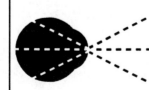

This Large Print Book carries the
Seal of Approval of N.A.V.H.

THE BLOODY TEXANS

KENT CONWELL

WHEELER PUBLISHING
A part of Gale, Cengage Learning

GALE
CENGAGE Learning·

Detroit • New York • San Francisco • New Haven, Conn • Waterville, Maine • London

GALE
CENGAGE Learning

Copyright © 2008 by Kent Conwell.
Wheeler Publishing, a part of Gale, Cengage Learning.

LIBRARY OF CONGRESS CATALOGING-IN-PUBLICATION DATA

Conwell, Kent.
    The bloody Texans / by Kent Conwell.
      p. cm. — (Wheeler Publishing large print western)
    ISBN-13: 978-1-59722-848-0 (pbk. : alk. paper)
    ISBN-10: 1-59722-848-6 (pbk. : alk. paper)
    1. Trappers—Fiction. 2. Scouts (Reconnaissance)—Fiction.
3. Wives—Death—Fiction. 4. Revenge—Fiction. 5. Texas
Rangers—Fiction. 6. Mexican War, 1846–1848—Fiction. 7. Large
type books. I. Title.
    PS3553.O547B58 2008
    813'.54—dc22
                                        2008032194

Published in 2008 by arrangement with Leisure Books, a division of
Dorchester Publishing Co., Inc.

THE BLOODY TEXANS

Slowly the evening shadows settled over the cabin deep in the forest, covering the brutality and savagery witnessed by the cold afternoon sun.

A north wind howled out of the dark, rolling clouds, battering the adobe huts and stick *jacales* of San Antonio de Bexar. Sheets of rain obliterated the far side of the narrow *calle.* Water cascaded off roofs, and in its rush to the Rio San Antonio, coursed down muddy streets cutting channels that crisscrossed like spider webs.

Inside a dimly lit bar, guttering candles cast eerie shadows across the rock-hard faces of two rugged men seated at a wood-slab table. One hunched thoughtfully over a clay mug half-filled with whiskey; the other stared intently at the first. Overhead, the dirty canvas ceiling sagged in several spots where water collected and dripped to the dirt floor.

A low murmur of conversation, punctuated by an occasional laugh, filled the shadowy room as roughhewn cowpokes poured cheap whiskey down their gullets, their protection against the winter night.

Sam Walker cleared his throat and spoke to the man bent over the mug of whiskey. "Forget about Cooper, Jack. If he wanted to

9

go with us, he'd be here."

John Coffee "Devil Jack" Hays lifted his cold, hazel eyes into the steady gaze of his friend. "Like hell I will. Nathan Cooper doesn't go, I don't go."

Sam clucked his tongue and shook his head at his old friend's cussedness. "That ain't what the governor said. He appointed you to take a ranger company to Zack Taylor down on the Nueces."

Hays leaned back in his chair and permitted a faint smile to play over his boyish face. "Well then, the Right Honorable J. Pinckney Henderson can damned well unappoint me." He paused, and his smile broadened. His tone issued a challenge. "You remember the Mier Expedition and Perote Prison. You really want to go into Mexico and face up to Santa Anna without Nathan, Sam?"

Sam downed the remainder of his drink and a look of pure hatred clouded his square face. "How could I forget? I lived in that lice-ridden prison. I buried a dime under the flagpole them greasers made us raise. With or without Nathan Cooper, I swore that one day I'd pocket that dime and see a Texas flag flying on that pole. And I reckon on doing that very thing." He paused and drew a deep breath. "If I had a choice, Jack, you're mighty right I'd want Nathan

Cooper, one arm and all. But if he was goin' with us, he'd be here now."

Jack Hays stared at the mug in his hands, his youthful face a study of concentration. "You're probably right." A new leak oozed from the canvas ceiling and began dripping steadily on the middle of the table. Absently, Jack shoved his empty cup under it. "Of course, we can do it without Nathan, but the whole job would be one hell of a lot easier with him. Even if he is getting long in the tooth and has a wooden arm, he's sure no cripple. He's rode the river more times than you and me can count. He fought pirates with Lafitte, trapped in the Rockies, and lived with them cannibal Karankawas." He paused and grinned. "I reckon he's what they call a white Indian. He's the most uncivilized white man I ever met. Or he was until he got himself married up. You got to admit, he was a big help out in Laredo in forty-one."

The mention of Laredo brought a smug grin to Sam's face. He patted the worn handle of his Paterson Colt. "Reckon I do. You, me, and Nathan had the only full grown Colt Patersons in the republic, thanks to Sam Colt." He refilled his clay cup. "I don't reckon I'll ever forget the face of that Mexican captain — what was his

11

name? I forget. I remember the face, but I forget the greaser's name."

Jack grinned. "García. Captain García."

Sam laughed. "That's right, García. You remember the expression on his face when you sent him back to Laredo with our demand for their surrender?"

A faint blush tinged Jack's ears. "Yeah. He'd been mighty happy to cut our throats right there, but he's like them Mexican honchos. They don't mind pushin' little people around, but let someone stand up to them, and suddenly they catch a case of the gallopin' grunts."

Sam laughed. "The *alcalde* from Laredo sure came out early next morning. Reckon he took your warning serious."

The faint smile on Jack Hays' face faded. He changed the subject. "I got doubtful feelings about this Mexico business Polk is stirrin' up."

The leather-and-plank door swung open, and a gust of rain swirled through the small room, drawing curses from the other cowpokes in the cantina. A tall, heavily bearded cowboy stepped through the doorway. His face was rock hard, and his eyes colder than the north wind outside. He looked around the room. When he spotted Jack and Sam, a grin split his square face. He stomped

12

across the floor and shook his head. "Only five more rangers showed up, Colonel. At this rate, we'll never get our full complement."

Jack Hays studied the newcomer, finally nodded, rose, and hitched up his gunbelt. "We got a couple weeks. You take care of things around here, Rip. I'll be back sooner or later."

John Salmon "Rip" Ford, adjutant to "Devil Jack" Hays, nodded tersely. "Where you going, Colonel?"

Jack looked at Sam Walker. "Well, Sam here's going to New York. Since Zack Taylor has requested four regiments of Texas Rangers in this here war, we're going to arm our boys with new Colt revolvers, and Sam is going to see that they get built."

Sam Walker gulped his drink. "Yes, sir."

"An' me," added Jack Hays, "I'm headin' to the redlands of East Texas. If we're taking on Mexico, I'd sure cotton to having Nathan Cooper on our side, and the only way he won't be at our side is if he's gone and got hisself killed on us." He grinned at Sam Walker and dumped the rain water from his cup. "Pour us another drink, Sam, and stick a full bottle in our saddlebags. It's a mighty cold night to be horseback."

CHAPTER TWO

His shoulder into the cold drizzle, Jack Hays struck the Injun Bayou-Aurora trace two miles below Nathan Cooper's farm. The sun was bright in a clear sky, but there was no warmth in its rays. The cold earth soaked up the heat, giving none back. A chill filled the forest. The sentinel pines were black and foreboding, sure as shooting a warning that Old Man Winter was priming himself for another blow.

An unbidden grin came to Jack's face when he thought of Nathan Cooper. "Damn. It'll be good to see that yahoo again," he said to his horse, a sixteen-hand piebald stallion. He shrugged inside the heavy mackinaw and tugged his wide-brimmed hat down over his ears.

With muscles of cold-rolled iron and a temper more volatile than a fifty-pound keg of black powder, Nathan Cooper's super-human strength and explosive disposition, complemented by his pure cussedness, proved an irresistible magnet for Jack Hays — he himself a fiery-tempered young man who, even at thirty, couldn't grow enough whiskers to shave.

Slender, but tough as a dried mesquite post, Jack rode alert, every muscle tense, like a wound spring ready to snap.

Ahead, the trail curved. Through the forest, the ranger spotted a neat, solidly constructed log cabin with a dog run. He relaxed and grinned, but the grin froze on his face when he failed to see any smoke coming from the chimney. Something was wrong! Raw days like today always called for a blazing fire.

Rounding the bend in the trail, Jack shucked his Paterson Colt and cautiously approached the cabin. He studied the farm, surveyed the animals in the corral behind the barn, the fallow fields beyond the corral, and the three new grave markers right next to four weather-grayed markers.

Jack knew the story of the four old ones. Cooper's brother, sister-in-law, nephew, and uncle were massacred by the Karankawas ten years earlier, in 1836, but the others, the new ones . . . He grimaced, beginning to understand Nathan's failure to show up in San Antonio. In the middle of the yard lay a mud-caked shovel.

He pulled up in front of the cabin and cocked his five shot ball-and-cap revolver. The door was half open. He called out. "Hello, the house. Anyone to home?"

From inside came the thump of an object striking the plank floor. Jack's eyes narrowed, and his finger tightened about the trigger. "Hello the house! Someone in there? Nathan?"

A thick silence poured from the open door, spilled across the muddy porch, and flowed to the ground, enveloping Jack and his stallion. The hair on the back of his neck bristled.

He glanced over each shoulder and stepped from his saddle. Ground-reining the piebald, he eased onto the porch and paused beside the open door.

At his feet, tracks of fresh mud crossed the porch and entered the house. He pressed his head against the logs and strained to pick up the slightest sound from inside. He heard nothing.

Moving slowly, Jack Hays peered around the doorjamb, the muzzle of his .36 leading the way. Abruptly, he froze.

The cabin was in shambles, the table overturned, clothes strewn about, the window on the back wall shattered. The single room reeked with the sweet stench of whiskey.

Holding his breath and tightening his finger on the dropdown trigger of his Paterson, the slight Texas Ranger peered into the doorway and scanned the empty room. An empty jug lay on its side in the middle of the floor, still rocking. He stepped inside, and a cold premonition swept over him.

Before he could react, a wooden forearm whipped around his neck and yanked his head up, forcing him to his tiptoes. The dim light flashed on a blade, and in the next instant, the ranger felt the sharp edge against his throat.

"Don't move a hair, mister," growled a deep voice in his ear. "Just you drop that hammer and toss that hogleg on the floor."

Jack did as he was told. When the six-gun clattered to the floor, the blade was yanked away and a hand slammed into his back, shoving the young colonel across the cabin.

He caught his balance and spun into a crouch to face his assailant.

A giant of a man with a black beard stared at him, his teeth bared in a snarl. His large hand held a bowie knife, its fifteen-inch blade glimmering in the fading sunlight.

Jack hesitated. When he saw the wood and leather prosthesis on the big man's left arm,

17

he relaxed, grinned, and took a step backward. "Nathan! It's me, Jack Hays."

Nathan frowned. He squinted his eyes, studying the slender man before him. After a few moments, recognition wiped the snarl from his face. The tension flowed from his giant body. He lowered the bowie. "Yeah, I remember, Jack. I thought you was one of 'em come back." He glanced over his shoulder into the yard, then arched an eyebrow at the younger man. "You by yourself?" His breath reeked of whiskey. Red spiderwebs marked the whites of his eyes.

"Yep. All by my lonesome. How —"

The frown deepened on Nathan's rugged face. He interrupted, "You run across anybody the last day or so?"

Jack knitted his brow, wondering just what in the hell had happened. He studied the bigger man in his woolen shirt and trousers with his red mackinaw hanging open. "No. Other than a couple Cherokees back on the Trinity where Sam Walker and me split up. He's heading to Galveston and then on to New York to get us some new Colts." He hesitated. "What's the trouble, Nathan?"

Nathan ignored Jack's question. He sheathed his bowie and closed the door. "Getting chilly. I'll build a fire. Put your piebald out in the barn."

18

The Texas Ranger remained motionless as Nathan struck a spark to a handful of tinder. A tiny tendril of smoke drifted up the mud-and-stick chimney. Jack Hay's patience snapped. "Nathan! What the hell's going on?"

His eyes fixed on the tiny flame before him, he replied. "Put the piebald up."

Hays studied his friend a moment. "First, tell me what's going on here."

Without a word, Nathan rose from his crouch and stared at the smaller man. Slowly, his gray eyes cut to a daguerreotype on the wall.

Jack studied the picture, a daguerreotype depicting Nathan, a beautiful young woman, and a small blond-haired girl about eleven or twelve. Jack furrowed his brow, remembering their names, Marie and Ruthie — Nathan's wife and the young niece Nathan had saved from the Karankawa chieftain, José Maria, back in '36.

A cold chill swept over the Texas Ranger, and he cut his eyes in the direction of the new grave markers. "Jesus, no," he muttered, looking back at Nathan.

His broad shoulders slumped, Nathan stared out the window at the new graves.

Jack laid his hand on his friend's shoulder and whispered, "Damn, I'm sorry, Nathan."

He felt he should say more, but he couldn't find the words. "I'll put my animal up."

Nathan nodded, fresh stabs of pain searing his heart.

While the ranger was tending his horse, Nathan plodded through the motions of adding to the fire, covering the broken window, and righting the overturned table. He went outside and sliced venison from the haunch hanging in the dog run.

When Nathan returned, Jack had slid a skillet on the fire and dropped in a spoonful of suet. Nathan handed him the steaks and reached for a bag of coffee. He squatted and dropped a couple handfuls of pungent grounds in the pot and slid it into the coals.

Jack plopped the steaks in the skillet. "Sorry about your trouble, Nathan," he said, keeping his eyes on the coffee and venison. "How'd it happen?"

Nathan remained silent, staring into the flames leaping in the fireplace. Outside, darkness crept through the forest, and a north wind sprang up, singing the chilling song of winter through the pines.

After a few minutes, Jack flipped the steaks with the tip of his knife and, talking just to hear himself talk, muttered, "You've got more important things on your mind now, but the reason I come up here was to get you to ride to Mexico with me and the rangers." He glanced at Nathan, who remained staring into the fire.

"Zack Taylor's down at the mouth of the Nueces. He's gettin' ready to move into Mexico. You see, them Mexicans got a burr under their saddle 'cause the United States took Texas into the Union. President Polk, he wants to set them straight, so he's sending Steve Kearney to California and us down to the Nueces."

The steaks sizzled and popped. Jack rummaged through the spilled dishes and came up with two tin plates and cups. He flopped a thick steak in a plate and filled the cup with syrupy black coffee. He rummaged through the cabinet and brought out a jar of cane molasses. "Here go," he said, placing them on the table, which was lit by the flames dancing in the fireplace. He prepared his own and scooted a chair up to the table. "Better eat, Nathan."

Jack Hay's words snapped Nathan from his trance. He looked around and nodded. Like all westerners, Nathan Cooper was a pragmatic man. He reached for the coffee. He hadn't eaten in two days, and a body had to have sustenance, especially if he was going carry out exactly what he had in mind.

CHAPTER THREE

The fire warmed the small cabin.

Jack sipped the coffee and sliced off another chunk of venison. "You got matters to tend to around here, Nathan, I'll give you a hand." He glanced in the direction of the graves, wondering who was in the third new one. "No sense in you being all alone out here — at least, not right now."

Nathan paused in cutting his steak. His eyebrows knit in sadness, and he looked at Jack across the table. "Alone?" After a moment, he added in a soft, anguished voice that rumbled like distant thunder, "I'm not alone, Jack. Them out there — as long as I got them, I won't ever be alone here." He studied Jack Hays, wondering if the young man understood what he meant.

Jack nodded and drew the back of his hand across his lips. "I reckon you're right, Nathan. I hadn't thought about it like that." He paused, started to speak, then decided better of it.

Several minutes passed in silence. Both men finished off the venison and syrup, mopping up the grease with johnnycakes. Jack rummaged through the cabin and found another jug, this one cork full of whiskey. He poured a half cup of coffee and topped it off with the whiskey, then he held the jug up to Nathan, who nodded. Jack filled his mug, glancing into his old friend's face. Nathan seemed to have aged twenty years. "What happened to them, Nathan? The grippe? Pneumonia?" He raised the cup to his lips.

A flame blazed up in Nathan's eyes. Anguish and pain had suppressed his anger, but Jack Hay's question forced it to the surface. "Scavengers. Rawhiders. That's who done it."

Jack slowly lowered the untouched cup. "Scavengers?" He paused, then added. "Not Injuns?"

Nathan's fingers tightened about the tin cup as the anger filling his chest began to fester and grow. "It was white men. White men did it."

Jack's brow furrowed. "Any idea who they was?"

The sudden fury, the sudden anger faded from Nathan's rugged face as he leaned forward, remembering. He stared at the picture on the wall, blinking against the tears. "No idea. I was over in Louisiana picking up some breeding stock. When I got back . . ." His voice trailed off, and his face crumpled in pain.

He closed his eyes and took a deep breath. He had lived side by side with death all his life, but it had never seemed as real, as personal as it now did. This could not be brushed aside, to be considered at a later date when time had dulled the sharp edges of the pain.

Nathan forced himself to continue, his tone flat, without emotion, as if he were reciting from rote memory. "When I got back, they were all dead — Marie . . . little Ruthie . . . but she wasn't so little anymore." With a hint of pride, he added, "Turned into a fine young lady with a young beau." He hesitated, feeling a rage once again beginning to grow within his chest. He nodded in the direction of the graves. "Her beau too. Artis." He paused, his eyes looking wistfully into the past. "Artis, he come here sometime back. Worked for me. Orphan boy. Good as they come. And now — all of 'em — dead. I couldn't find no trace of the killers. A norther blew through and wiped out their sign. I got no idea which way the murderin' bastards headed." What he didn't tell Jack was that he had found flesh under Marie's fingernails, short as they were from hard work. One of the men, maybe more, had the hell scratched out of him.

Taking a deep breath, he stared into the shadows above him. As Jack looked on, twenty years faded from his old friend's face, replaced by a grim determination.

Nathan stuck his hand in his pocket and pulled out a leather pouch. "They left this," he said, tossing the bag to Jack Hays. "Cut tobacco. That's not Injun."

Jack stirred the tobacco with his finger. "Injuns might have stole it."

Nathan's lips twisted in a sneer, and in a tone cold as the north wind beginning to howl outside, he said, "Injuns would have carried off everything. Nothing is missing, just busted up. It was white men." The anger, the fury suppressed by his anguish and pain exploded, filling him with a burning rage. His eyes bored into Jack's. He laid his plate-sized hand on the handle of the bowie knife hanging from his belt. Through clenched teeth, he growled, "I know it in my gut."

The youthful-appearing Texas Ranger leaned back in his chair and sipped at his coffee and whiskey. He looked Nathan squarely in the eyes. "Reckon you plan on hunting them down. I figure I'll ride along with you. With luck, we'll catch the bastards before I got to be back to San Antone."

For the first time in two days, a faint grin tugged at Nathan's lips. "I'm obliged, Jack. But you best reconsider. Laredo in forty-one was a Sunday picnic compared to where I might be taking you."

With a nod, Jack chuckled. "Hell, you know me, Nathan. Nothing I like better than a good fight. I always figured I'd never make twenty, but here I am, going on thirty. Ten years more'n I expected. When we starting?"

For several seconds, Nathan studied the younger man, seeing himself back in the 1830s. Finally, he nodded to the south. "Come morning, we'll light out for Aurora. That's where Marie's pa lives. I reckon that's where we start, by telling him. First thing in the morning."

The north wind wailed and moaned throughout the night. Before sunrise, Nathan and Jack were on the south road to Aurora, a young settlement on the shores of Sabine Bay. Nathan had shed his woolens and donned his buckskins — his killing clothes, his wife had always joked, for he always wore them into the forest to bring back meat for the family. He would smile at her gentle teasing. She knew as well as he that buckskins made no sounds in the forest, which allowed him to slip even closer to his game.

Midmorning, the wind picked up, bringing with it a light dusting of snow. Nathan scooted deeper into his fur-lined coat, aware that the weather would keep them from reaching their destination before dark.

He glanced at Jack Hays. Though fifteen years Nathan's junior, if Nathan had his druthers of any man to ride shotgun, it would have been Jack Hays. Deceptively slight, deceptively small, Hays was not a colonel of the Texas Rangers by mistake. Nathan had seen him outshoot, outfight, and outcuss every last man jack of them.

"We'll pull up on the edge of the woods tonight." He glanced at the thick gray clouds from which the snow was falling heavier now. "Doesn't look like this'll blow over before we reach the marsh prairie." He'd spent winter nights on the marsh prairie. It was an experience to be avoided.

Jack Hays pulled his hat down over his eyes and nodded. "Lead on, Macduff."

They camped in a hollow on the lee side of

27

a small hill covered with loblolly pines, with trunks five feet thick and so tall, their tops were lost in the clouds. While Nathan fashioned a lean-to and covered it with a bear hide, Jack built a fire. Despite the drift of snow, they were soon bundled in their soogans, soaking up the comforting warmth of the fire, gnawing jerky, and enjoying six-shooter coffee generously laced with whiskey.

If the circumstances had been different, it would have been a night to enjoy. A layer of snow covered the forest behind them and the marsh ahead. Nathan knew from experience that within hours after the snow ceased, the south winds would melt it.

Jack looked up at his broad-shouldered companion. "How do you figure running them down, Nathan?"

Nathan was leaning back against his saddle, his blankets drawn up under his arms, his hand cradling a steaming cup on his chest. He stared at the flames, lost in the dark corridors of his memories.

When Nathan failed to answer, Jack nodded to Nathan's left arm. "See you got a new arm down there."

Jerked from his thoughts, Nathan glanced at his arm. "Yeah. Couple years back." He held up his left arm, from the middle of the forearm down, fitted with a wood and leather prosthesis with an iron T. "Stuck the crossbar on it. Handy to throw a half hitch around."

"Good idea," said Jack. He sipped his drink.

The sweet smell of hot coffee and whiskey swirled around Nathan's head. He sipped the coffee. "Whoever the bastards were, I figure they either headed to Aurora or back to Injun Bayou. You didn't pass anyone coming from Liberty, so that's out. Reckon they probably went to Injun Bayou, but Marie's pa, Barney Willis, he lives in Aurora. He needs to know. We'll go there first. Then we'll go to Tevis Bluff — Beaumont, they call it now — and on over to Liberty before swinging back to Injun Bayou."

He paused, then grew reflective. In a low, rumbling voice, he said, "She was mighty damned good for me, Jack. Kept me civilized, that woman did. Before her, there was powerful lot of Injun in me, wild Karankawa Injun. She had a way of smoothing it out. Making it fit in with the white man's way." He parted his lips to say more, but then seemed to think better of it.

A gust of wind swirled several snowflakes under the lean-to. Jack sipped his coffee, uncertain how he should respond. He

29

cleared his throat. "Well, I reckon we'll run across them one place or another."

Nathan stared at the cup resting on his massive chest. "I reckon. Even if I got to tear down the gates of hell to get to them."

CHAPTER FOUR

A hundred miles to the north, the snow blew deep and thick. Hunched in their saddles in a thicket of oak a half mile from Nacogdoches, the five rawhiders peered at the dim lights of the small village. Frank Selman rested his gnarled hands on the saddle horn and leaned forward.

Behind him rode two rough-dressed hombres in heavy coats and two Mexicans wearing battered sombreros pulled down against the gusting snow. Under their Saltillo serapes, the Mexicans wore ragged *chaqutas* and *calzoneras.*

"What do you think, Frank?" asked Red, who was huddled deep in his mackinaw.

The bearded man sneered, his thick lips parting to reveal two missing front teeth. "Find us a cantina to hole up in 'til this storm blows over, then we'll strike out for Mexico, and some of that Yankee gold."

"*Si, si,*" said Luis Salado. "*Y una joven, niña*

en una cama caliente."

"Hell, Luis," retorted Red, "we'd all like a young, beautiful girl to share a warm bed with."

Frank grunted, studying the two men and the fresh scratches on their faces. "Didn't you fellers get enough back at that cabin?"

Red sneered. "I never get enough."

The storm abated before sunrise. Within an hour, a salty breeze blew in from the Gulf of Mexico, pushing the temperature up twenty degrees. By the time Nathan and Jack polished off a couple of mugs of coffee and stomped out the fire, the gray of false dawn rose in the east, and the snow started to melt.

"We ought to reach Aurora by noon," Nathan remarked, swinging into the saddle. His horse, a red roan with Kentucky blood, snorted and pranced. Nathan sat tight in the saddle as the animal humped his back and worked out the kinks from the cold night.

The ride to the Neches River north of Aurora was made in silence, broken only the squeak of saddles and the sucking slosh of hooves in gumbo mud and water. Nathan was lost in a world of planning, calculating.

He tried not to think of Barney Willis' reaction when the older man learned of his daughter. Instead, he tried to put himself in the place of the killers, to travel the trails they followed. There were three trails, one through Aurora to Liberty, one from Injun Bayou to Liberty, and the other from Injun Bayou to Nacogdoches.

In his mind's eye, Nathan traced the narrow trail from Aurora to Beaumont, then on to Liberty. More than once, his hand caressed the familiar handle of the bowie knife at his side.

He promised himself that whoever the son of a bitches were, their days were numbered.

Just before noon, the two riders spied several thin columns of smoke drifting into the blue sky. The smell of salt in the air grew more pronounced. Nathan studied the countryside dotted with head-high stands of dry cane. Behind, traces of snow still lay in patches. Ahead, the patches grew smaller until they disappeared altogether.

The trace became more circuitous, winding its way on high ground around bayous with black gumbo banks covered with the almost-human tracks of raccoons and the more mammal-like tracks of the mink and otter. The sky was filled with swirling gulls stealing food from each other and black skimmers swooping low over the water, their lower bills submerged, scooping up small fish and crustaceans.

"River ahead," announced Nathan. He looked at Jack. "You swim?"

"Not my favorite pastime," replied Jack. He hesitated, then added. "I get by."

Nathan grunted. A few minutes later, he reined up. "Here we are, the Neches."

Jack's jaw dropped open. The Neches was a swirling, treacherous river almost a quarter mile wide. He looked at Nathan in disbelief. "This? We're going to swim this?"

Without hesitation, Nathan urged his roan into the muddy water. "Just slip out of the saddle and hold on to the horn. And keep your powder dry," he added.

Jack paused, then a grin played over his boyish face. "What the hell," he said, driving the piebald into the river, but wishing he was back in San Antone or on the Nueces facing the Mexicans, rather than in the cold water of the muddy Neches.

Fifteen minutes later, they emerged on the south shore of the Neches and followed a winding trace through the canebrakes. Despite the bright noonday sun, Jack shivered aloud.

Nathan muttered, "Hang on, Jack. We'll

be at Barney's in ten minutes."

Jack shook his head. "Ain't you cold, Nathan?"

"A mite," the big man said. "I just put it out of my mind. Kronks taught me that."

"I reckon it was some kind of different living with them Karankawas," Jack said.

But Nathan did not hear the remark. He was lost in his own quandary of how to tell Barney of the tragedy. Before he left the farm, he had planned to tell the older man straight out. The closer he got to Aurora, the more reluctant he grew to hurt his old friend. But he knew full well that no amount of preparation or hedging could soften this kind of shock.

A few minutes later, they broke out of the canebrakes and spied Sabine Bay. Smoke drifted from the mud-and-stick chimney of a neat cabin with a split-shingle roof, the one Nathan had put on ten years earlier when he was recuperating from the loss of his forearm.

Barney Willis, a cannonball of a man with a grin as broad as his face, strode onto the porch when Nathan and Jack reined up. "Howdy, Nathan, howdy." He waved a callused hand and glanced around, searching for his daughter and the young woman he had come to look upon as his grandchild.

Climbing the porch, Nathan took his hand. "Hello, Barney." He hesitated, searching for the words.

The older man frowned when he spotted the buckskins Nathan wore. He hadn't seen Nathan in buckskins for years. "Where's Marie and Ruthie? They come with you or you leave 'em at home?" He paused and chuckled. "Hell, does a man good to get out sometime without the womenfolk." He laughed. Then he looked into Nathan's face. The grin faded. "Nathan?"

Barney glanced at Jack Hays. The young ranger colonel dropped his gaze to the ground. The older man looked back at Nathan. His forehead knit in a frown. "What's goin' on, Nathan? What's wrong?"

Squaring his broad shoulders, Nathan took a deep breath and drew himself to his full six-foot-six height. He hurt inside, just about as bad as he'd ever hurt in his life. "You best grab aholt of something, Barney. You're fixin' to get hit right between the eyes mighty hard."

Tears blurred Nathan's vision, and he scrubbed his eyes with a rough knuckle. "They're dead, Barney. Marie and Ruthie, they're both dead, killed by a passel of cut-throats who just happened by."

The older man stared at Nathan in disbelief. He glanced at Jack Hays, who continued to stare at the ground. Barney looked up, his ruddy face pale, his dark eyes flickering on the edge of panic. His voice broke. "This ain't no joke, Nathan. This sure as hell ain't no way to joke."

Nathan swallowed the burning lump in his throat and laid his hand on his old friend's shoulder. "No joke, Barney. I wouldn't joke like that." His bottom lip quivered, and he stared heavenward in an effort to get a rein on his own emotions. He squeezed Barney's shoulder. "Let's go inside. I'll tell you what I know."

Barney Willis sat staring at the fire, his eyes red and swollen. Nathan sat beside him, gazing at the floor between his moccasined feet.

The older man coughed, then whispered, "That winter ground is mighty damned cold."

His own eyes fixed on the fire, Nathan replied, "I bundled them up good, Barney. They ain't cold."

Jack Hays had boiled a pot of coffee. He filled two cups partway and topped them off with Barney's corn liquor. "Here you go, boys."

Several minutes passed. Both Nathan and Barney were lost in their own thoughts.

Finally, Barney sipped his coffee. "Any idea where they be?"

Nathan grunted and scratched an itch on his knee with the iron T. "Makes no difference. I'll find them."

"Reckon I'm going with you," Barney immediately replied.

Jack glanced in surprise at Nathan, but the big man just nodded. "Figured you would. It could be mighty rugged."

Barney's eyes grew cold. "I've wrestled fifty-foot logs on this river for the last twenty years. Now, some bastards kilt my daughter. You don't got to talk to me about rugged."

Nathan turned up his coffee and drained it, then glanced at the window through which the pale afternoon sun shone. "We leave now, we can reach Tevis Bluff by dark. If they're not there, then we'll head on to Liberty." He glanced at Jack. "I don't figure they went there, or you might have seen them. But no sense in taking any chances. We'll sleep a couple hours outside of Liberty, then ride in about midmorning."

Barney gulped his coffee and starting packing.

Jack shook his head at Nathan and

grinned. "I always did like the way you operate, Nathan Cooper. You don't waste no time."

CHAPTER FIVE

In a cantina on the west side of Nacogdoches, Frank Selman and three of his men sat around a rough-hewn table filling their bellies with beans, tostados, enchiladas, and chiles, washing the entire greasy mixture down with tequila. The fifth gang member, Luis Salado, was too busy with three laughing senoritas and a bottle of tequila to concern himself with grub.

Red glanced at Luis, then grinned wickedly at Frank Selman. "How long we hanging around here, Frank? I got an itch."

Selman shrugged his massive shoulders and flexed arms the size of tree trunks over his head. He dragged the back of his hairy hand across his thick lips. "Damn, Red. Weren't that wildcat back on the Sabine enough for you?" He glanced at the deep furrows on Red's face. "I figured you had enough of women for a few days."

Red laughed. "Not yet, Frank. Not yet."

Frank Selman grunted, "Well, make do tonight. We're pulling out in the morning. Two days in this place is enough. Them lawmen from New Orleans could still be tagging after us."

"You certain about that job in Mexico, Frank?"

Shoveling beans in his mouth, Selman nodded, his cheeks bulging from the excess of food. He rolled a tortilla, filled it with chiles, poked it between his lips, and choked the entire mouthful down in two large gulps, washing it down with cheap tequila, which he noisily swallowed. "Two hundred a month for a gunnie? You bet, I'm certain. Word came straight from some greaser padre."

The four hardcases grinned at each other.

"That's more'n I make in two years," said the other white man, Otis Sims.

Frank tilted his plate and scraped the last of the beans and beef into his spoon. He swallowed them whole, leaned back in his chair, patted his belly, and belched.

His hunger satisfied, Selman glanced around the cantina, spotted several darkskinned senoritas with broad, teasing grins. He shoved back from the table and grinned lecherously. "Okay, boys. Have fun. Come sunrise, we're hittin' the San Antone road."

41

He nodded across the room to Luis Salado. "Alfredo, make sure that cousin of yours knows. We ain't waitin' around."

Alfredo Torres nodded. "*Si.* Me, I too wait around a few days." A lecherous grin spread over his lips. "I enjoy the senoritas as does Luis."

Selman shrugged. "Your funeral."

Neither man had any idea just how prophetic his words were.

Barney's small sorrel stayed right with the red roan and piebald despite the rough travel. Two hours after leaving Aurora, the three men rode into Beaumont, the small settlement on the bend of the Neches where the river flowed in from the north.

Only a few pale lights punctuated the winter dusk. One came from a clapboard-and-log saloon with a weathered sign hanging askew. A barn lantern hung from one corner of the sign. The name, Tevis Bluff, was marked out with a stroke of dark paint, and BEAUMONT was printed in faded whitewash just beneath.

Tying up at the hitching rail, Nathan dismounted and drew his pistol, a Paterson Colt presented him by Sam Colt back in '39. With his iron T, he pushed open the leather and wood-slab door and stepped inside, followed by Barney and Jack.

At the bar, a wizened man looked up, grinned, then spotted the leveled Colt. His grin faded.

Nathan scanned the dingy room. Empty. On one end, a fire danced in the hearth, casting flickering shadows the length of the low-ceilinged inn.

He glanced over his shoulder and nodded to Jack and Barney. Holstering his Colt, Nathan bellied up to the bar, rough planks laid between two empty whiskey barrels. A dirty canvas was tacked to the edge of the thick planks, draping to the rough floor to provide some semblance of a civilized bar.

"Yes, sir?" mumbled the innkeeper, his eyes on Nathan's Colt.

"Whiskey."

Without hesitation, the innkeeper reached under the bar and brought up a bottle of Yellowstone whiskey.

Jack Hays whistled. "Damn, it's been quite a spell since I seen any of that good stuff."

Neither Nathan nor Barney replied. With cold eyes and a set jaw, Nathan downed the first drink, then glared at the innkeeper. "I'm looking for some men. Three, four, five — maybe more, but I don't think so. Any strangers come through here?"

The innkeeper shook his head hurriedly.

"No, sir. Not that I recollect."

Unable to constrain his impatience, Barney spoke up. "We want 'em bad, mister. I find you're lying to us, I'll come back here and cut you open and feed your worthless carcass to the fish."

The innkeeper stared at Barney in fear, but the fear gave way to recognition. "Hey, ain't you Barney Willis, from down in Aurora?"

Barney glanced up at Nathan, then nodded to the innkeeper. "I know you?"

The shriveled man shook his head. "No, sir. I only come here a year or so back, but I remember seeing you down to Aurora one time when I was in the Sabine Fur House. You was talking to Charley Wyeth."

"Could be," Barney replied. "But like I said, I don't remember you."

The bartender grinned sheepishly. "Hell, Mr. Willis. I ain't the kind nobody remembers, but it's the gospel truth there ain't been no strangers through here the last couple days. Before that a couple drummers, but that's all."

Nathan nodded, and allowed a terse smile. "Much obliged, mister. Sorry to have come down on you like we did." He downed the last of his whiskey and turned for the door. "Let's go, boys. Next stop, Liberty."

44

Nathan's big roan led a killing pace down the narrow trace until the moon set. Then they pulled into a windbreak and made camp. Jack tended the horses while Nathan and Barney built the fire and raised a makeshift lean-to. Barney nodded to the slight ranger. "He the kinda hombre who'll fight with us when we catch them bastards? He don't look more than a boy. Don't have much to say."

Nathan looked up from feeding tinder to the fire. A broad grin split his face. "Back in forty-one, that boy there headed a column of rangers all the way from San Antone down to Laredo, where he ran up against a Mexican army three times the size of his force. He charged and routed them, and sent them scrabbling back to Laredo. That boy treed the whole village of Laredo. Next morning, the *alcalde* begged Jack to spare the town and promised him anything he wanted."

Barney arched his eyebrows. "Sure don't look like it."

Nathan chuckled, the first time he had laughed in days.

As false dawn spread over the forest, they

were on the trail once again. At noon, they pulled up in a grove of oaks and studied the small community of Liberty, a collection of clapboard shacks and log cabins on the east bank of the Trinity River.

Always cautious, Nathan remained in the timber as he circled the village, coming in from the west.

Catfish entrails, gamy and rank, pestered by buzzards, lay heaped on the riverbanks on the outskirts of town. Along the muddy streets and under the ramshackle cabins, razorback hogs rooted, squawking chickens scratched and pecked around doorways where scraps had been thrown, and flimsy corrals held spavined horses and broomtail mules, all starving, their ribs as prominent as the tines on a pitchfork. The overpowering pungency of wet manure and putrefying meat enveloped the village, smothering it like a rotting blanket.

The first two inns were boarded up. At the last one, Jack and Barney remained outside as Nathan shoved through the wood-slab door, pausing just inside to scan the dark room.

He made out the figure of a lanky man leaning over the bar, his long, slender fingers wrapped around a dirty glass halffilled with cheap whiskey. He and the barkeep looked around. Immediately, the lanky man's gaze shifted to Nathan's wooden arm. Nathan stopped at the opposite end of the bar.

The old barkeep limped the length of the bar. "Stew's all gone. You got to settle for whiskey or beer."

"Ain't hungry, ain't thirsty. I want information," Nathan replied. His gaze flicked past the innkeeper and caught the man at the bar staring at him. Immediately the man dropped his own gaze to the glass in his hands. "Seen any newcomers the last week or so?"

The old man hesitated. "You the law?"

Nathan resisted the urge to grab the small man by his grimy shirt and shake the information from him, but he understood the old man's natural reticence concerning the law in the young state. "No. I'm not the law. Now, you see any strangers come through the last few days?"

"Well . . ." The old man paused, thinking. His forehead wrinkled in thought. "Nope. None at all. Fact is, Joe Ed down there," he said, nodding to the rail-thin man at the opposite end of the bar, "he's been just about my only customer this last week. Weather like this, most folks stay to home in front of a hot fire."

Nathan studied the bone-thin man a moment, the angular face, the downcast eyes deliberately avoiding him. The hair on the back of his neck tingled. He gave the old innkeeper a curt nod, then left, telling himself that tonight, he'd best sleep with one eye open and one hand on his Colt.

Outside, he shook his head at Barney and Jack. "No luck." He swung into the saddle and paused, looking to the north.

"What's on your mind, Nathan?" asked Jack.

Pointing with his iron T, Nathan explained, "Seventy or so miles north of here is the old San Antone road from Nacogdoches. El Camino Real, the Royal Road, the old padres used to call it. Those we came after didn't ride this way. That means they probably made for Nacogdoches. We might be better off cutting north here and taking the road into Nacogdoches. We can circle around to Injun Bayou the back way." He looked at Barney. "Then back to the farm."

Barney Willis sat motionless in his saddle, bundled to his neck in his mackinaw, his slouch hat snugged down on his ears. The heavy-set man cleared his throat and looked in the direction of the farm. "You don't mind, Nathan. I . . . I'd kinda like to go by the farm first."

The icy chill fled Nathan's eyes. He knew exactly how the older man felt. "I don't mind at all, Barney."

After they had crawled into their soogans that night, and the campfire had burned low, Barney whispered to Nathan. "I just had to see her gra . . . her . . ." He paused, unable to speak the word. An anguished groan drifted through the cold night. "Just see where she is, Nathan."

Nathan nodded, glad for the darkness that hid his own tears. "I know, Barney. I know how you feel."

Jack Hays listened to the poignant discussion. Tears clouded his eyes. He too was glad it was dark.

As the fire burned low, Nathan silently slipped his Colt from the holster and laid it across his chest.

CHAPTER SIX

The night was cold, and the wind moaned through the treetops like mournful ghosts. The fire had burned down to coals, wolf eyes winking in the darkness.

Nathan jerked awake, immediately alert. He lay motionless, staring into the shadows surrounding the camp, searching for the source of the sound that had awakened him. Slowly, he wrapped his fingers around the butt of the Colt, cocking the revolver with infinite patience so as to make no sound.

From the forest behind them came the *hoo, hoo-hoo, hoooo-oo* of a horned owl. Moments later, a second call came from the darkness before them.

Jack Hays stirred. Barney continued to snore.

Straining his ears, Nathan picked up the faint shuffle of feet over leaves off to the left. Then a branch cracked to their right.

"How many you figure, Nathan?" whispered Jack.

"Four, maybe five."

Jack remained silent. He heard a faint rustle from across the fire. When he looked, Nathan's soogan was empty.

In the forest, Nathan crouched behind a loblolly pine, his keen eyes searching the darkness between him and the camp. Suddenly, two shadows slipped from one tree to another and dropped to their knees.

A grim smile twisted his lips. He figured the lanky man back at the bar would pull something like this. It seemed half the men in Texas were always trying to steal what the other half worked for. No wonder the damned state was so violent. Sometimes Nathan wondered just why in the hell the United States wanted such a lawless territory.

Nathan watched and waited. One of the kneeling figures gave the signal again, and again a reply came from beyond the fire. Nathan shook his head in disgust. Not only were they lawless, they were also stupid, imitating a call they didn't understand.

Staying in a crouch, Nathan eased toward the two men.

When he was less than five feet from them, two shots rang out from the camp.

The two men jumped upright and raised their six-guns. Nathan calmly slammed the muzzle of his .36 into one's temple, and smashed the iron T into the back of the other's head, slamming the man's face forward into the scaly trunk of the pine.

Both men collapsed. Nathan snagged the back of one's coat with the iron T and twisted his fingers into the other's collar, dragging both unconscious men to the fire, where Jack stood looking down at the two bushwhackers he'd shot.

Holding a torch near one of the dead men's faces, Nathan identified him as Joe Ed, the man back in the bar in Liberty.

"What were they after?" asked Barney.

"Whatever we had," answered Nathan. "Horses, guns — owlhoots like this steal whatever they can lay their mangy hands on."

Jack Hays eyed the two unconscious men. "What about these two, Nathan?"

For a fleeting moment, Nathan remembered some of the painful tortures of the Karankawas, but then, thinking of Marie, he dismissed them. He shook his head. "Hadn't rightly given it much thought."

Jack arched an eyebrow. "You should've let me take care them." He patted the worn handle of his Paterson. "I had 'em in my sights when you cold-cocked them."

Barney threw a puzzled glance at the boyish-looking young ranger. Then he frowned at Nathan.

Nathan understood Barney's confusion. He remembered his own shocked surprise at the sudden violent attacks of the Texas Rangers and the give-no-quarter, take-no-quarter mindset driving each of the cold-eyed men, all following the example of their young leader.

Having lived with the Karankawa, Nathan witnessed that very philosophy implanted into even the youngest child. But to see it employed by white men had come as a surprise. He grunted. "Should turn 'em over to the law, but I don't feel like dragging them along with us."

One of the unconscious men moaned.

"Set him up," Nathan said.

Jack propped the bushwhacker against a pine.

"You hear me?" asked Nathan. He stared down at the groaning outlaw.

"Y — Yeah."

Nathan shucked his bowie and squatted in front of the man. Touching the tip of the deadly blade to the bushwhacker's chin, he tilted the man's head back. "You best pay careful attention to what I'm saying."

The man's eyes bugged out of his angular face. "I . . . I hear, mister. I hear."

"I don't plan on dragging you after me." He hooked a thumb at Jack Hays. "My friend there wants to plant your carcass in the ground. I'm inclined to let him, but I am a fair man. I figure to leave you two here. When I come back, I'm stopping off in Liberty. If I find any trace of you two, I'll carve you up and throw you to the catfish. You hear?"

The frightened man tried to nod, but the tip of the knife pressed into his flesh. A bubble of blood gathered on the tip. "I promise. We'll — you ain't goin' to find us nowhere. Me, at least. That's a promise."

Nathan stared at the wild-eyed man. With only a gentle nudge, he could drive the blade into the man's brain. A surge of adrenaline coursed through his body, and he felt his breath quicken. Slowly he lowered the bowie, resisting the almost overpowering urge to take the man's life. He stepped back and sheathed the knife. He glared at the bushwhacker, who had pressed his fingers to the bottom on his chin. "See that you keep it."

The bushwhacker nodded. "Yes, sir. Don't worry, I won't break it."

The second bushwhacker awakened just as Nathan, Jack, and Barney rode away. "Damn. My head's killing me," he moaned, touching his fingers to the knot on the back of his head and the bump on his forehead.

The first bushwhacker gave his compadre a warning look. "You best shut your damned mouth unless you want to get yourself kilt dead." Without another word, he turned back into the forest toward his pony.

When the second one saw Nathan's broad back so close, he grabbed for his revolver, but his holster was empty. He looked over his shoulder at his departed compadre. "Hey, what's going on?"

His partner didn't look back. He just kept walking.

Jumping to his feet, the second bushwhacker ran after him. "I said, what's going on?"

"Joe Ed and his brother are dead. We should be, but we ain't. That hombre told us to get out of the country, and that's damned well what I plan to do."

The second bushwhacker snorted. "Well, hell. He don't scare me none."

The other man shouted over his shoulder

without missing a step. "Well, he sure as hell scares me."

Later on the trail, Barney glanced at Nathan. "How'd you know they was out there, Nathan? I didn't hear nothing 'til Jack started shooting. Scared the bejeebers out of me."

"Yeah. You was awake when I woke up, Nathan," said Jack. "What'd you hear?"

Nathan glanced at his two friends. "Owls."

Barney frowned. "Owls?"

"Yep. Like most outlaws, those old boys got sawdust for brains. They never figured owls talk, but they just hoot. Well, owls don't waste their breath like a lot of humans. When they talk, most of it means something."

Jack arched an eyebrow.

Nathan continued. "You listen, and you can hear that the male has a higher voice than the female. He always talks first. Usually, a female answers, and a lot of that talk is romantic gibberish. So when I hear a hooty owl with a deep voice calling out first, and then a high-pitched one answering, I figure something's going on I need to pay attention to."

At that moment, a single owl hooted.

Barney asked, half believing, half disbelieving. "What about that one, Nathan. What's he saying?"

With a cryptic grin on his grizzled face, Nathan said. "It's a female, and she's letting everyone know she's settling down for the day."

At sundown, the three rode up to the farm. The cabin was cold and empty, and a suffocating aura of desolation lay over the entire two hundred acres. To the south, the swamp waters reflected the gray sky overhead.

Jack built up the fire and put coffee on to boil while Nathan and Barney stood at the gravesites. The young colonel glanced out of the window, then turned back to the fire. He shaved jerky into a pot of water for a broth.

In the East Texas forest, nighttime comes abruptly, but neither Nathan nor Barney moved a step from the graves. Inside the cabin, Jack sipped the coffee and refilled his bowl with broth.

Much later, Nathan and Barney came inside, their faces drawn with pain.

Jack nodded to the cheery fire. "Coffee's hot. I threw together a thick broth. It'll get us through the night."

With a short nod, Barney reached for the coffee. Nathan nodded at Jack and spoke in a monotone. "Reckon we need some meat. I noticed the haunch on the dogtrot was gone. Wolf or bobcat must've worried it off."

"Yep," Jack replied. "Jerky soup ain't as filling as red meat, but it'll keep your stomach from yowling."

They rode out early next morning, pausing on the small hill beyond for a last look back. The seven markers stood in the shadows cast by an ancient white oak. Barney coughed. When he spoke, his voice was strained with emotion. "Damn, they look lonely down there."

Swallowing at the burning knot in his throat, Nathan turned back to Injun Bayou. "The sooner we get on with it, the sooner we get back to keep 'em company."

Just before noon, they rode into Injun Bayou, a small settlement on the Sabine River. Nathan's earlier guess had been accurate. Five strangers had ridden through less than a week past.

Isaac Goldstein, the local innkeeper and hosteler, frowned at the tragic news and pointed north with a bony finger. "They just rode straight through, Nathan. They didn't stop and talk or nothing. Two of 'em wore sombreros, and one of the others had a thick beard." He hesitated. "If we'd known, we mighta stopped them for you."

Nathan forced a grin. "Thanks, Isaac. I don't know how long I'll be gone. Take a look at our place whenever you get a chance."

"Don't worry none, you hear? I'll take care of it just like it's my own."

Swinging back into the saddle, Nathan turned his roan north on the road to Nacogdoches.

CHAPTER SEVEN

An hour before sundown on the third day, Nathan pulled up on the south bank of the Angelina River. Jack and Barney reined up beside him.

A blustery wind howled across the rolling hills, all of which were covered with thick buffalo grass now that the piney woods of East Texas were beginning to thin into the vast grasslands of the central section of the state.

The gray water of the Angelina ran smooth and deep. Nathan rode upriver, searching for a ford. Just above an S-bend, he found a short stretch of white water where the river tumbled over shallow rocks.

"We cross here," he said, dismounting and leading the roan across the rugged riverbed.

On the far shore, he pulled into a copse of oak. Dead wood littered the ground. "I reckon this is as good a place as any to spend the night and dry our boots."

Sometime later, after they filled their stomachs with coffee and roasted rabbit, after the sun had dropped behind the horizon and the stars sprinkled the black sky with handfuls of sugar, after the last blue jay tucked its head under its wing, and after his two compadres slept peacefully, Nathan lay staring into the night, trying to imagine the faces of the men for whom he searched.

Three white, two Mexican — perhaps tomorrow, he would find them. If not — Taking a deep breath, he turned on his side and stared at the winking embers in the banked fire. If not, he told himself, he would keep looking. Ten years, twenty years. No matter. He would not rest until he found the men who killed his wife and niece — and his niece's betrothed.

He fell into a deep slumber, only to jerk awake in a cold sweat early next morning. He stared into the darkness, trying to push the nightmare from his head.

Unable to sleep, Nathan rose well before sunrise, stirring the fire and putting coffee on to boil. Barney and Jack rolled from their soogans. The rabbits from the night before had been gnawed to the bone, so jerky and hot coffee had to satisfy their hunger.

Within minutes, they pulled out, topping a small rise just as the orange sun peered over the forest behind them. The sky was clear and blue. The wind had let up, but the air was crisp with a chill. Ahead, like a rumpled gray blanket on a bed, the grassy prairie undulated in a series of rises ending in a tree-covered hill on the horizon.

His breath frosty in the crisp air, Nathan said, "Best I figure, Nacogdoches is just the other side of that hill yonder."

"How far you make it?" asked Barney.

Jack Hays replied, "Ten, maybe twelve miles. Two hours."

They kicked their ponies into an easy lope.

Exactly two hours later, the three rode through the trees on the crest of the hill and emerged on a grassy plain. The squat village of Nacogdoches sprawled on the next rise. Thin columns of smoke drifted into a sky as clear as glass.

Situated on the northwestern corner of the vast East Texas forest, Nacogdoches was no different from every other green-stick and rawhide village scattered throughout the state, with two notable differences: it was larger, and sitting on the Camino Real, it was the main entry point for the Anglo-American colonization of Texas.

Usually, a village had a single street. Nacogdoches had three, three mud-choked, malodorous streets lined with tottering shacks that were atrophied by the scorching summer sun and shriveled by the frigid blasts of winter.

The three-inch snow from the previous week had melted, leaving behind streets of sludge — a pungent, soupy mixture of ankle-deep animal manure, human waste, and garbage — destined to maintain its watery consistency until late spring when the winter storms and spring rains abated.

The town was awake, but traffic was random, slowed by the weather and the glutinous mire. Most families, unless there was some kind of emergency, were content to remain inside by a warm fire and pass the day as they might. The few hardy souls slogging through the soupy muckholes the locals called streets were mostly Mexican vendors making deliveries, ragged youngsters with armloads of branches for the fires, or businessmen scurrying to open their shops for the few customers who might brave the elements.

Reining up at the first cantina, Nathan led the way inside, stomped up to the candlelit bar, and ordered a whiskey. The cheerful little innkeeper's face crumbled into a sad frown. "No whiskey, senor. Only tequila."

Nathan glanced at Jack and Barney. Both men shrugged. "Tequila's good," replied Nathan.

The Mexican innkeeper grinned and slid a bottle and three glasses on the bar.

Nathan reached in his pocket and nodded to the three-quarters-full bottle. *"¿Cuatro?"*

"Four bits, senor."

Barney shoved his hat on the back of his head and reached for the bottle. He growled. "Cheap. Must be a small worm in the bottom." He filled their glasses and tossed his down in one gulp. With a shiver, he reached for the bottle and refilled his glass. "Damn, that's raw, but it warms a man."

Jack grunted. "Not as much as that fire," he said, carrying his glass to the fireplace and turning his back to it, soaking up the heat from the roaring fire and drying his damp clothes.

His glass of tequila in hand, Nathan studied the small innkeeper. "Been any strangers around the last nine or ten days?" He sipped the tequila.

The innkeeper's shifty eyes cut from Nathan to Jack and Barney, then back to Nathan. He shrugged. "See no one, senor. No one comes to Manuel's cantina."

Nathan caught the furtive look. He

touched a finger to his massive chest. "No law. I look for men who kill my wife. White man and Mexican. Three white, two your kind." He touched the iron T to his cheek. "One, maybe more, will be scratched up, probably on his face."

His lower lip protruding, the small innkeeper shook his head. "*Si. Qué una compasión.* What a pity." He shrugged. "I can do nothing, senor. I do not see them." His face became animated, and he poked his finger against his chest. "But if Manuel José Escobar Fuentes see those of whom you speak, he will send word to the senor."

Nathan studied the small man. He seemed too contrite, then too eager. "Cantinas? *¿Cuántos?* How many cantinas in town?"

Immediately, the innkeeper held up four fingers. *"Cuatro."*

For several moments, Nathan stared at the innkeeper who drew his tongue over his dry lips. Nathan dropped his hand to the hilt of his bowie. The innkeeper gulped. Nathan nodded. "Much obliged."

He took his glass and joined Jack in front of the fire. Barney followed with the bottle of tequila.

"You think he was telling the truth?" Jack asked, glancing past Nathan and Barney at the Mexican innkeeper who was busily scrubbing the bar.

Scratching at his heavy beard with the iron T, Nathan considered the question carefully, all the while keeping an eye on the busy little man. Finally, he replied, "I'm not sure. I got a feeling he knows something, but he's hanging on to it like a starving coyote."

Barney started to push past Nathan. "Hell, let's make him talk."

Nathan laid his prosthesis on Barney's arm. "Not right now, Barney. Let him think we believe him. When we leave here, Jack can hang back and keep a eye peeled while you and me try the other cantinas." He arched a questioning eyebrow at the ranger colonel.

The slightly built ranger downed his tequila, shivered mightily, and poured himself another. "Sounds right good to me." He nodded to Barney and grinned. "Course, I feel like Barney there. I wouldn't mind kicking that little greaser's butt until he talks."

"Patience," Nathan grinned. "Patience."

Barney frowned. "How do you figure they might have scratches on their faces?"

A shadow of pain flickered in Nathan's eyes as he cleared his throat. He knew his reply would dredge up fresh pain for Barney, but it couldn't be helped. "I found blood and skin under Marie's fingernails. She scratched the hell out of at least one of them."

Barney's round face grew hard and cold. He squeezed his eyes shut.

Ten minutes later, they "adiosed" the innkeeper and rode away. Around the first corner, Jack reined his piebald behind a large, sprawling live oak and waited while Nathan and Barney headed for the next cantina.

Within minutes, a young Mexican boy dashed from the cantina and raced through town. Jack followed at a distance on his pony, staying a block over, glimpsing the boy from time to time across vacant lots or between buildings.

The boy ran through the back door of another cantina. Jack pulled up. He grinned to himself.

Nathan and Barney visited two more cantinas and came up empty-handed.

"One to go," said Nathan.

Barney grunted and, standing on his left foot in the stirrup, shifted around in his saddle to face Nathan. "Why'n the hell don't we just go back there and make that little greaser talk?"

"Give him time, Barney. If I'm right, he probably led Jack to them. If not, then we'll go back and see if we can show him the error of his ways."

As they approached the next cantina, Jack pulled out of a thick clump of wild jasmine behind a log cabin. He nodded to the cantina and motioned to the back door. "They're inside."

His eyes narrowing, Nathan muttered. "We'll go in the front. Jack, watch the back." The rage he had suppressed these last several days began to simmer. He tied the red roan to the hitching rail and stared at the door. He flexed his fingers, then opened the slab door.

A flickering oil lamp lit one end of the dingy room, a fireplace the other. Nathan stepped inside. Barney followed and closed the door. A half-dozen tables filled the room. Three dark-skinned Mexicans sat hunched over a table in the corner. The sullen look on their faces, the hate etched across their faces, served as a warning to Nathan. He scanned the room. The other tables were empty. The three Mexicans were the only patrons of the cantina.

Behind the bar, a cold-eyed Mexican glared at him. Perched on the end of the bar with one knee crossed over the other was a young senorita with a sultry smile and a seductive arch to her eyebrows. *"Buenos días,* senors," she said, her voice filled with gaiety.

With feline grace, she sprang to the floor and waved a slender hand to an empty table. "We have frijoles and chiles and the best tequila in the whole village of Nacogdoches."

With a terse shake of his head, Nathan erased the smile from her face. "I'm looking for some men."

Barney stepped to his side.

Nathan gestured to the seated men with his iron T and spoke to the young woman in a voice loud enough for the Mexicans to hear. "Senorita. These three. They live in Nacogdoches?"

The three Mexicans' faces grew hard.

She replied immediately. *"Si. Si,* they live here long, senor. Very long."

The three relaxed.

Nathan nodded. "What are their names?"

"Oh, senor. That one is Alfonso Morales. This is his cantina," she said pointing to the first. "Next to him is Carlos Benitas. The other is Pablo Ruiz. Long these three live in Nacogdoches, senor, as *la madre y el padre* before them."

Nathan and Barney exchanged puzzled

glances. Had Jack made a mistake? Nathan didn't believe so, but anything was possible. He studied the three surly Mexicans a few more moments, then left.

Behind the log cabin from where Jack watched, Nathan gave him the disappointing news.

Jack insisted. "A kid ran in there, Nathan. He carried word to someone about something. Hold it." A faint grin curled his lips. "Well, damn, would you look at that?"

Nathan shifted in the saddle as one of the Mexicans slipped out the back door and scurried up the muddy street. Easing behind the thick growth of jasmine, the three watched the slight man pause in front of a barn, then slip inside.

Moments later, the doors swung open and another Mexican astride a large pinto burst through the open doorway and raced for the outskirts of the small village. The rider's sombrero flopped against his back, held by a rawhide lanyard. The morning sun struck his swarthy face.

Nathan's eyes grew hard when he spotted the dark-scabbed furrows on the fleeing Mexican's cheek, furrows made by Marie's fingernails.

CHAPTER EIGHT

Instantly, Nathan drove his heels into the flanks of the roan. The great red animal leaped forward into the street, nostrils flaring, its mighty muscles contracting and expanding powerfully. The mud sucked at the animal's hooves, making popping sounds.

A handful of citizens rushed into doorways and onto the street as the Mexican spurred his pinto frantically. Seconds later, those in the street jumped aside as a giant white man forking a red roan raced past.

The Mexican glanced over his shoulder, and his eyes bulged in fear. He dug his cruel spurs into the pinto, cutting one-elevens and drawing blood. The game animal reached down deep, pulling up every last remnant of strength and of courage.

But such courage was useless, for the red roan ate up the distance between them within seconds. By the time the Mexican

71

caballero reached the outskirts of the small village, Nathan was at his side.

When the frightened man looked around and saw Nathan, he grabbed for his belt pistol.

Using the iron T, Nathan snagged the Mexican's vest and yanked him from the saddle. The rider slammed to the ground on his back, flipped over twice, and slid through the mud, stunned despite the snow-softened soil. He blinked, trying to orient himself.

Nathan swung down and stood over the dazed Mexican. His eyes blazed when he saw the deep scratches on the man's face, three parallel ruts gouged out of the man's flesh, three furrows made by fingernails, Marie Cooper's fingernails before she was raped and murdered.

Jack and Barney reined up. Behind them, a handful of citizens hurried out to see what the trouble was. In the lead was the sheriff.

"What's going on out here? Who the hell are you jaspers?" The big-bellied sheriff staggered to a halt beside the prone Mexican. Red-faced and gasping for breath, he looked up at Nathan.

Without taking his eyes off the Mexican, Nathan replied. "You know this man, Sheriff?"

The sheriff shook his head. "Never seen him before. Now, what's going on here?"

The prostrate Mexican bleated, "*Por favor,* sheriff. I have done nothing. I — I do not know what this gringo wants."

Nathan drew his hand back sharply, silencing the whining man. He held a tight rein on his anger. "This man, and four more, raped my wife and niece and then murdered them along with my niece's intended. I aim for this one to give me the names of the others before I kill him."

The Mexican's eyes grew wide. He grabbed for his pistol, but Nathan stomped on his arm. He screamed in pain.

The sheriff shook his head. "Who in the hell do you think you are? You can't take the law in your own hands."

Nathan kept his eyes fixed on the screaming Mexican as he replied in a voice cold enough to freeze water. "Nathan Cooper. That's who I am, and there ain't a lawman alive who can stop me from killing this pile of dung at my feet."

The sheriff glared at Nathan, trying to stare the big mountain man down, but the intensity in Nathan's eyes caused the sheriff to take an inadvertent step back. Suddenly, he was very uncomfortable.

Jack Hays spoke up. "Sheriff, I'm Colonel

Jack Hays of the Texas Rangers, commissioned by Governor J. Pinckney Henderson to enlist men for the war with Mexico. Cooper is one of my men. He has orders to chase these men down."

The last statement was a bald lie, but Jack had learned the cynical lesson long ago that only about 10 percent of the human race could ferret out lies mixed with truths.

Confused, the sheriff looked from Hays to Cooper while the Mexican continued to sob and beg the sheriff to intervene.

Nathan spoke again. "I'm asking you for the last time, Sheriff. Who is this man?"

The sheriff swallowed hard. "I never seen him before." He looked around at the group of curious onlookers, spotted the Mexican innkeeper. "You, Morales. Who is he?"

Morales shrugged and tried to play dumb. "Sheriff, I do not know this man. As *Dios* is my witness."

Nathan fixed the Mexican innkeeper with a savage glare. He felt the blood boil in his veins. "Well, God ain't your witness now. You got me to answer to. This hombre come busting out of that barn after you sent word to him. Now, you tell me what I want to hear, or I'll cut your throat and then go after your family."

Morales didn't hesitate. "He ride in four,

five days back with four others. He calls himself Alfredo Torres. The others, they leave, but this one," he said, his tone suddenly filled with scorn, "this one is a whoremonger. All he wants is to pester my girls and pay nothing."

Nathan, his foot still on Torres's arm, turned his cold eyes back to the prone Mexican, but he spoke to Morales. "Where did the others go, innkeeper?"

"Yeah, Morales. Where did they go?" chimed in the sheriff.

The innkeeper looked at the sheriff and shrugged. "I do not know, Sheriff. By *la Madre Santa,* that is the truth. All I know is they take the road west." He nodded down the Camino Real and made the sign of the cross.

Keeping his icy glare on Torres, Nathan spoke in a soft, deep voice, but one that left no doubt in anyone's mind that he was in no mood to argue. "Take your people and go back to town, Sheriff. I'll take care of what needs to be done here."

Torres begged. "No. Senor Sheriff, do not —" He screamed as Nathan twisted his heel into the Mexican's arm.

The sheriff looked at Jack Hays.

Hays arched an eyebrow and in a wry voice, said, "I'd do like I was told, Sheriff."

He did.

Nathan took a step back. "Get up," he demanded of the Mexican.

Sobbing uncontrollably, the bedraggled figure struggled to his feet, clutching his arm to his oversize belly. The scabs on his face had broken open from the fall, and fresh blood trickled crimson streaks down his muddy cheek and dripped from his jaw.

Nathan's eyes narrowed into dark pinpoints of pure hatred as he visualized this man abusing Marie. It was all he could manage to keep from slicing the whining man to pieces in the middle of the road where they stood — but he needed information. In a strained voice, Nathan said. "Who was with you?"

Torres looked fearfully at the three cold-eyed gringos. "I go nowhere, senor. I know nothing of what you speak."

Nathan's hand lashed out and slapped the Mexican across the face, spinning him to the ground. Barely containing his fury, the enraged mountain man jerked the stunned Mexican to his feet and shoved him into his pony. "Mount up."

Without a word, Torres did as he was told.

Deftly, Nathan tied the frightened man's hands to the saddle horn and grabbed the reins.

The four riders headed west down the Camino Real with the reins of Torres's pony wrapped snugly around Nathan's iron T.

CHAPTER NINE

Overhead, clouds thickened, blocking the warm rays of the sun. A cold wind blew in, a portent of a coming front. A few miles down the road, they forded a small creek. Barney glanced at Nathan. "Reckon I wish I'd listened to you when you wanted to cut north at Liberty. Likely we'd have all them no-accounts by now."

Nathan grunted. "Maybe. Maybe not. Truth is, it don't matter all that much because sooner or later, I'll find them." Ahead he spotted a tall pecan. "That'll do," he said, reining his roan off the muddy trace.

Torres' eyes grew wide. "Please, senor. I beg you. I do not know of what you speak. I, Alfredo Torres, have done harm to no one."

Nathan reined up. "I reckon no woman did that to your face, huh?"

The Mexican caballero grinned wickedly. "*Si,* senor. In Nacogdoches. Maria Consuela. She works at Morales' cantina."

"Not likely," Nathan snorted, swinging to the ground and tossing a loop over a sturdy pecan limb. "Is that why you lit a shuck out of town?" He grabbed the Mexican, yanked him to the ground, and quickly threw a loop around the stunned man's ankles and snugged it tight. Then he tied the man's hands behind his back with rawhide, after which he tossed a rope over a limb several feet above them. He nodded to Jack. "Jack, how about you and Barney give me a hand with a few armloads of dry wood. I don't want our friend here to catch a cold."

Alfredo Torres watched in horror as the three gringos quickly gathered a large pile of dried timber.

Very deliberately, Nathan laid a small fire under a large limb, then unsheathed his knife and began shaving curls of wood into the middle as tinder. "Of course, all you have to do is tell me who was with you."

Torres shook his head frantically. "But, senor, I do not know of those you speak."

Jack Hays stepped forward. "You're a liar. The saloon keeper said you came in with that bunch last week."

Shaking his head emphatically, Torres pleaded. "*Si,* I come with them, but I do

79

not ride with them. They pulled in at the hitching rail just as I entered the cantina."

Barney glanced quizzically at Nathan who continued shaving curls of firewood into a pile. Without looking at the frantic Mexican, Nathan grunted. "Too bad. Shame a jasper's got to die just because his memory went bad." He paused, studied the small stack of wood, then nodded. "That ought to get us started." He glanced at Jack and Barney. "All right, boys, give me a hand."

Alfredo Torres began to scream as the rope dragged him through the mud and then raised him off the ground. They tied him off four feet above the laid fire. The panicking man twisted and jerked on the ropes.

Barney frowned. His ruddy complexion paled. He looked at Nathan, his eyes reflecting his disbelief at his son-in-law's intentions.

Nathan squatted by the fire. "Bouncing around like that won't help you none. Make it last longer." He paused, retrieved his flint from his parfleche bag and struck a spark to the tinder. Moments later tendrils of smoke began rising.

Torres began to squall. Then he wet his pants.

Nathan arched an eyebrow. "Who was with you?"

The Mexican shook his head.

A tiny flame leaped up. Nathan fed more tinder. "Let me tell you what's going to happen to you. First, that greasy hair of yours is going to burn off. Then your skin will blister, and when the blisters break, there's nothing to protect your skull. The heat will bake it and suddenly — pop! Like a chicken egg, your head will explode and dump your brains all over the fire." He paused, then added, "But before that happens, you'll hurt worse than you ever thought possible, amigo."

Barney swallowed hard, unable to believe Nathan was going to carry out his threat. Killing someone in a fight was one thing, but to deliberately torture? This was a side of Nathan he'd never seen — the Karankawa side, his daughter had once told him.

Marie had always laughed that the buckskins were Nathan's uncivilized dress. And now, the significance of the big mountain man donning such apparel was not lost on the older man.

Torres began to sob, but refused to give Nathan the answers he sought. The heavily muscled man added more fuel. The fire grew hotter. Torres' hair began to spark, and when a black lock caught fire, he squealed, "I tell you, I tell you. *Por favor.* Cut me down."

Barney sighed with relief, then froze as Nathan growled. "Tell me first."

Nodding frantically, Torres blurted out, "*Si, si!* Frank Selman, he was our leader." And the others!"

Jerking his head from side to side, Torres sobbed. "Red Davis, Otis Sims, Luis Salado. *Por favor.* Cut me down. *Por el Mary Virgen,* cut me down."

Nathan kicked the fire apart, and in the same motion, slashed the rope, sending Alfredo Torres headfirst into the burning coals.

The terrified man struck on his shoulder and rolled frantically from the remnants of the fire, scattering the coals. A few caught his clothes and began burning tiny holes. He screamed.

Nathan simply stared down at the man while Jack calmly poured water from his canteen on the smoldering dots on Torre's clothes.

Arching an eyebrow, Nathan shrugged his shoulders. "You're a more forgiving man than me, Jack."

The sun dropped behind the ancient pines, ushering in a north wind edged with tendrils of ice. With Torres propped against the trunk of the pecan, Nathan learned that the five hardcases' plan was to go to San Antonio, there to join a priest by the name of Padre Celedonia de Jarauta, who was the leader of a band of guerrillas.

Nathan glanced at Jack across the small fire they had rebuilt to boil coffee. "You heard of that jasper?"

Looking up from cleaning his Paterson Colt, Jack nodded. His eyes narrowed and a grim smile played over his thin lips. "He's one of those firebrands that be pushing the war with the U.S."

Barney looked into Nathan's eyes. "That means them killers is going to Mexico. I say let's follow after them. Hell, if we hurry, we might catch up to them down in San Antone."

Nathan nodded. "This Selman. What does he look like?"

Torres' words tumbled over one another. "Big. Like you. Big black beard. Wears a red mackinaw." He touched the tip of his tongue to his two front teeth. "No teeth here."

"What about the others? Red Davis?"

The Mexican grimaced. "Tall as that gringo," he said, nodding to Jack Hays. "Red hair. The other, Sims, he is tall and skinny. He got no teeth and a scar on his

83

face, across his eye. Luis, he have mustache."

Barney grunted. "Don't reckon we'll have trouble recognizing them jaspers. I mean the white men. Those Mexes, they all look alike."

Pursing his lips, Nathan studied the cowering Mexican. "Where were you to join up with them?"

Torres gulped. "Bastrop, senor."

His eyes narrowing, Nathan laid his callused hand on the bone handle of his knife. "I reckon we best get started."

Barney grunted. "What if they ain't there?"

With a raw grunt, Nathan growled. "We'll follow as far as we got to. All the way down to Mexico City."

"Hold on, Nathan," Jack Hays said, pushing to his feet and holding out his hands to either side.

Nathan looked around sharply, his grizzled face twisted in an impatient frown.

Jack continued. "You know as well as me, given the conditions between Mexico and the United States, two gringos wandering into Mexico is a sure way to find yourself on that staircase to hell." He shook his head. "No way you two can dodge the Federales down there more than a day or so."

Barney and Nathan exchanged puzzled looks. Barney cleared his throat. "What do you have in mind?"

Jack stroked his beardless cheek. "I started to tell you a minute ago." He nodded to Alfredo Torres on the ground. "You know who you're after. You know they want to join up with this Padre Jarauta."

Nathan shrugged. "So?"

The grin on the slender man's face grew wider. "What I didn't get a chance to tell you was that this Padre Jarauta and his Jarautaristas have joined up with General Canales." The slight ranger paused, his eyes narrowing at Nathan as he added, "Canales, the man responsible for the execution of Captain Ewen Cameron." Jack paused. "Remember Canales, Nathan?"

With a guttural snarl, Nathan responded, "That butcher? I'll never forget that one."

"So, you want those men. I want the jasper they're joining up with, Jarauta. Four companies of Texas Rangers have been ordered to engage Canales and Jarauta. If you don't find them in San Antone, come with me, both of you. Join the Texas Rangers for six months, and we'll track those blood-thirsty killers all the way to Mexico City — all the way to Panama if we have to."

For several moments, Nathan and Barney stared each other, pondering Jack's suggestion. Barney cleared his throat. "What do you think, Nathan?"

Gently tapping the iron T on his left arm into the dead trunk on which he sat, Nathan pondered what to do. On the one hand, revenge, retribution would come faster with just the two of them in pursuit. On the other, with the hostilities between the two countries, their chances of ending up in a dingy Mexican jail for the next twenty years or in front of a firing squad was a hell of a lot more likely on their own than with an enlistment in the Texas Rangers.

Nathan nodded. "If we don't find them in San Antone, I reckon I'd be inclined to go with you. It might take a spell longer, but I got no pressing business at home. What about you, Barney."

Barney grinned. "Me neither." He paused, turning to stare at the hog-tied Mexican. His eyes narrowed. "What about this one?"

Pushing to his feet, Nathan slid the bowie from his sheath with a satiny sound. "I got my own ideas."

Torres eyes grew wide. He began to blubber.

Having ridden from town just before Nathan's arrival, Luis Salado had waited a few miles out of Nacogdoches for his cousin. When Torres failed to show up, Luis had ridden back to find him.

In town, he learned of Torres's capture, so he headed back to Bastrop to meet the others. From the trace, he spotted a fire deep in the woods. He left his pony a quarter of a mile down the road and slipped in close to the fire, thinking he might lay his hands on some easy money.

He lay silently, his black eyes taking in the scene before him. A cold chill ran down his spine. He had no intention of exposing himself just to help Torres, cousin or not. As soon as the opportunity presented itself, he would slip away.

CHAPTER TEN

Nathan took a menacing step toward the hogtied Mexican. Barney glanced at Jack Hays, but the cold-eyed ranger's face showed no emotion. Barney rose. "Hold on, Nathan."

The heavily muscled mountain man looked around at his father-in-law, his slate gray eyes blazing with impatience.

Torres looked up at the older man hopefully.

"I reckon I feel the same way you do, maybe more so because I raised my girl from the crib on. I nursed her through all them childhood sicknesses. But, while it'd warm my heart to send this jasper to hell, you and me both know Marie wouldn't want us to kill him personal. She'd want the law to do it."

Nathan's eyes grew dark. "The law? Like the sheriff back in Nacogdoches? You know as good as me, an hombre can't place no trust in the law. This is the only way to be certain."

Torres cringed against the trunk of the pecan. When he did, he winced as a coal he had scattered when he fell into the fire minutes earlier burned his hands. He jerked his hands aside, and then an idea born out of desperation popped into his head.

Jack Hays spoke up. "You forget, Nathan. This one's a greaser. Turn him over to the sheriff when we get to Bastrop, and he'll get hung. Probably before a trial. But your hands will be clean of him."

Flexing his fingers about the handle of the bowie, Nathan shook his head. "Then why waste time?"

Barney laid his hand on Nathan's shoulder. "Because you know as well as me that Marie wouldn't want his blood on your hands unless you got no choice." He paused. "It's getting dark. At least sleep on it tonight. In the morning is soon enough."

His black eyes pleading, Alfredo Torres looked up at Nathan.

Nathan hesitated, struggling against the furnace of bloodlust boiling his blood, a thirst for revenge he had learned well from the savage Karankawas. Still, Barney was right. Marie always believed in the law. Her quiet determination had acted as a soothing

89

salve on his impulsive anger.

Jack and Barney waited expectantly.

Before Nathan Cooper met Marie Willis back in '36, he would have ripped out the Mexican's throat without hesitation, then kicked his limp body aside and promptly boiled himself a cup of coffee.

She had changed him, tempering the savagery and cruelty instilled in him from his years with the Karankawa. In a sense, he told himself, a return to that savagery would be like slapping her in the face.

He drew a deep breath, then blew out through his lips. "Reckon you're right, Barney. Marie always went out of her way to give a hand to them that needed it. Even vermin like this one."

Jack and Barney grinned at each other.

Alfredo Torres sagged back against the tree trunk, his bound hands searching for the dying coal. He clenched his teeth when he found it. Delicately, he tried to place the rawhide binding his wrists on the smoldering coal.

While Barney set about putting together supper, Nathan and Jack led the horses down to the creek to fill their canteens and water the ponies. By now, night had settled over the forest.

■ ■ ■ ■

From where he lay hidden, Luis Salado realized this was his chance to slip away. He started to slip back, then froze as Torres leaped to his feet and jumped the older gringo.

Nathan jerked around as a yelp broke the silence, followed by a string of curses and then two booming reports of a Colt. He swung onto his roan and raced back to the camp.

Barney stood clutching his arm and staring into the darkness of the surrounding forest.

"Barney!" Nathan leaped from the saddle and hit the ground running. His keen eyes swept the camp, taking in the smoldering rawhide and the blood staining the sleeve of Barney's flannel shirt.

The older man spun, his face a mask of rage. "That damned little greaser caught me by surprise, Nathan. I had just took off my mackinaw when he grabbed my knife, and if I hadn't jumped back, he'd have laid me open like a hog. As it was, he just scratched my arm. More blood than anything." He pointed the muzzle of his Colt into woods. "He headed thataway."

Muttering a curse, Nathan bolted into the dark forest.

Jack ran into camp just as the shadows of the pines swallowed Nathan. "Nathan! Not tonight. Wait until morning. He won't get far."

Barney shook his head and muttered, "Waste of breath, Jack. Here, give me a hand with this arm."

For a moment, the two peered into the forest, which had grown silent as death. With a shake of his head, Jack rolled up Barney's bloody sleeve.

The older man cast a glance at the forest. "I'd sure hate to be in that greaser's boots about now."

Jack chuckled as he poured whiskey on the wound down Barney's forearm. "Reckon you're right. Nathan's got a head hard as an anvil. Why, I could tell you stories about him back in forty-one."

Barney grimaced. "Maybe so, but I could tell stories back in thirty-six that would turn the marrow of your bones to ice. You knew he spent time with the Karankawas?"

Jack nodded. "Yes."

"That man was a savage bear. Spent a couple years with them after leaving LaFitte, the pirate. Went trapping after he left the

Kronks. Years later, they stole his niece. That's when he lost part of his arm. Shot up, cut up. He tracked them Kronks for months, but he got the little girl back. Ruthie. That was her name." He paused and fought back the tears in his eyes. "At least the little thing had ten years or so to enjoy this old life."

Jack nodded, having heard the stories of Nathan Cooper several times. He snugged the knot on the bandage. "There. Good as new in a couple days."

With a groan of relief, Barney plopped down and leaned up against a dead log. He nodded to the whiskey. "A drop or two of that snake poison ought to be a boon to us tonight." He glanced at the dark skies beyond the sentinel pines. "Looks like this could be a night to put the hounds in the barn."

From his hiding spot, Luis Salado remained motionless, fearful of discovery, yet too curious over his cousin's fate to back away.

The fire had burned low when Nathan ghosted from the darkness into the firelight. Jack and Barney sat near the fire, sipping coffee.

A scalp dangled from the belt about

Nathan's waist. Without a word, he knelt by his saddlebags and deposited it inside his parfleche bag.

"Got things took care of, huh?" Barney muttered.

Nathan looked over his shoulder and nodded. "That's one of them."

Luis Salado's eyes grew wide when he saw the black scalp. His heart thudded against his chest, and he pressed his swarthy face into the ground to still his trembling muscles. Silently, he muttered a soft prayer. Later, after the three gringos slumbered, he slipped back to his horse.

That night, Nathan awakened with a start, drenched with cold sweat. He squeezed his eyes shut, trying to push the nightmare from his head, the same one he'd dreamed back on the banks of the Angelina River.

The weather along the Old San Antonio Road battered the three for several days, forcing them to lay over at a small tavern where the road forked south to Bastrop and west to Austin.

They sat around the fireplace that night sipping whiskey and laying plans in soft undertones. "I'm already a few days late,"

94

Jack said, "so I reckon tomorrow, I'll head on in to San Antone."

Leaning back in his chair, Nathan nodded. "We'll ride on down and see what we can find at Bastrop." He glanced at Barney, who nodded his agreement. "If we don't show up in San Antone in a few days, that means we found the other four."

To his relief, those nights in the tavern, Nathan slept peacefully, spared the horrifying nightmare.

At a table in the Colorado Saloon in Bastrop, Frank Selman pondered the identity of the big mountain man of whom Luis Salado had spoken, the one who had killed and scalped Alfredo Torres. He knew the hombre wasn't the law. The law didn't scalp. Studying the golden liquid in his glass, he reckoned the jasper had to be some kin to the three back at the cabin. That was the only explanation for the savagery. He figured Torres had told the jasper everything he knew.

Selman pursed his lips. The smart thing to do was light a shuck out of Bastrop just in case the hombre did ride in.

The chilling story of Torres' death had not seemed to bother his two partners, Red Davis and Otis Sims, for they were laughing

95

and whirling two Mexican *putas* about the puncheon dance floor. Both men had guzzled too much whiskey, and Selman was having second thoughts about the two accompanying him down to San Antonio, where he was going to join up with Padre Jarauta.

He scratched at his thick, black beard. Those two liked women too much, and from all he'd heard, many of the Mexican women traveled with their soldier husbands. And neither Red nor Otis had ever given any indication that the sacred vows of marriage were an obstacle to their own brand of fun.

In his gut, he knew there would be trouble. If he were smart, he'd distance himself from those two. He glanced out the rear door where the fourth member of his bunch, Luis Salado, slept in the barn. Now Luis, he could trust. For a Mexican, he displayed uncommonly good sense, better than Otis or Red. "Beats all," Selman muttered under his breath as he stared at the golden liquid in his whiskey glass. "I never reckoned I'd prefer the company of a greaser over my own kind."

With both arms around a lissome senorita and a bottle clutched in his hand, Red Davis shouted at Selman. "Come on, Frank.

96

Join in the fun."

Selman shook his head, drained his glass, and pushed to his feet. He pointed to the rear of the saloon. "I'm getting some shut-eye. You two best do the same. We're pulling out early in the morning."

As Selman closed the door to his room behind him, he wondered if maybe he should pick up Luis and the two of them ride on out. Head up to Austin instead of Gonzales. Maybe throw off the mountain man. It might be a tad farther, but it might be worth the time. Leave Red and Otis to whoever that big jasper was.

The next evening, Nathan and Barney rode into Bastrop just as darkness settled over the small village of log cabins and clapboard buildings. The only businesses open were two saloons, The Handlebar and The Colorado, one on either end of the muddy street that stretched two blocks.

Nathan hailed a farmer driving a wagon down the street. "Hate to bother you, partner, but where can a body find a place to bunk without fighting off the bedbugs?"

The bone-thin farmer grinned and pointed to the end of the street. "The Handlebar, I reckon. From what I hear, they change linens at least once a week whether

97

they need it or not."

Nodding thanks, Nathan and Barney continued down the street.

Tying up at the hitching rail, they ambled into the Handlebar, a dimly lit saloon and hostel with a roaring fire at one end of the room and a bar at the other. Several guests sat around the tables, feeding their gullets, quenching their thirst. None of them fit the descriptions given by Alfredo Torres.

The proprietor, John Tinsley, who resembled a cannonball, grinned amiably and welcomed them when they entered. For a dollar each, they could share a room, and for another dollar, stall their horses in the barn out back.

After dropping their bedrolls off in their room, Nathan and Barney headed back to the bar for a drink and a couple of plates of grub to put themselves around.

The food was plain, but filling, son-of-a-bitch stew with a dessert of plum duff, all washed down with several cups of steaming black coffee.

Around a mouthful of stew, Nathan mumbled, "Once we fill our bellies, I reckon it'll be time to start asking questions."

CHAPTER ELEVEN

After dinner, Nathan and Barney drifted to the bar, which unlike most make-do bars out on the frontier, sported a polished top and a brass foot rail.

The bartender, a jasper so skinny that if he'd had only one eye, he'd have looked like a needle, approached. "Evening, gents. What'll it be?"

"Whiskey."

Barney pulled out a cigar and offered one to Nathan, who declined. "Don't know what you're missing, Nathan. Nothing beats a good cigar and glass of whiskey after a solid meal."

"Never picked up the cigar habit."

"Here you go, gents," said the bartender, sliding two glasses brimming with whiskey in front of them. "Four bits a drink."

Nathan slid a small gold dollar on the bar. "Obliged."

The amiable bartender grinned at them.

"Where you be passing through from?"

"Back east."

"Heap of folks back yonder. Pretty wild out here." He surveyed Nathan from head to toe and added, "But from the looks of you old boys, mister, I don't reckon that bothers you none." The smile remained on his face.

Nathan sipped his whiskey. "We're looking for four men, three white, one Mexican. One has a beard, one red hair, one no teeth, and the Mexican we don't know."

For a fleeting second, the bartender studied Nathan, then shook his head. "Ain't seen them, partner. You might try the Colorado up the street. We're the only two saloons. Folks like you're talking about come to town, they usually hit us or the Colorado."

The small pendulum clock on the wall chimed once. Nathan glanced at the clock. Ten thirty. He downed his whiskey in one gulp. "Let's us take a walk, Barney."

Nodding, Barney finished off his whiskey and flipped the rawhide loop off the hammer of his Paterson Colt. "I'm with you."

Outside, the temperature had fallen, but the wind had lain, so the icy cold wasn't as penetrating. The sky remained overcast. The

100

night was black as pitch, the only light coming from a few lanterns hanging along the street between the two saloons.

A half-dozen heads turned as Nathan and Barney entered. They paused just inside to survey the room without seeing those whom they sought. After a moment, Nathan led the way to the bar, where a fat man wearing no shirt, just his longjohn top, watched through narrowed eyes.

Nathan plopped a gold eagle on the rough plank bar, then laid his iron T on it. "I'm buying information, barkeep," he stated in a low, but icy voice. "Four men, three white, one Mexican." He described them once again.

The bartender eyed the ten-dollar gold piece hungrily. "They was here. Pulled out this morning."

Barney caught his breath. "Where to?"

Lifting his eyebrows, the obese man replied, "Didn't say. Maybe Gonzales, maybe La Grange, maybe Austin. Take your choice."

Nathan studied him several seconds, his iron T still on the gold eagle. In a voice that left no doubt as to his determination, he said, "Any chance of someone around here knowing more about those jaspers?"

Swallowing hard, the bartender nodded at

two girls sitting at a table with two cow-pokes. "Them two gals was right friendly with the redheaded jasper and the skinny one with no teeth. They might know."

With a nod, Nathan pulled his prosthesis off the coin and with Barney following, made his way across the room.

The two cowpokes scowled up at them when they stopped at the table.

Nathan nodded. "Pardon me for butting in, boys, but it's worth a round of drinks if I can ask your lady friends a question. Then we'll be gone."

The two cowboys sized up the big man, and decided they didn't mind at all. "I got no problem," said one. "Jim Bob?"

He laughed nervously. "For a free drink, I sure ain't."

"Obliged," replied Nathan. He looked at the two curious senoritas. "The old boys you was with last night, the redhead and the skinny one. They say where they was heading?" He pulled out a gold eagle.

The girls eyed it greedily. "*Si*. Austin. They leave this morning."

Nathan nodded. In a voice cold as ice, he pointed to his cheek. "Did any of them have claw marks on their faces?"

One of the senoritas nodded. "*Si*. The redheaded one, he have them."

■ ■ ■ ■

The night remained overcast, offering not even a glimmer of light by which they could travel until false dawn, when an impatient Nathan Cooper and Barney Willis rode out of Bastrop, heading northwest to Austin.

Midafternoon, they reined up on the crest of a limestone hill and looked down on the small village, still in sad repair, although it was now the capital of the state.

"Don't look like much," Barney muttered.

"Well, believe it or not, that shabby collection of buildings down yonder has been the capital of the state for the last month or so."

A horse-drawn ferry carried them across the Colorado River, after which they followed a well-worn road to the top of the next hill.

Nathan reined up.

"What now?" Barney pulled up beside him.

"Reckon we'll find us somewhere to bed down, then get a lay of the land."

Austin, the capital of Texas since February 19, was about twice the size of Bastrop. Otherwise, a jasper could not tell much difference in the two villages.

From the activity on the street, Nathan figured the small town probably held three hundred or so citizens. At the end of the first block, he spotted a livery.

A wizened old man hobbled out to meet them. Leaning on his cane, he cackled, "Howdy, boys. What can I do for you?"

Nathan nodded. "Looking for a place to bed down for the night. Any suggestions?"

He pointed to the barn behind him with his walking cane. "The hay in here's cleaner than any of them saloons around here. Dollar to stable your hosses. Throw your soogans in the loft for free."

Barney grinned. "Don't reckon we can do no better'n that, Nathan."

Swinging down from the roan, Nathan agreed, "Don't reckon so."

The old man, Moses Payne, showed them the stable and the loft. "Roof is tight, so if it rains, you won't get wet. From the sign, I don't reckon we'll have a cold spell for another few days, so you old boys ought to be right comfortable."

Nathan noticed three ponies in the livery. As he uncinched his saddle, he nodded to them. "Good looking ponies. They for sale?"

Moses shook his head. "Nope. Customers. Three old boys rode in yesterday."

Barney and Nathan locked eyes.

Casually, Barney said, "We was to meet some fellers here. One has large beard, one's a redhead, and the other's got no teeth."

"Don't reckon they be the ones." He nodded to the three horses. "Those boys come down from Fort Worth heading to San Antone. They plan on joining up with the Texas Rangers down there and go to Mexico."

Nathan grunted and tossed his saddle up on a rail. "Where's the nearest place to get some grub?"

"Take your choice." The old man pointed down the main street. "Four saloons and one hotel. One'll kill you as fast as the others."

For the next two hours, Barney and Nathan prowled the muddy streets of the small village, learning nothing, even though they offered rewards for information.

Barney paused outside the door of the Golden Touch Saloon and stared at the sun dropping below the western horizon. "How do four jaspers just up and drop out of sight like this, Nathan? Someone must have seen them."

Nathan pondered his father-in-law's observation. "Sure seems that way." Drawing a deep breath, he added. "I reckon it's time to put ourselves around a steak and head back to the livery. Maybe we can figure out what to do next."

An hour later as they left the hotel after their steak, a young senorita approached from the shadows. She halted in front of Nathan and tightened the shawl over her head when she saw the iron T where his left hand should have been. She drew a deep breath. Her black eyes glittered in the light from the hotel as she tried to keep from looking at his arm. "You look for the gringo with red hair?"

Barney looked sharply at Nathan who touched his own cheek. "With scratch marks here?"

She nodded. *"Si. Si."* She touched her own fingers to her cheeks. "Very deep scratches, senor."

Nathan suppressed the excitement pounding in his blood. "You know where he is?"

"No, senor. Not now, but I know where he is going." She paused. "You will pay for information?"

"If it's good."

She smiled seductively. "He spend the night with me. He goes to Bexar. He leave early this morning."

Nodding slowly, Nathan asked, "Anyone with him?"

The young girl frowned, then shook her head. "I see no one, senor."

A grim smile played over Nathan's lips. He retrieved a gold eagle from his pocket and tossed to her. *"Gracias."*

She nodded. *"De nada."*

CHAPTER TWELVE

At sunset two days later, Barney and Nathan rode into the ranger garrison on the outskirts of San Antonio de Bexar, where ten years earlier 183 patriots held off 2,400 Mexicans for thirteen days.

When the massacre was over, all of the patriots except one were dead, along with 600 Mexican soldiers killed and wounded.

Ranger headquarters was a cluster of adobe huts surrounded by a dozen wood-stick *jacales* and three split-rail corrals.

Jack Hays, a broad grin on his youthful face, hurried to meet Nathan and Barney. He shook their hands vigorously and invited them into his quarters. He gestured to some rough-hewn chairs. "Sit yourselves." He uncorked a bottle of Old Crow and poured three tumblers full. "What's happened since I left you?"

Barney grunted wryly and rubbed his

posterior. "Not much, other than a heap of saddle sores."

Jack handed them a drink and frowned. "Sorry to hear that."

"It isn't all bad. One of them is here," Nathan explained. "We followed them up to Austin where we lost three of them. The fourth, the redhead, he's in San Antone."

Barney sipped his whiskey. "Yep. And we figure them others is here too."

Jack nodded thoughtfully. "That fits in with some of the intelligence we've been picking up. Seems like Jarauta has been recruiting gunnies hereabouts to go into Mexico with him and Canales. Paying two hundred a month we hear, but we can't pin it down for certain."

Nathan chuckled. Skepticism filled his voice. "Those old boys are dumber than I thought. Even if they go down there with Jarauta and Canales, they won't come out with two hundred a month. Canales will kill them first."

With a crooked grin, Jack Hays remarked, "Then just sit back and relax, Nathan. Let Canales do the job for you."

Nathan's eyes grew cold. "That's one job I want to take care of myself."

Nodding slowly, the ranger colonel replied, "I don't blame you." He paused, then added, "Reckon you'll be prowling the San Antone streets after those old boys. Take care. There's about eight hundred souls in Bexar, and about seven hundred and ninety-nine are Mexicans. There ain't no love lost for gringos down there."

Barney drained his whiskey. "We don't aim no hurt at nobody except those four hombres."

"Maybe so," said Jack. "But Mexicans are a mighty suspicious and clannish bunch, especially towards the Anglo. Wisest move you could make is spend the night here and start your search in the morning. It's harder than tying a knot in a bobcat's tail to get a lay of the land down there at night."

Nathan rose and stretched his arms over his head. "That's the best offer we've had today, Jack. Where do we stable our horses?"

As they swung into their saddles next morning after a breakfast of beans and tortillas, Jack reminded them, "You're welcome back tonight. And if you run into trouble, give a shout."

A half-dozen dirt streets intersected by a half-dozen more made up San Antonio de Bexar proper. On either side of the muddy streets were block-long adobe walls with an

110

arbor in front. Doorways cut into the adobe led to the various businesses.

Merchants selling everything from goats to corn to melons displayed their goods under the arbors; bazaars filled the plazas; senoritas lounged around the wells; laughing vaqueros sat in the shade of arbors in front of adobe cantinas drinking their tequila and, in the poorer establishments, pulque.

Rickety *carretas* with large slab-wood wheels pulled by lazy oxen or tiny burros rattled down the streets, cutting deep ruts into the mud. Wings flapping, startled chickens darted from in front of the carts, then quickly resumed clucking and scratching. Wiry-haired pigs grunted and rooted along the sides of the adobe buildings. The stench of mold and manure hung in the air.

All eyes turned on Nathan and Barney as they rode into town. Several vaqueros sitting beneath the arbor of a cantina watched as the two gringos rode into the livery across the street.

Nathan reined up and eyed the diminutive liveryman. "*¿Cuánto?* How much?"

The small peon in baggy white blouse and pants shuffled his feet. "Two pesos."

"Sounds fair," said Nathan. Dismounting, he handed the reins to the smaller man and

111

dropped eight pesos in his hand. "We'll be back for our ponies after dark. Anything happens to them, I'll burn this place down. *¿Comprende?*"

Clutching the coins greedily, the frightened liveryman nodded emphatically. "*Si, senor.* I watch. Pablo, he watches well."

Leaving the livery, Nathan and Barney headed for the first cantina. The laughing vaqueros suddenly grew silent, the smiles on their faces turning to frowns of suspicion.

Noticing the sudden silence, Nathan muttered to Barney, "Pay them no mind. Let's go inside."

The cantina was dark and warm. Twelve-inch-thick adobe walls held heat in the winter and repelled it in the summer. Thick logs four feet apart spanned the room to support the ceiling. Thin poles laid side by side covered the logs, and in turn, several layers of smaller limbs crisscrossed the poles, which were then covered with a foot of dirt.

A slight Mexican watched from behind the bar as the two gringos entered. In one shadowy corner, two older men sat at a small table, cradling cups of pulque in leathery hands.

Nathan nodded to the small bartender. *"Buenos días."*

The slight man nodded. "*Buenos días,* senors. How may I serve you?"

"We're looking for four men, senor." Nathan replied, then quickly described them. When he finished, the bartender shook his head.

"I do not know of these of which you seek, senor. I am sorry."

After Nathan and Barney left, one of the older peons scurried up to the bartender. "Diego! That one, the one with one arm. He is the one of which my brother told us last night. He is the one who takes the scalp of Rico Torres' brother, Alfredo."

The bartender's eyes narrowed. "You are certain, Agustin?"

The old man nodded emphatically. "*Si.* Senon was told in the plaza yesterday by the one who witnessed the one-arm man taking the scalp. He, Luis, was forced to fight off the gringo to save his own life."

Diego eyed Agustin narrowly. "Luis, you say. Not Luis Salado?"

"*Si.* Luis Salado."

Diego lifted a skeptical eyebrow. "Luis has never shown courage. He is a mouse who would run before he fights. He is known as a teller of lies."

Agustin shrugged. "*¿Quién sabe?* All of

which I speak is what I was told."

Diego nodded. "*Si.* I understand. We must spread the word. If that gringo is the one of which Luis speaks, then he must be avoided. We must tell him nothing."

The answer was the same for Nathan and Barney in every cantina, every meat shop, every granary, every vegetable stand, and every general store. It was a long morning.

Barney removed his hat and stared up at the cold winter sun directly overhead. He ran his fingers through his thinning hair. "I don't know about you, Nathan, but I'm beginning to get the feeling nobody ain't going to tell us nothing. They all look mighty suspicious-like."

Nathan chuckled and rolled his massive shoulders. His slate gray eyes scanned the muddy street, aware of the black eyes following them. "Don't give up, Barney. I've never seen a gold double eagle fail." He glanced around. "You can't tell. Why, someone might be watching us at this minute, waiting to catch us when no one is around."

Barney grunted, and in a wry voice, remarked, "From what I've seen of them, what they're waiting to do to us ain't what I would consider joyful."

Nathan arched an appreciative eyebrow. "I'm impressed. I didn't figure you'd caught the looks they been throwing at us." He paused and patted his belly. "I don't know about you, but I'm ready for something solid. Those beans and tortillas this morning don't hold a jasper too long."

"You ain't getting no argument out of me," the older man laughed. He looked around the plaza, clearly puzzled. "Any idea where to go?"

Nathan nodded to a general store and cafe, one of the few businesses with wood clapboard walls and glass windows. "Let's see what we can find in there. Overton's."

A white man about Barney's height, but fifty pounds lighter and wearing a stained white apron, nodded when the two entered through the open doorway. "Howdy, strangers. My name's Tim Overton. This here is my place of business. Now what can I do for you?"

Nathan studied the man's slender face as he replied. "A question or two, if you don't mind."

The store owner's smile flickered, but remained steady. He glanced past Nathan's shoulder and spotted four grim Mexicans at the door looking in. He smoothed the few strands of thinning hair over his bald head.

115

"Well, boys, I ain't much in the business of questions. If I was, reckon my family would be starving. But seeing you're my own kind, I'd be obliged to offer any help."

Despite the amiability of the storeowner, Nathan sensed shiftiness. He described the men for whom they searched. When the slight merchant shook his head, Nathan shrugged. "Hope you help us on the next one. My partner and me are looking for someplace to get us a solid meal of steak and potatoes. The thin rations of these folks around here don't go too far."

Overton chuckled. "Reckon I know what you mean." He shot a warning glance at the four dark-complexioned peons at the door. "Through that door back there is my café. I got me a cook who fries up the best steaks in this part of Texas. He'll load you a plate of steak and potatoes you'll be hard-pressed to finish. I've even got a keg of beer to wash it down with."

Barney glanced at Nathan in delight. Nathan nodded to the merchant. "Sounds good."

Overton called out, "Antonio!"

A thin voice came from the rear. "*Si*, Senor Tim."

"Fix these old boys a heaping plate of steak and potatoes."

As Barney and Nathan filed through the doorway to the cafe, Tim Overton threw a warning glance at the surly caballeros in the doorway.

With a brief nod of understanding, they broke apart and disappeared.

Despite the hair bristling on the back of his neck, Nathan kept his eyes forward. Whatever was going to happen would not be here, or now.

CHAPTER THIRTEEN

Nathan paused in the doorway and scanned the room. In one corner, two men hunched over plates of frijoles were seated at a table. The other tables were empty.

The furniture was rough hewn, but sturdy. The room was snug and warm, heated by the fireplace in the rear wall. Nathan slid into a chair next to the wall.

Overton hadn't told any stretcher about Antonio's magic with steak and potatoes, and the beer drawn from a keg cooled in the nearby San Antonio River was an unexpected pleasure.

After the meal, Barney leaned back and pulled out a black cigar. He puffed contentedly until he noticed Nathan slowly ease his Colt from its holster and lay it in his lap. A frown knit the older man's forehead.

Nathan muttered, "Don't make no sudden moves. Nothing going on right now, and if I can, I don't plan on letting it happen at all."

With a brief nod, Barney whispered, "What?"

A tiny smile ticked up a corner of Nathan's lips. "Something. Just wait for my move." He glanced across the kitchen at the cook. "Antonio!"

The Mexican cook looked around, a broad grin on his face. "*Si*, senor."

Nathan flipped him a coin and with his iron T, patted his belly. *"Muy bueno. Delicioso."*

The rotund cook caught the coin with a fat hand and nodded amiably. *"Gracias,* senors. *Gracias."*

"And Antonio," Nathan added. "Would you ask Senor Tim to come back a minute?"

Antonio nodded vigorously and disappeared through the doorway. Moments later, Tim Overton entered, an affable smile on his thin face. "Well, boys. How was it?"

"Just like you said. Of course, I didn't have any idea what you set up for dessert, but I don't reckon it's nothing I'd care for," Nathan replied as he pulled his Colt from under the table. "Now, if you want to see the sun come up tomorrow, you best hope there's nobody waiting out front for us, especially those young caballeros I spotted in the doorway."

Overton's face froze. His eyes grew icy, but when he looked down the muzzle of the Paterson .36, he made up his mind fast. He licked his lips. "You boys are making a mistake."

Nathan grunted, "Partner, I've made so damned many mistakes in my life that one more won't hurt." He pushed to his feet. "Ready, Barney?"

With a grim smile on his face, Barney rose, Colt in hand. "I never been readier."

Nathan approached Overton. "Let's go. It's your hand now. Play it out the way you started, and I'll bust your spine with lead plums."

The slight merchant gulped, then stumbled toward the front. Still several feet from the door, Nathan halted. "Go on, Overton. Call them off."

For a moment, Overton hesitated. He reached out for the pickle barrel to steady himself, then stumbled to the doorway. "Back off, caballeros, back off. He's got a gun on me."

"Now," Nathan growled softly. "Step outside."

Overton did as he was told.

Nathan and Barney stepped out beside him. The street was deserted, but Nathan felt eyes from the darkness behind the open windows staring at them. In a cold voice that left no question in Overton's mind that the big mountain man meant every single word, Nathan said, "I've had enough lead dug out of me to fight the Alamo all over. We're going to keep searching for these jaspers, and if we get jumped, I'm coming back for you, and that thin patch of hair you're wearing will go on my belt." He paused, his gray eyes burning into the slight merchant's. "You best believe me, Overton. For your own sake, you best believe I'm not lying."

Tim Overton stood trembling under the arbor in front of his store, knees shaking, and his stomach churning with fear as the two Texians turned their backs on him and walked away.

After they disappeared around the corner, he hurried down the street to the cantina of Castel where Red Davis was enjoying the young senoritas.

The remainder of the afternoon was as fruitless as the morning, but the tension hanging in the air had grown thick as molasses on fried johnnycakes.

When they pushed through the doorway of one cantina, Barney muttered under his breath, "I keep expecting a sharp blade through my ribs every second, Nathan."

"I was half expecting it too," the big mountain man replied.

"You know some of them greasers is following us."

With a wry grunt, Nathan muttered, "What did you expect? They're trying to build up nerve, find the right moment — but maybe they won't."

Barney frowned at him. "They won't? Why not?"

"Overton. I don't know who he is, or what sort of position he has around here, but he's important. And apparently, he took my promise to heart."

As the sun dropped below the stark black line of the western horizon in a blaze of gold and red, Barney plopped down on a bench outside a meat shop and rubbed his feet. The rancid smell of butchered goat and beef filled the air. "I don't know about you, but I'm just about wore out. That offer old Jack Hays made this morning looks mighty fetching. A hot meal, a couple drinks, and a bed would suit me just fine."

Nathan looked around. Across the street was a plaza slowly coming to life as the night's shadows began creeping in, chilling the small village. Several children played about the rock-walled water well. Under the tall, spindly mesquite, the yellow glow of dangling lanterns punched holes in the encroaching darkness, and gay voices echoed from the shadows of the bazaars surrounding the plaza.

"Tell you what, Barney. I reckon we've done a good day's work. Let's pick up our ponies and head back out to the ranger garrison."

Despite most of the population having returned to their homes for the night, many eyes watched the two gringos make their way along the dark streets.

As they approached an unlit plaza further down the street, Nathan's animal senses screamed a warning. Without breaking stride, he muttered from the corner of his lips, "Someone's up ahead, Barney."

The older man caught his breath. His eyes searched the darkness around them. "I don't see nothing."

"There. The plaza. They're waiting for us. Get that Colt ready. And when the trouble starts, act fast."

Two *carretas* sat in the plaza, several yards apart, and just as Nathan and Barney reached the midpoint between the rickety carts, a rush of feet broke the silence.

Surprising his attackers, Nathan bolted

toward the shadows converging on him. Using the muzzle of his Colt like a club, he slammed one shadow across the temple, dropping him like a sack of corn seed. In the same motion, he sidestepped and hooked the T into the clothing of the second assailant and spun, whipping the surprised jasper off his feet and sending him tumbling head over heels to the muddy street. The third shadow jerked to a halt, then turned and vanished into the night.

Nathan spun to go to Barney's aid, but the burly man was looking down at a limp body on the ground. He relaxed and with a chuckle, muttered, "You do all right for an old man."

Barney stared into the darkness that was Nathan's face. "Go to hell," he laughed.

During the last three blocks to the livery, Barney muttered under his breath, "I got me the distinct feeling we're still being followed."

Nathan chuckled. "Don't worry. They're just watching. After back there, they don't have the stomach."

The ranger garrison was a quarter of a mile beyond the last adobe, a few hundred yards past a small creek. By now, the crescent moon had risen, casting a dim glow over the stark landscape. A few clouds moved past, and in the moonlight, the mesquite threw spindly black shadows like witch's fingers against the bluish ground.

In the distance, a rabbit squealed in terror as a hunting owl carried it away.

The shoes of their ponies echoed hollowly off the wooden bridge, a staccato report that almost smothered the soft voice at the end of the bridge. "Senor."

Nathan stiffened, wondering if his ears were playing tricks.

The voice broke the silence again. "Senor. *Por favor.*"

"Whoa, boy," Nathan said, reining up and looking around.

The trembling voice hesitated. "You are the gringo that takes scalps?"

"Maybe," Nathan growled.

The voice hastily said, "Then you are the one. Do not dismount, senor. No one must know I am here, but one of those you seek, the one with red hair. I know where he is."

CHAPTER FOURTEEN

Barney reined up beside Nathan, staring into the shadows of his face. Nathan nodded imperceptibly, then said, "How much?"

"No, senor. The one with red hair, he rape and beat my sister. He is with her now. I fear for her life. When I hear a gringo *el Diablo* searches for that one, I thank *la Madre Santa.*"

The hair on the back of Nathan's neck bristled. Keeping his eyes fixed on Barney, he replied. "Where is he?"

"You know the cantina across from the Alamo where you were today? Castel's?"

"Go on."

"He is in the last room at the top of the stairs. My cousin, Platon, owns the cantina. He is the one who tells me where my sister was taken."

For several seconds, Nathan pondered the information. Finally, in a cold voice, he replied, "If this is *la mentira, una artimaña*

126

— a lie, a trick — I will destroy the cantina; I will find you and your family, and I will take all of your scalps."

A distressed voice replied feebly, "I do not lie, senor. My name is Santo Esquivel. I am well known. You will have no trouble finding me."

A grin curled Nathan's lips. *"Gracias,* amigo. *Muchas gracias."*

"Be careful, senor. The redheaded one, he has gringo friends at the cantina."

Slowly, Nathan turned his roan about and headed back to San Antonio. Barney pulled up beside him. "What if it's a trap?"

After a few moments, Nathan chuckled. "I got a gut feeling he was telling the truth, but if it is a trap, those old boys are going to be mighty remorseful of the day they was born."

At the first adobe on the outskirts of town from which a light shone, Nathan pulled up and offered a gold eagle for a small lantern and a clay *olla* filled with oil.

Barney laughed. "You ain't thinking what I'm thinking you're thinking, is you?"

Nathan grinned at his father-in-law. "I reckon I be thinking just that. We'll take our time. See how the land lays. This jasper's on the second floor. If there's a way to get in from above, I will. If not, then we'll burn the damn place and kill the bastard when he tries to escape."

With a grunt, Barney nodded. "That's what I always liked about you, Nathan. You never beat around. You always got right to the nut-cuttin'."

"I got a feeling," he replied, "that when we ride in, there won't much time for anything but hot lead and cold steel."

Slumped over their ponies, they wound their way deeper into the village, always staying in the shadows. From time to time, clouds moved overhead, casting welcome shadows over the streets. Strains of guitar music drifted over the village, punctuated with gay laughter and festive cries.

From where the two Texians sat on the ponies in the shadows of an adobe at the corner of the block, the cantina was the only two-story building around. The windows were all shuttered.

Whether there was another exit, they couldn't tell, but Nathan's patience was running too thin to spend more time scouting the area. Without taking his eyes off of the cantina, Nathan muttered. "You know what to do. When we bust in, I'll throw the oil, grab my hogleg, and head up the stairs. You toss the lantern. It'll take a few seconds to catch fire. By the time those hombres figure out what's happened, I'll be upstairs." He looked around at his father-in-law. In a grim voice filled with finality, he added. "You might have to kill somebody."

Barney nodded. "I'll carry out my end. Kill the worthless trash, Nathan. You hear me. Kill him."

Leaving their horses tied in the shadows, the two Texians shuffled across the dusty street and paused on either side of the heavy door of the cantina.

Nathan looked at Barney, who drew a deep breath, and nodded.

Stepping inside the cantina, Nathan paused, accustoming his eyes to the shadows of the small room.

A grizzled cowpoke in front of the fireplace jumped to his feet, shucking his six-gun. "I know you. You're the one what killed Torres and scalped him. Well, I'm going to send you to hell."

"Not if I send you first," Nathan shouted, hurling the clay *olla* at the gunman and shucking his Colt. In the next moment, he put two lead plums in the gunman's chest,

129

knocking him back into the fireplace, where the flames exploded.

And then, without hesitation, Nathan leaped up the stairs like a cougar.

Behind him, Barney hurled the lantern, igniting the remainder of the oil and turning the dead gunman and the interior of the cantina into an inferno.

More gunfire rang out; men cursed; women screamed.

A single, frantic shout rang out: "Red!"

Barney glimpsed Nathan disappearing at the top of the stairs. By that time, a half-dozen frantic patrons were scrambling to escape the roaring fire. Barney dropped into a crouch behind an overturned table and waited.

The commotion downstairs emptied the rooms above.

Hanging lanterns lit the hallway on the second floor. When Nathan reached the top of the stairs, a flood of screaming customers and courtesans shoved him back.

Pressing up against the wall, he peered over the panicking crowd for a head with red hair. A sense of despair washed over him, crushing the hopes that had grown within him in the last hour.

Suddenly, he spotted a tassel of red hair.

The face turned toward him, and their eyes met. Nathan saw the fear in the eyes of the man called Red.

When he spotted Nathan, he turned and fled.

With a growl, the large mountain man shoved stumbling people aside and burst through the crowd after the fleeing man.

At the end of the hall, Red slammed through a door and disappeared into the night.

Nathan drew up at the open door. Clouds had covered the moon, and the night was black as pitch. Suddenly the clouds parted, and Nathan spotted Red racing across the rooftops. Without hesitation, he shoved his Colt in the holster, shucked his bowie, and dashed after the fleeing man.

The smaller man was as agile as a young bobcat, leaping walls between roofs. At the end of the block, he swung over the side and dropped to the ground.

Nathan hesitated when he reached the end of the building. He caught a fleeting glimpse of Red Davis disappearing around the corner building in the next block, heading for the plaza. Nathan leaped to the ground, nine feet below, his muscular legs absorbing the shock. Seconds later, he rounded the corner and squinted at a shadow disappearing into the plaza among the darker shadows of *carretas* and small herds of goats.

Without warning, the night grew black as clouds covered the moon. Nathan dropped to one knee at the corner of a building, peering into the darkness and straining his ears for the slightest hint of Davis' movements.

Across the plaza came the soft bleating of goats, the rumbling of stomachs as cattle regurgitated their food, and the faint creaking of mesquite limbs squeaking against each other with the breeze.

Squinting his eyes in an effort to penetrate the darkness, Nathan struggled desperately for some indication of where Davis had disappeared. He froze as he heard a faint squeak of wood against wood. A chill ran up his back.

Overhead, the clouds broke. Nathan pressed up against the adobe wall, scanning he plaza. There was no movement, no sound. Behind him, he heard the screams from the burning cantina and the pounding of frantic footsteps fleeing the inferno.

From time to time came a familiar scratching sound, but try as he might, Nathan couldn't place the soft noise. He studied the plaza. It was walled in on three sides, and he had seen no light to indicate Davis' flight into one of the surrounding buildings.

Chances were that Davis was still in the plaza.

Then his mind began winnowing through what had taken place in the last few minutes: goats, cattle, and two *carretas,* one by the water well, the other on the far side of the plaza.

Nathan listened intently. The squeaking he had earlier heard — could it have been one of the rickety carts?

A few minutes later, he heard the same faint, but familiar sound — the unmistakable grating of wood against wood. The slight breeze couldn't trigger such movement, only a heavier weight, such as a man's boot shifting on wood. He peered in the direction of the *carreta* by the well.

After several seconds of silence, the soft grating once again drifted across the plaza. Flexing his finger about his Colt, he eased forward into the shadows toward the sound. Only a few feet ahead, the dark silhouette of the *carreta* took shape.

Overhead, the clouds parted.

Suddenly, teeth bared in a savage snarl, Red Davis leaped to his feet in the *carreta* and fired at Nathan. An orange plume illumined the night.

As soon as Nathan spotted movement, he

threw himself aside and touched off a shot.

Davis jerked his head around, screamed, and grabbed his right eye. He spun and fell into the well with a loud splash.

Holstering his Colt, Nathan pulled his bowie and rushed to the well, but by now, lights were coming on around the plaza. He hesitated, his fingers flexing about the handle of his knife. He had sworn to take five scalps, but there was no time to fish this one from the well.

CHAPTER FIFTEEN

The sound of hooves jerked Nathan around as Barney reined his sorrel to a halt. He was leading Nathan's roan.

"We best light a shuck out of here," Barney drawled, nodding to the windows around the plaza lighting up.

For a moment, Nathan hesitated, then sheathed the bowie and swung into his saddle.

Five minutes later, they reached the outskirts of town and left the small village behind.

Next morning, Barney peered out the window of the barracks as Jack Hays and a small contingent of Texas Rangers met with the sheriff of San Antonio. He glanced over his shoulder at Nathan, who was sitting on his bunk sharpening his knife. "They be too far away to hear what he's saying, but from the look on the sheriff's face, he's mighty put out about something."

With a chuckle, Nathan muttered, "I reckon he didn't take too kindly to one of his buildings getting all burnt up last night."

Barney turned around and pulled out a cigar. "Well, whatever he was so het up about, he's said his piece. Him and his boys are riding off back to town."

Nathan grunted. "Reckon we'll find out soon enough."

At that moment, Jack Hays, followed by two grinning rangers, pushed through the door. With a wry note in his voice, he said, "Hope you boys enjoyed yourselves last night in town. I don't reckon it'd be any too smart on your part to go back in."

"Oh? That what the sheriff said?"

Hays laughed. "That and heap more." He paused, looking at Nathan expectantly.

"Well," Nathan began, sheathing his bowie and buckling his gunbelt about his waist, "I reckon that old boy had best get himself accustomed to us, because there's three more jaspers hiding out in San Antone that Barney and me are going to dig out."

Jack shook his head. "They ain't there no more, Nathan."

Barney frowned. "What's that?"

The slight ranger colonel hooked his thumb over his shoulder at one of the iron-jawed rangers behind him. "Boys, this here is John Henry Brown and Jesse Zumwalt. They rode in yesterday with orders and intelligence I figure would be of some use to you."

Nathan and Barney nodded. "What kind of intelligence?" Nathan asked.

"You tell him, John Henry. You two was there."

John Henry Brown hitched up his gunbelt and limped forward, his rugged jaw covered by a week-old growth of wiry whiskers. "Me and Jesse here was coming in with orders from the governor for the colonel here and his men to report to Fort Isabel down on the coast when we spotted a passel of Mexicans heading our way. We hid out until they passed, about forty of them. What got our attention was one of the gringos riding with them, an owlhoot with the handle of Frank Selman. I know him from New Orleans."

Nathan stiffened. "Selman? Black beard?"

John Henry glanced briefly at Hays, then replied, "Yep, and with him was Tomas Cristobal."

"Cristobal?" Nathan frowned at Hays.

With a terse nod, Hays explained. "Cristobal is Padre Celedonia de Jarauta's right-hand man. If Selman was with him, then

137

you can bet your last plugged nickel those others you're after are on the way to Mexico."

"Are you right certain it was this Cristobal jasper you saw? I'd hate to take off in the wrong direction."

For a moment, the ranger's eyes blazed. He nodded and laid his hand on his leg. "Cristobal is the one who gave me this gimpy leg. There ain't no way I'll ever forget that greasy face of his."

Barney spoke up. "Was another white man with Selman?"

John Henry frowned at Jesse. "I didn't notice. You see one, Jesse?"

The slender ranger thought a moment, then nodded. "A skinny one. Riding alongside the one with the beard."

Barney turned to Nathan with a grim smile. "Looks like the three of them are still together."

"Looks that way," replied Nathan.

"What I told you earlier is coming about, Nathan," Hays remarked. "Those three have gone to Mexico to join Jarauta, who I heard has also hooked up with Mariano Parades, the ex-president of Mexico. You want those three, then you got no choice. Two Texians all alone in Mexico now will get themselves killed. We're pulling out for the mouth of the Nueces River in the morning."

Nathan hesitated. "The Nueces?"

"Yep. From the latest intelligence reports, Jarauta and Parades are somewhere between the Nueces and Matamoros. They haven't joined up with Canales yet, as far as we know. We're ordered to scout the country between the Nueces and Point Isabel for sign of Canales."

"What's at Point Isabel?"

"General Zack Taylor and fifteen hundred American troops. Soldiers and marines."

Barney frowned at Nathan. "What are U.S. troops doing there?"

"I got no idea. Jack?"

Devil Jack Hays grinned slyly. "U.S. troops are always where there's a war."

"But we ain't at war with Mexico," protested Barney.

Hays' grin grew wider. "Not yet, but there's been a heap of saber rattling."

The frown on Nathan's face deepened.

Jack explained, "Governments ain't no different than men. They got a bellyache, they're going to complain. Mexico claims the U.S. shouldn't have annexed Texas. The president as much as told Mexico to go to hell when he sent Zack Taylor and troops to the border, which is the Nueces River."

Barney scratched his head. "So how'd Taylor get to Point Isabel?"

"Last July, the Mexican army attacked Taylor and he drove them back across the Rio Grande. And now, that's where the U.S. wants to make the border. The Mexes say no." He shrugged. "It don't take a genius to figure out what's going to happen next."

Nathan laughed. "Don't reckon it does."

Barney buckled up his gunbelt. "Well then, Colonel Hays. How do we go about signing up with that group of cowboys you call rangers?"

The next morning, Colonel Jack Hays and a dozen rangers, including Nathan and Barney, forming Hays First Regiment of Texas Mounted Volunteers, rode out of San Antonio across 140 miles of South Texas prairie thick with large patches of spiny chaparral, rattlesnakes, wild hogs, rangy longhorns, sudden thunderstorms, deadly lightning, and a dozen other ways to send an hombre stumbling down the stairway to hell before he knew what hit him.

During the seven-day duration of the journey, the twelve-man regiment swelled as more volunteers caught up with them, one of them the company adjutant, Rip Ford. Hays laughed when he explained that Ford's nickname, Rip, stood for rest in peace, for he was unforgiving of his enemies and quick with a handgun, a deadly combination that made for a good Texas Ranger.

When they reached Point Isabel, twenty-five miles from Fort Texas and Matamoras, Sam Walker was waiting. He reported that a thousand specially designed .44 Colts were being manufactured for the rangers. Also waiting was another Texas Ranger regiment under the command of Colonel George T. Wood that had been formed by Governor J. Pinckney Henderson.

Rangers continued to report. Ben McCullough rode in leading fifty rugged rangers. By the end of April, the ranger companies were at full strength, almost a thousand strong — a thousand unruly, restless hardcases more accustomed to fighting than sitting.

Hays and Wood had their hands full controlling the independent-minded rangers. A good day was when they didn't have to break up more than a half-dozen fights.

Nathan and Sam Walker were appointed scouts for Hays' regiment; Barney was appointed aide to the adjutant, Rip Ford. "Look, Barney," Hays explained after taking the older man aside, "I know you want to be out there with Nathan, but I need someone here who can read and write." He paused and looked square into Barney's eyes. "You understand what I'm saying? Besides, you'll have your fill of fighting. Old Rip never misses a fight."

"That being the case," Barney replied, "I don't reckon I mind at all."

The rangers bivouacked on the gulf side of the army encampment, for the prevailing winds were from the south, carrying the odors and stench of the mile-square encampment north over the saltgrass prairie.

The first night in camp, Nathan awakened in a cold sweat from the nightmare, the first he'd had in weeks.

For the next three nights in a row, he had the same dream, the same one he'd had that night on the Angelina, and again the night he scalped Torres.

He was standing just inside the forest at his home, watching as the five scavengers massacred his family and burned their bodies. His feet were rooted to the ground, and when he screamed, no words came from his lips. All he could do was helplessly look on.

On the fourth morning, a distant sound like thunder jerked him from his nightmare. He sat up abruptly. Pushing to his feet, he drew a scoop of water from the barrel and poured it over his head.

From behind, a wry voice said, "Bad dream?" At that moment, the thunder boomed again to the west.

Ignoring the question, Nathan turned to Jack. "That what I think it is?"

The slight colonel nodded and pointed to the general's tent. "Cannon fire. Old Zack wants to see me. I'll be back directly."

A grim smile played over Nathan's lips. "I hope so. All this waiting is making me mighty edgy. I'm ready to pay a visit to Jarauta and Canales."

Jack grinned. "It might be sooner than you imagine. I got a feeling we're about ready to hitch up the wagons."

Watching Jack walk away, Nathan couldn't help remembering the nightmare. Four nights in a row. Why? From his years living with the religious beliefs of the Karanka-was, he knew the dream was a premonition, but of what?

General Zachary Taylor was short and heavy, with pronounced wrinkles and gray hair under a enlisted man's forage cap. He wore a faded green coat over gray trousers two sizes too large for him. He looked up from his desk when the slight ranger colonel entered the tent, and nodded. "Howdy, Jack. Have a seat."

Hays nodded, familiar with the general's homespun ways, a demeanor that would be an asset in Old Rough and Ready's run for the presidency three years later. "Obliged, General."

Taylor gestured to the cannon fire. "I'd like to know what that's all about."

With a crooked grin, Hays replied, "Hell, that's no problem, General. We'll find out for you."

The older man chuckled. "I reckoned you could." Hays rose, but Taylor stopped him. "One more thing, Jack. The army thrives on discipline. Your rangers don't have any. They're setting a bad example for my marines."

Devil Jack laughed. "The only discipline we got, General, is when we fight. I reckon that'll have to satisfy you and the army."

After Jack rode away, Nathan stared across the prairie in the direction of the cannon fire. Barney came to stand at his side. "What's all this about that Canales Mex? I heard you and Jack talking about him once before."

Nathan's gray eyes turned to ice as he stared into the past. "Friend of mine from around Goliad named Ewen Cameron got on the wrong side of Canales a few years back. He was one of them old boys of the Mier Expedition. You remember it?"

Barney nodded, his face hard, his eyes cold. "The black bean episode. What Texan don't?"

"Yep. A hundred and seventy Texians drew beans. Seventeen of the beans were black. Those that drew the black ones were shot. Cameron drew a white one, but Canales persuaded Santa Anna to execute him anyway." He paused and looked around at Barney. "Seems like sometime earlier, a Mex stole Cameron's horse. Cameron got it back, but Canales sided with the Mex and court-martialed Cameron. Cameron was acquitted, and Canales never forgave him. When he saw the chance to get back, he did. That's what the Canales business is all about."

"He got that much influence with Santa Anna?"

Nathan nodded grimly.

Squatting by the fire, Barney poured a cup of coffee and offered it to Nathan. "We'll catch up with them sooner or later."

Nathan squatted and took the coffee. "I'm not made for sitting around, but I reckon this is one time we've got to. With conditions like they are between the two countries, those old boys over there would shoot first, then ask questions."

Thirty minutes later, Devil Jack Hays, accompanied by Sam Walker, swung down from his piebald stallion. Walker remained in his saddle. Jack grinned at Nathan. "You got your wish."

Nathan frowned.

Hays continued. "Old Zack wants you and Sam to ride down to Fort Texas across the river from Matamoras and see what's going on. Seems like there might be a little trouble."

CHAPTER SIXTEEN

A wiry jasper, Sam Walker stood a couple of inches shorter than Nathan, but his muscles of banded steel were a close match to the mountain man's.

Pulling out of camp, they headed west, staying down in the *hondonadas* washed out by runoff rainwater. The Gulf Coast prairie was flatter than a wet saddle blanket. Keen eyes could pick up movement at considerable distances, but down in the gullies, only their heads appeared above the waving grass.

The thunder and roar of cannon fire grew louder. Midafternoon, Walker reined up. "Them Mexicans is sure lambasting Fort Texas. We best go on foot from here, Nathan. A mile or so yonder ahead is a rise. Beyond is Fort Texas and the Rio Grande. Them Mexes figure all this land back to the Nueces belongs to them, so I wouldn't at all be surprised to find a heap of them around that ridge yonder."

Tying their ponies in a *seco hoyo* with a small trace of water standing, they moved forward in a crouch along the winding *hondonadas.*

His hearing honed keen by his years in the mountains, Nathan, who was behind Walker, suddenly shoved the smaller man into the side of the gully and whispered harshly, "Quiet!"

Moments later, voices drifted across the prairie, then slowly faded away.

Sam glanced back at Nathan and grinned. "Be right back."

He shimmied through the scrub to the crest of the ridge. Moments later, he returned. In a muffled voice, he said, "The fort is a half mile or so beyond. The Mexicans have it surrounded on three sides. We best wait here until dark. I figure the artillery will take a break then, and that's when we slip inside."

The bombardment ceased at sundown. Two hours after night had settled over the Gulf Coast prairie, the campfires surrounding the encampment called Fort Texas burned low. There was no breeze, and the pungent odor of wood smoke lay over the prairie.

Muffled voices drifted across the waving

148

grass, and from time to time, silhouettes of soldiers appeared in front of the dancing flames.

Staying in the shadows along one side of the gully, the two scouts ghosted along the sandy bed, noting the numerous footsteps in it. "Regular road down here," Walker muttered.

A chill ran down Nathan's spine. He glanced at the rim of the gully above their heads. A jasper could be standing two feet back from the rim and be out of sight. He drew a deep breath and laid his hand on the handle of his bowie.

The gully twisted and turned like a snake.

The snap of a twig jerked Nathan around. He froze in the shadows, peering over their back trail, but seeing no movement. He turned, and from the corner of his eye spotted a shadow on the rim. The starlight glittered off the brass on the soldier's uniform as he jerked his Brown Bess musket to his hip and aimed it at Sam Walker's back.

Like a mountain cougar, Nathan leaped up and swung his left arm, the iron T catching the belt of the soldier and yanking him abruptly from the rim.

Startled, the soldier didn't have time to shout before he landed on his head, snapping his neck.

Walker spun, his Colt cocked. His keen eyes quickly took in the situation. He grabbed the soldier's feet and dragged him into the shadows. "Thanks," he muttered.

"De nada."

The ridge fell behind, and the gully grew shallow, forcing the scouts to drop to their stomachs. Ahead, the dark shadows of a series of earthworks rose from the prairie. Walker paused, and gave the call of a western meadowlark, a flutelike bubbling.

Moments later, the call was answered from the earthworks. Walker responded, then scurried forward in a crouch. Nathan followed.

Five minutes later, they squatted around a small fire, sipping coffee and listening to the fort's commanding officer, Captain James Hayden. "So far, we're holding out. We're going to need some help likely in the next day or two. We got word that a Mexican general by the name of Arista is coming with five thousand troops."

Walker whistled softly and surveyed the earthworks. "How'd you manage to get a patrol out, Jimmy?"

Hayden shook his head. "No need. They sent an emissary in today, a white man along with five Mexican officers. We were told to surrender or we'd suffer the same fate as those Texians at the Alamo and Goliad."

A twinkle of amusement glittered in Nathan's eyes. "So what did you tell them?"

Hayden laughed. "Well, I didn't answer like Travis. I didn't want to waste powder or a ball, so I just told them to go to hell. That seemed to perturb the white man considerably, a jasper who called himself Selman."

Nathan froze, stunned, and then his heart thudded against his chest, sending excitement and anticipation coursing through his veins. "Selman? Black beard? Missing some front teeth?"

Hayden frowned. "You know him?"

His eyes growing cold, Nathan replied. "Never seen him yet."

Walker looked around at the ominous threat in Nathan's tone. "Personal?"

With a terse nod, Nathan replied, "Mighty personal."

Turning back to Hayden, Walker asked, "When's Arista getting here?"

"After I told them where they could spend eternity, they warned me I only had a couple days to think it over."

Nathan drained his coffee and muttered. "Reckon it's time for us to get back to the colonel, Sam."

Walker grunted. "Reckon so." He nodded to Hayden. "Take care."

Hayden frowned. "Be careful out there. Those Mexicans are thick as horseflies in May."

After carrying Sam and Nathan's report to General Taylor, Colonel Jack Hays listened as Taylor laid out his plan. "We'll move out this morning to relieve our force at Fort Texas. If we're lucky, we can make it before Arista arrives. We've had reinforcements enough to leave a force behind at Point Isabel. We'll camp tonight on the plains of Palo Alto."

After his officers departed, Taylor instructed Hays to put half of his rangers on the north flank and the other half on the south. "If by some chance we meet Arista before reaching Fort Texas, I want your undisciplined roughnecks to cause that greaser general so much trouble in the rear, he'll have to pull some of his front line soldiers back."

When Nathan heard the news, he cornered Hays. "I want to ride point, Jack."

Hays studied his friend. "Sam told me about Selman."

Nathan nodded tersely.

A crooked grin played over the slight man's face as he looked up into Nathan's cold gray eyes. "Don't do nothing foolish, you hear?"

With a chuckle, Nathan replied, "Can't afford to. After him, there's still two left."

Nathan and Sam Walker rode point on the south flank of the 2400-man army while Barney accompanied Rip Ford on the north flank.

"Watch yourself," Nathan had warned his father-in-law before pulling out.

Barney chuckled. "You're the one best take care." He grew solemn, and he offered Nathan his hand. "Don't go taking no wild chances if you spot one of them bastards, you hear me?"

The big mountain man took it soberly. "I'm not that dumb."

That night, the U.S. Army of Observation camped on the edge of Palo Alto. Across the brushy plains, to General Taylor's disappointment, glowed the distant fires marking the Mexican camp.

Arista had intercepted Taylor before he could reach Fort Texas.

Walker and Nathan were sent out to reconnoiter during the night. They returned at midnight with a report that even though Arista had left fifteen hundred men at Matamoras, he still outnumbered Taylor's twenty-four hundred by a thousand men.

"Which really doesn't make it a fair fight," drawled Devil Jack. "Our thousand rangers can take care of a bunch of Mexicans like that before breakfast every morning."

Taylor grinned at the braggadocio. "Well, Colonel, you and your boys are damn well going to have a chance to show us."

Squatting around a fire sipping coffee and chewing on hardtack and bacon, Nathan fought against the restless itch urging him into action. He'd had little sleep during the early morning hours after his scout, for he'd kept imagining his confrontation with Frank Selman and the other two scavengers.

To his disappointment, the first shots fired the next day were from the Mexican artillery, but it was well out of range. Taylor moved forward, his plan to keep his light artillery moving while the thick brush hindered the heavier weapons of Arista's force.

By the time one of Arista's batteries relocated, Taylor's lighter, more mobile artillery had wreaked its destruction and

154

moved to another location.

Astride his roan, Nathan waited impatiently for orders to move forward. Throughout the day, the pounding of cannon fire reverberated over the plains.

In frustration, General Arista sent his cavalry out to flank the U.S. artillery, a move that a thousand Texas Rangers cheered, for as soon as the Mexican cavalry appeared in the heavy brush on the plains, the bloodthirsty rangers charged.

"What the hell!" General Taylor shouted. "Those damned idiots are riding right into our cannon fire."

Major Sam Ringgold, who had come up with the innovative idea of mobile artillery, paused. "What now, General? You want us to hold fire?"

Taylor frowned, his craggy face contorted in anger. "Hell no, Major. Keep firing. If what I've heard about those rangers is true, they can even dodge cannonballs."

Leaning low over the neck of his roan ahead of a dozen other yahooing rangers, Nathan swept around a tangle of thorns and mesquite and burst upon a startled battery of artillerymen, who threw up their hands and exploded in every direction.

Gunfire racketed like a string of Fourth of July firecrackers. Blinding smoke filled the air, but seconds later, Nathan burst from the smoke and came face-to-face with a patrol of General Arista's elite cavalry and Jarauta's guerillas.

Near the rear of the Mexican patrol, a face appeared for a fleeting second, a grizzled renegade with a thick black beard.

Selman!

Nathan blinked, and Selman vanished in the dust of the charging cavalry.

Using his legs to guide his roan, Nathan rose in his stirrups and squeezed off two shots, knocking the first two cavalrymen from their saddles. Behind him, other rangers began firing.

Teeth clenched, he drove into the charging cavalry, firing his Colt with deadly accuracy. His eyes searched frantically for Frank Selman, but failed to spot him again, as he swept past the Mexican patrol. His Colt snapped on a spent chamber. He jammed the sidearm in his holster, grabbed his bowie, and wheeled his pony about and reengaged the enemy.

In the next instant, dozens of horses slammed into each other. Men cursed at the top of their lungs as the bright sunlight glinted on flashing blades; sidearms roared; thick acrid smoke covered the battlefield; horses squealed and pawed the air while their riders fought desperately to stay in the saddle.

Suddenly, a lancer appeared in front of Nathan with an upraised saber. The sun flashed on the blade. Nathan threw up his left arm, deflecting the blade with the iron T and slashed with his bowie, laying open the Mexican's arm like a hog.

And then it was over.

The Mexican cavalry vanished.

Frank Selman remained hidden behind a thick growth of mesquite and porcupine sedge grass, peering through the dust at the big man with wooden arm. His eyes narrowed. That was the jasper of whom Luis Salado had spoken, the savage mountain man who had killed, then scalped Alfredo Torres and probably Red Davis. Peering through the dust, he shucked his belt pistol, but the big man had ridden into the crowd of Texas Rangers.

Watching the rangers milling about, Selman muttered, his black eyes cold as ice, "Come on, big man. Ride this way." He cocked the hammer of his sidearm.

The other rangers pulled up around Nathan, their eyes scanning the brushy plains while their fingers nimbly reloaded their weapons.

Nathan studied the retreating cloud of dust, sorely tempted to pursue it in the desperate hope of finding Frank Selman. Now that he had seen the man's face, he would never forget it.

Remaining motionless, Selman watched coldly as Nathan emerged from the ring of horses surrounding him.

Nathan clicked his tongue and started the roan after the retreating cavalry, when a shout from behind drew him up.

CHAPTER SEVENTEEN

Nathan wheeled his roan about and spotted Colonel Jack Hays signaling his rangers to pull back and regroup.

A hundred yards distant, Selman muttered a curse and dug his spurs into his pony, sending the startled animal after the retreating cavalry.

By now, the sun was nearing the horizon.

As Nathan rode up to Hays, the slight colonel gestured to the retreating Mexicans. "Nathan, you and Sam keep an eye on them. See what they're up to. We got us a couple boys doing the same on the north flank."

Sam glanced to the south. "What about Perote, Jack? When are we heading down there?"

Hays chuckled. "We'll get there, Sam. And you can have the honor of digging that dime

159

out yourself."

Nathan counted over two hundred dead and wounded Mexican soldiers on the battlefield of Palo Alto. Women following their men knelt and wept by the dead ones. Others tended their wounded, glancing up impassively as Sam and Nathan rode past.

From a vantage point in the middle of a mesquite tangle covered with berry briars, the two scouts watched as Arista's army retreated toward the river, setting up defensive positions in an old bed of the Rio Grande called Resaca de la Palma.

Taylor studied the map where Nathan indicated Arista had established his defense. Ben McCullough, thoroughly familiar with South Texas, shook his head. "Prying him out of there, General, will be harder than separating two coats of paint — damn near impossible."

Hays stepped forward. "Maybe not, Ben."

The plan was simple.

Weigh into Arista with the light, mobile artillery while the rangers hit either flank.

"The way I see it," Nathan muttered to Barney when the older man later questioned the plan, "that Arista jasper made a heap big mistake putting his back to the river. Once the Mexicans start to retreat, and they will, the current of the river will completely disorganize them. Why, hellfire, it'll be like shooting fish in a barrel." What Nathan didn't reveal to his father-in-law was that he had his own plans. With luck, that night, he would kill Frank Selman.

Well after dark, Nathan slipped out.

Thirty minutes later, he lay in thick sedge grass beneath a palmetto on a small bluff overlooking the old riverbed and studied the Mexican encampment. He knew he would never recognize Luis Salado or Otis Sims, but if he could spot Selman, perhaps one or both of the killer's compadres would be with him.

Studying the camp, he guessed white renegades made up almost a quarter of the men below, but throughout the evening until the fires burned low, he failed to spot Frank Selman.

Selman, Sims, and Luis Salado huddled at the edge of a fire in the middle of the encampment, whispering. Sim's eyes were wide with fear. "You sure it was him, Frank?"

Selman tore off a twist of tobacco rope. "Hell, yes. How many men you reckon be running around wearing a wooden arm? It was him, no doubt in my mind."

His voice trembling, Salado muttered. "He comes for us, do you think?"

Rolling his eyes, Selman grunted. "What other reason?"

"*¡Dios!*" Salado muttered. "First, Torres, then Davis . . ." His words trailed off.

Sims blurted out, "We don't know about Red for sure. He might have just stayed back in San Antone."

Selman sneered. "No way old Red would have stood around in San Antone this long. If the sheriff hadn't run him out, then some mighty angry husbands would have." He paused to squirt a stream of tobacco on the dying fire. "I got to go along with Salado here. That one-armed jasper done kilt old Red."

Disappointed, Nathan eased back into the shadows. He rose into a crouch and ghosted back through the palmettos toward the plain of Palo Alto.

As he rounded a tangle of mesquite, he came face-to-face with a Mexican sentry. In the starlight, Nathan saw the sentry was nothing more than a boy. Before the young man could shout, Nathan, his big fist doubled around the handle of his bowie, clipped the sentry on the point of the chin. The boy dropped without a sound.

Squatting, the mountain man studied the slack features of the unconscious youth in the dim starlight, realizing he was just about the age of Artis, the young man who had courted his niece, Ruthie.

He shook his head, then disappeared into the night.

"No sign of them, huh?" Barney peered over the edge of the coffee cup.

"Nope, but they're there. I reckon there's four or five hundred renegades with that bunch."

Midmorning, artillery boomed from the river. Taylor answered, and two hours later, hordes of Texas Rangers, teeth bared, standing in their stirrups, and revolvers belching flame, with Nathan Cooper in the forefront, struck from both flanks in wild abandon, scattering the frightened soldiers and driving them back across the Rio Grande.

A bearded face flashed, for the moment freezing Nathan on the back of his horse. Suddenly a slug tugged at his shirt and the face vanished in the midst of the retreating soldiers.

Nathan spurred his roan into the muddy water, only to be drawn up abruptly by Jack Hays. "Hold it, Nathan. Hold it. Don't go no farther."

Anger flashed in his gray eyes as Nathan wheeled the roan about.

Jack shook his head. "Don't go no farther."

Nathan yanked on the reins and shouted above the cacophony of the battle. "Selman's over there. I spotted him."

"I don't care," the slender colonel shouted. "There's been no declaration of war. You cross that river, and you're playing right into Mexico's hands."

Teeth bared in frustration, the big mountain man jerked his roan around and stared helplessly as the disorganized and fleeing Mexican soldiers scattered and disappeared into the thorny thickets of Mexico.

That night, a spring storm blew in. For the next two days, Nathan and Barney were confined to their tent, pacing the floor between their cots until the ground was harder than a banker's heart.

During that same period of time, Jack Hays and Rip Ford had their hands full preventing the rangers from busting open each others' skulls.

Taylor's square face seemed to tremble with anger. "I thought you could control those devils, Hays."

With a slight shrug, Hays replied, "I told you before, General. Put those old boys in front of Mexicans or Indians, and you got yourself the best fighters in the world, but give 'em a few hours spare time, and they'll do more hurt to each other than the Mexicans ever could."

Old Rough and Ready pointed a knotted finger in the direction of the rangers. "Then give them something to do. Make up some kind of duty."

Jack rolled his eyes. "Might as well send them home, general. Those old boys are as tough as whang leather. They treat their ponies like kept women, tend their Colts like new babies, and worship their coffee with the fervor of a zealot, but they ain't going to wiggle a toe to do made-up work." He paused, and with an easy grin added, "They're kinda like a box supper, general. You buy the box, and you got to take what comes with it even if she's got no teeth."

For the next few days, it was a toss-up between the stormy weather and boredom as to which would touch off the rangers' stretched-thin tempers.

And then, two days running, intelligence came that salved the impending explosion.

Taylor received word that war had been

165

declared on Mexico, and the next day, Sam Walker rode in with spotty reports of Arista's army moving inland.

"Whether that means Linares or Monterrey or Reynosa, we'll just have to get out there and find out," Hays decided after hearing Walker's report and studying the map. He glanced at Nathan, then back to Walker. "Any sign of Canales or Jarauta?"

Outside, the wind and rain battered the tent, causing the sides to flutter and pop.

Walker met Nathan's eyes and shrugged. "We heard he might be everywhere from Linares to up around Reynosa, but the truth is, I figure some of Canales' spies was just trying to get us to chasing our tails." He paused, then added, "He might be a greaser, but he didn't pick up the moniker the Chaparral Fox for doing what folks expected of him."

With a curt nod, Hays ducked out of the tent. "Come on, boys. Let's see the general about this."

General Taylor nodded slowly, his lips pursed, his steady eyes studying the map before him. He laid the tip of a knotted finger on a small dot on the map. Keeping his eyes on the dot, he said. "Colonel Hays, you and your band of hellions head for

Linares here and try to cut Arista's sign. Colonel Wood and his regiment will head for Reynosa."

Outside, Nathan ducked his head into the rain as he and Hays slogged back to their bivouac area. Above the pounding rain, Hays shouted, "Soon as the weather breaks, we'll pull out."

Nathan shot the smaller man a quizzical glance.

Hays gave him a crooked grin. "I know what you want, Nathan. I want it too, but another day or two until the weather is fit for traveling won't hurt nothing. Selman and his sidekicks are out there. I guarantee you by the time this is all over, you'll have from them what you want."

A flash of hate glittered in mountain man's eyes. "I never figured otherwise."

CHAPTER EIGHTEEN

The narrow road to Linares twisted over a rolling prairie that had hungrily soaked up the rain. Patches of chaparral ranging from a hundred yards to over a quarter mile in width dotted the countryside. Most of the chaparral was scrub oak, thick with bushes and covered with spiny vines mostly impenetrable by nothing larger than coyotes or rabbits.

The first day out, men and horses were lively, ready to work off some of the boredom of being penned up in their tents and corrals for almost a week.

A poisoned water hole at the first camp failed to dampen the enthusiasm of their mission, but three more days and three more poisoned holes had most tempers on a razor's edge.

After making camp for the night, Hays sent Nathan and Walker ahead. "We're running low on water. See what you can find."

The night was cool, and the starlight illumined a countryside teeming with live creatures. In the distance, hawks screed and moments later rabbits squealed.

Off to the left, a male owl hooted. A female, in a lower pitch, answered twice. And back to the north, coyotes howled.

Walker chuckled. "Appears a lot going on out here."

Nathan grinned. "All except what we're looking for. I — Hold on." He reined up and squinted into the night. His heart thudded against his chest. "Over there. A fire."

To the southwest, a tiny light flickered off and on in the darkness.

Walker muttered. "Canales? Arista?"

After several strained moments, Nathan muttered, "Not just a single fire."

"Who then?"

Disappointment in his voice, he replied, "Maybe a *pastore.*"

Walker nodded. "Sheepherder. Yeah." He studied the dark countryside about them. "Reckon sheep's about the only thing that can live on that scrub out there."

The two rangers moved cautiously, but when they were a quarter of a mile from the fire, the baying of a dog broke the silence of the night.

They continued easing forward, taking

169

care to remain in the fleeting shadows cast by spidery mesquite and tangled briars until they were in shouting distance.

Nathan sniffed the air and frowned. "They're not sheepherders."

Walker frowned. "How do you know that?"

With grin, Nathan replied. "The smell. You can smell sheep a mile away."

"So, who do you think they are?"

"No idea, but we'd be smart to figure they're somehow hooked up with Jarauta or Canales." He cleared his throat and shouted, "*Hola*. Amigos."

Three dark shadows appeared by the fire, then two disappeared into the night.

Nathan chuckled. "They're not stupid. I'll go in. You watch from out here."

Walker shucked his carbine. "Stay in sight."

Riding in easily, Nathan held up his wooden arm. "*Significo no daño. Busco agua.* I mean no harm. I look for water." He laid his hand on his canteen.

The slight Mexican dressed in a baggy white blouse and pants eyed Nathan suspiciously, but pointed down the road. "*Uno milla*. One mile. Water."

At that moment, two more peons emerged

from the darkness on either side of Nathan, one with a machete and the other a worn ball-and-cap pistol.

"Hola." Nathan nodded without moving a muscle.

The two nodded in return. One, upon spotting the prosthesis on Nathan's arm, frowned, but remained silent. The other spoke. *"¿Americano?"*

"Si." Nathan nodded. "I come to fight with General Canales. You know of Canales?"

For a moment, the frown on the man's face deepened then faded into a smile. He pointed northward. *"Si, si.* The general, he visits the rancheros from Monterrey to Reynosa for men to help him fight *Americanos.* Many *Americanos* fight for him. Many hundred."

Nathan nodded to them. "You Canales?"

The three glanced at each other, then the first shook his head. "No, senor. We are poor travelers."

With a slight tug on the reins, Nathan backed his roan away slowly. He nodded. *"Gracias,* amigos. *Gracias."*

When Walker heard of the water, he wheeled his horse about. "Let's get back to Jack with the news."

Nathan stopped him. "First, let's make

171

sure water's there. I don't trust those three. Besides, it's been years since I've prowled this deep into Mexico, but some of these holes will be bubbling over one day and drier than a tobacco box the next day."

A few minutes after Nathan disappeared, the three peons broke camp and raced across the desert with news for Padre Jarauta that the devil Texan with one arm was searching for him.

The bottom of the waterhole was cracked and dry. Walker grunted. "Good thing you figured on taking a look."

With a shrug, Nathan wheeled his roan about. "Let's hope we can find some water holes between the Linares road and the Monterrey road."

Topping a rise before the sun rose, Nathan nodded to a dark line on the northern horizon. "Chances are, that's where we'll find good water."

Walker frowned. "The mountains? How far do you reckon it is?"

"Hard to say. Years back in the Rockies, I've stared at a mountain for a week before finally reaching its foothills. Best I recollect, these mountain ranges down here are the size of those back north. I'd reckon it'll be a good day's ride for Jack and the boys."

Walker eyed the dark silhouette skeptically. "You want to ride over? Jack's waiting on us."

Nathan shook his head. "No. Let's tell him what we know. Let him decide."

Hays listened impassively as the two rangers reported in. When they finished, he looked from one to the other and drew a deep breath. After slowly releasing it, he muttered, "Looks like we head north on short rations. At least we got us a handle on Canales."

Nathan nodded. "The Mexicans said Canales had a right considerable number of Americans with him."

Devil Jack snorted. "Not Americans. Traitors."

The northern trek from the Linares Road to the Monterrey-Reynosa Road twisted through some of the most hostile, most desolate countryside in Mexico.

By the time they rode into the foothills of the Sierra Madres, both horses and men were exhausted.

Setting up camp near a series of springs with sweet water, the rangers looked forward to a few days' rest, but their night was shattered when, from a mountain ridge far above, a hail of gunfire raked the camp, sending rangers ducking behind boulders and ponies tearing away from their picket ropes.

Otis Sims smiled grimly as he and his men calmly fired their ball-and-cap rifles into the cluster of rangers camped below. He had picked his point of ambush carefully. There was no way for the rangers to lead their horses up the slope, and by the time they rode around the hogback ridge extending a mile into the desert, his small party would have vanished in the snarls and tangles of the chaparral below.

The dozen or so guerillas fired and reloaded three times, then, as planned, scurried along the trail that curved around a wall of limestone and down the far slope to their tethered ponies. The last to leave, Sims leaped to his feet, fired a fourth shot, quickly reloaded, and headed around the limestone wall.

The toe of his boot snagged on a fissure on the ridge floor, sending the gangly man stumbling forward. He threw out his hand to break his fall, but his face slammed into the hard rock, momentarily stunning him.

■ ■ ■ ■

Down below, while the rangers returned fire, Nathan quickly led a handful of the enraged cowpokes up the mountainside. The rangers were suited for battle from the back of a pony, not pushing their way through the clawing confines of brush-filled arroyos; they were accustomed to the pounding of a saddle and not to the leg-pumping, heart-bursting scramble up a steep mountain slope. By the time Nathan reached the ridge, he was several yards ahead of the nearest ranger.

On the ridge, Sims rolled over and blinked his eyes, trying to gather his wits. At that moment, the scrape of metal against rock came from the far side of the column.

Panic surged through his veins. He leaped to his feet, looked around desperately for a place to hide, and spotted a narrow fold in the limestone wall. Quickly, he slipped into the fold and held his breath.

By the time Nathan topped the limestone ridge, the guerillas had vanished. From the far side of the wall of limestone echoed the pounding of retreating hoofbeats.

Nathan raced along the trail, ducking around the corner and sliding to a halt. He squinted into the night. Balloons of dust rose behind the pounding hoofbeats of the ponies far below. He muttered a curse.

Sims peered around the corner of the fold behind which he had hidden. The lanky man's heart leaped into his throat when he spotted the iron T on the end of the large man's left arm.

That's him, he told himself. The bastard who killed Red and Alfredo. His eyes narrowed. He eased from behind the fold and slipped his Hawken to his shoulder. Quickly, he cocked the hammer and squeezed the trigger.

Nothing. Misfire! In desperation, Sims grabbed the barrel of the Hawken and swung it like a club.

Nathan spun at the sound. For a fleeting moment, he couldn't believe his eyes. Then his head exploded, and he collapsed.

Sims grabbed his knife, but a voice just around the vertical column called out, "Nathan! Where are you?"

Otis Sims grimaced, then vanished down the trail leading to the base of the mountain.

CHAPTER NINETEEN

Back in camp, Nathan squatted by the fire, dabbing a wet rag on the egg-sized knot on the side of his head. He growled between clenched teeth. "It was Sims, Barney. I'd swear to it. A scar across his right eye."

A cruel grin played over Barney's lips. He scratched at his fleshy jaw. "Looks like we might be getting close."

"Looks thataway." Nathan cocked his head at Jack Hays. "They was heading north. Toward the Monterrey-Reynosa Road."

With a terse nod, Hays rose, poured the remainder of his coffee on the fire, and grunted. "Reckon we best get some shut-eye if we're planning on moving out early."

The sign was obvious. Nathan could have followed it at a gallop, but Hays held back, not wanting to tire their remounts. Reining in his impatience, Nathan followed Hays' orders, instinctively recognizing the wisdom of the slight colonel's decision.

Besides, he told himself, no telling what we'll run into along the way. But they encountered no obstacles throughout the entire ride to the Monterrey Road. There the guerillas' trail turned east, toward Reynosa.

Two hours later, Nathan reined up, staring at the ground. The guerillas' trail turned north off of the Reynosa road. Hays nodded. "Let's go."

Suddenly, Sam Walker shouted, "Colonel. Over there. Ain't that Rip?"

Hays peered at the four riders heading toward them. "Looks like him. What in the hell is he doing out here?"

Nathan shook his head. "I got no idea, but the way those old boys are forking their ponies, they must have some kind of burr under their saddles."

Five minutes later, the four rangers reined up. With Rip Ford rode Joe Barlow. Ford grinned. "Howdy, Jack, Sam, Nathan."

Jack Hays grunted. "What are you doing out here?"

Ford hooked a thumb over his shoulder. "The general sent us to find you. He wants all the rangers to report to Reynosa."

Nathan shot Jack a threatening look.

Eyes blazing fire, Hays jabbed a finger at the ground. "We can't. We've been following Jarauta's sign. It turns off the road here."

Ford shrugged. "I don't know about that, Jack. All I'm doing is giving you Taylor's orders. He wants you back in Reynosa."

Nathan grunted. "You mean the old man expects us to give up the chase?"

Joe Barlow grinned. "Beats me. Don't know what's behind them orders or nothing, just that Taylor wants all rangers to gather up in Reynosa. For reasons known only to him, he don't want no one chasing after Jarauta right now."

Hays slammed the heel of his hand against his saddle horn viciously. "If he don't want us to run them greasers down, then why in the hell did he send us after them in the first place?"

Barlow shrugged. "Colonel Wood said the same thing. Fact is, soon as he got the orders, he headed down to Matamoras to talk to the general."

Devil Jack spat back. "If the general is looking for trouble, he'll damn well find it with a thousand idle Texas Rangers loafing about."

The ranger encampment lay across the river

from Reynosa. That first night around a small fire, Hays tried to pacify Nathan. "We shouldn't be here more than a few days."

Nathan growled, "I don't figure on getting sores on my butt by sitting around here until Taylor makes up his mind. As far as I know, Jack, them three I'm looking for might be no more than ten miles from here. No general on this earth is going to stop me."

At that moment, gunfire broke out on the north side of the camp followed by peals of laughter.

Hays grinned. "Just old boys letting off steam." He paused and added, "Give it a few days. Colonel Wood ought to be back first thing in the morning. We'll have a better handle on the situation then."

Nathan and Barney looked at each other. Barney nodded almost imperceptibly. Running his fingers through his long hair, Nathan nodded. "Jack, there's a fire burning in my belly that ain't going out until those other three jaspers are dead. Waiting around just makes that fire all the hotter."

And Colonel Wood's report the next morning was like dumping a bucket of coal oil on a fire. "No orders. No fighting orders that is," Wood howled in frustration. "Just stay put. That's what the general said. Just stay put."

A handful of rangers including Nathan, Barney, Hays, and Walker stood around the colonel's fire, listening to him rant and rave. He paused, his eyes cutting to the river and the dozen or so rangers whooping and hollering in drunken revelry as they rode back in from a night carousing in Reynosa.

Walker's eyes blazed. He looked at Jack. "Maybe you best see the general." He gestured to the returning rangers. "What the old man don't understand is these rangers got to have some place to tear loose. If it ain't on the Mexican army, these fellers will find another way."

Hays rode out thirty minutes later after eliciting a promise from Nathan and Barney to do nothing foolish until he returned. Nathan had frowned. "Foolish? Like what?"

Jack shrugged. "Like deserting. You're still enlisted in the Texas Rangers."

Nathan grinned at his long time friend. "You know better than that, Jack. If I want to desert, I'll desert, and ain't no one going to be able to do nothing about it." He gestured to the wild country beyond the camp. "I'll just vanish out there like a puff of smoke and come back whenever I feel like it, if I feel like it."

The big mountain man grew serious and added. "Tell Zack he's got more problems than me and Barney. He's got a thousand itchy rangers that'll blow this place apart like a twelve-pound cannon if they keep sitting around and doing nothing."

As if to punctuate his remark, a peal of thunder and a crack of lightning exploded above them. Moments later, the sky opened up and dropped a torrential rain that continued throughout the remainder of the day and into the night.

Hays returned the next day, having failed to sway the general. "He says he's waiting for intelligence to pinpoint Arista and Canales. Then we'll move. Until that time, we're to sit here on our butts and wait."

Despite the inclement weather, a steady stream of rangers rode back and forth across the river to Reynosa, disdaining the ferry because it was too slow. The small village had become the center of around-the-clock revelry.

For forty-eight straight hours, drunken rangers roamed the muddy streets, chasing the young women, tearing up cantinas, and then — just for fun — shooting off the heads of chickens and leaving them flopping in the mud.

When the senorita-loving, whiskey-guzzling Texas Rangers weren't hurrahing Reynosa, they were fighting among themselves. Half a dozen suffered wounds serious enough to put them in the infirmary.

Two days later, the rain ceased, and no sooner had the sun risen than a small contingent of anxious Mexicans crossed the swollen river on the ferry and approached the camp. The *alcalde* implored Hays and Wood to control their men. The village was running out of chickens and virgins.

Hays promptly loaded the five men into a wagon and had them driven to General Taylor with instructions to tell him exactly what they had told him. "Maybe this will make the old man see what I was talking about," Hays said as they watched the wagon disappear into the chaparral.

The next morning, Hays squatted around the fire with his adjutant, Rip Ford, and Ford's aide, Barney, and his scouts, Nathan, Walker, and McCullough discussing options, now that Taylor seemed to be content sitting on his tail, doing nothing.

McCullough nodded to the chaparral and

drawled, "Well, would you look at that?"

Dressed in full military regalia, Major William Polk, brother of the president, rode from the chaparral into camp on a prancing white horse. He sat stiff-backed in his saddle, as if he were wearing wooden underwear. He looked scornfully upon the handful of rawboned rangers squatted about the fire.

"I'm looking for Hays and Wood."

Hays rose. "I'm Hays. Wood's in his tent over yonder."

Curtly, Polk replied, "Send for him." He paused, then added stiffly, "The general sent me to straighten out this situation" — he swung down from the saddle — "to get to the bottom of the trouble here."

Hays frowned. "Situation?"

"The decided lack of discipline, Mister Hays." He nodded to the tent behind Hays. "Is that yours?"

Hays eyed the major. If ever he'd seen someone heading for a fall, this jasper was it. "Reckon it is." He nodded to Nathan who quickly fetched Colonel Wood.

Polk brushed past Hays and stepped into the tent. "Come in."

Hays followed, nodding to his men.

Inside, Polk stood on one side of the table, Hays and his men on the other. At that moment, Nathan and Colonel Wood entered. Wood recognized Polk. He nodded. "Major."

Polk nodded briefly. He curled his lips in distaste at the grimy collection of men staring back at him. *Backwoodsmen, hicks. No wonder the general is having trouble.*

He squared his shoulders. *This motley group of ill-dressed misfits will present no problem. Discipline. That's all it will take. Discipline.*

Contempt evident in his voice, he eyed the men staring back at him. "In the U.S. Army, every man is expected to do exactly what he is told or suffer the consequences." He paused for effect, to let his words sink in to the thick brains of the cretins staring at him.

Before he could continue, Hays spoke up. "We're not in the U.S. Army, Major. We're civilian scouts on six-month enlistment."

Polk stiffened. Not to be deterred, he continued, "Regardless, you are expected to do as you are ordered. And that means discipline will be enforced."

Nathan spoke up. "There wouldn't be need for any of that, Major, if we'd just get back to what we were doing and track down those Arista and Canales hombres."

Anger darkened Polk's face. "And who are

you?" He demanded arrogantly.

"Name's Cooper, Nathan Cooper, Major," the big mountain man said, stepping forward with a slight grin on his face.

Polk studied the buckskin-clad man with half an arm missing. With a hint of superiority in his tone, he replied, "Well, Mister Cooper. If you knew more about military discipline than the backwoods where you obviously come from, you'd know that my way is the best. And that's exactly what we will do."

Frustrated by days of inactivity, Nathan's patience snapped. Struggling to control his voice, he replied, "Forget it, Major. You just go ahead and play soldier boy. Me and my partner, we just resigned from your army." Over his shoulder, Nathan muttered, "Let's go, Barney." He turned to leave.

Surprised by the audacity of the man in buckskins, Polk grabbed Nathan's shoulder and spun him around. "That's desertion, and I'll have you shot."

Faster than the eye could follow, Nathan whipped out his bowie and sunk it in the table only six inches from Polk's belly. His gray eyes burned into the stunned major's. "Nobody grabs me or tells me what to do. Next time, Major, you'll be looking at your guts spilling out on the table." He paused.

"You understand me, soldier boy?"

Hays and the other rangers froze, stunned by the suddenness and ferocity of Nathan's move.

Polk gulped. Sweat beaded his forehead. Slowly he nodded.

Nathan paused another moment. "You best, Major. I say something once, I don't say it again." For several seconds, he stared hard at Major Polk, than yanked the bowie from the table and left with Barney following.

After the tent flap fell back in place, Polk began to bluster. "I'll have him shot. Call the guards. I want that man arrested."

Hays' soft, calm voice stopped him. "That's not a smart move to make out here, Major. Pull something like that, and you'll likely have a thousand Texas Rangers fighting to tear you apart. No sir, I reckon the smartest thing you could do, Major Polk, is ride on back. Make up whatever story you want. I'm not a rogue wolf like Nathan Cooper, but I am mean and unforgiving, and I have a heap more influence with Old Rough and Ready than you do, even if your brother is president."

After Polk rode out, Sam Walker sidled up to Hays and whispered, "Now what?"

187

A grin played over the slight colonel's lips. "Now, two things. First, you know the general about as good as me. Go tell him I'm putting out a few exploratory patrols to make sure Arista or Canales don't surprise us. Be right certain you say 'exploratory' and 'surprise.' And second, I got to try to talk Nathan Cooper into staying."

CHAPTER TWENTY

Hays found Barney and Nathan in their tent rolling up their bedrolls. "What's going on? You-all boys leaving before the action?"

Barney peered at him from under his brows suspiciously. "What's that supposed to mean?"

"Sam's on the way to Taylor. The old man will pitch a fit, but he can't do nothing about it. I told Sam to inform the general we had word that Jarauta and Canales were somewhere on the road between Reynosa and Monterrey, and I was sending patrols out to verify the information."

A frown wrinkled Nathan's broad forehead. "When did you hear that?"

His youthful face pure innocence, Devil Jack replied, "Why just a few minutes ago. Old Joe Barlow came up to me and asked if I figured Jarauta and Canales were on the road to Monterrey."

Nathan lifted an eyebrow. "That ain't

exactly the same thing, Jack."

Barney snorted. "Hell, Jack, I knew there was some reason I liked you. You're just about as sneaky as I am."

Later that morning, Nathan and Barney rode out with ten other rangers, Joe Barlow and Poney Hall among them. "Find Canales or Jarauta" was the only order Hays gave, the same order he gave to the other five patrols he ordered out.

Steam rose from the muddy road as the blistering sun baked down on their shoulders. Nathan and Barney led the small band along the Reynosa to Monterrey Road to the cutoff Jarauta's guerillas had suddenly taken north a few days earlier.

Less than a mile off the road, Nathan reined up and leaned from his saddle, studying a pile of horse biscuits on the ground. The pounding rain had broken them open, pooling their contents in dark circles.

Joe Barlow pulled up beside Nathan. "What do you expect to find after all that rain, Cooper?"

The big man grinned. "There'll be sign. Washed out tracks, horse biscuits like these, no telling what sort of falderal tossed aside."

He glanced at Barlow. Like most rangers,

the steely-eyed hombre was rawboned hard, wiry as whang leather with a square jaw shaded with a few days' growth of beard. "How come you and Poney are along? Colonel Wood get fed up with you two yahoos?"

Barlow chuckled and pulled out a rope of tobacco. He tore off a chunk and offered it to Nathan who declined. "You might say so. When we heard Hays was sending out patrols, we asked Wood if he was doing the same. He wasn't so inclined, so we just moved over to Hays' band of renegades." His grin grew wider.

With a wry note in his voice, Nathan replied, "I reckon the colonel was some put out at that."

Barlow shrugged. "What's he to do? I volunteered for this job, and I can damn well unvolunteer. Besides, Poney here knows this country considerably. It won't hurt none to have someone along who's got a idea where we are."

Later, Barney nodded to Barlow. "I like his grit, Nathan. He's our kind of man."

Nodding, the big mountain man replied. "Can't argue with you on that."

Two hours later, the small patrol cut off the road and into the chaparral desert. The trail, despite the torrential rain, was not too difficult to follow. Even heavy rain could not erase all sign left by the size of Jarauta's contingent of guerillas.

The trail kept in a westerly direction, and Monterrey was to the west.

On three different occasions that first afternoon, Barney pointed out one or two sets of tracks leaving the main party. "What do you figure, Nathan?"

Pursing his lips, Nathan peered to the north, the direction the last two sets of tracks headed. "Hard to say. Might be some of these old boys had business back at their own *jacales.* Might be they're running errands for these fellers we're tracking."

Back to the southwest, a blue line of mountains appeared over the horizon. Barney nodded to the sign. "Appears that be where this bunch is heading."

With a short nod, Nathan continued studying the trail. Abruptly he reined up. A frown knit his brow. Barlow pulled up beside him and glanced at the prairie before them. Other than a few piles of horse biscuits, the rain had washed out all sign. "What do you see?"

Without answering, Nathan swung down and with the toe of his boot, broke apart several of the horse biscuits. Pursing his lips, he nodded.

Barney grunted, "What is it, Nathan?"

Swinging smoothly back into the saddle, Nathan muttered, "Looks like this bunch of renegades got themselves some reinforcements along the way. From the sign, no shirttail jaspers, either."

Poney Hall and Joe Barlow pulled up. "How do you figure that? It might have been them who had dropped out along the way coming back."

Turning his gray eyes to Poney, Nathan shook his head. "Nope. Look." He gestured to the horse biscuits he had kicked apart. "Full of grain."

Poney frowned. "So?"

"So, most of the horses we been following had nothing to graze on except mesquite beans and sedge grass. These others been stabled where they've got a goodly supply of grain."

Barlow pulled out a bag of Bull Durham and built a cigarette. "How far do you figure they're ahead of us?"

"A few days." Leaning forward, Nathan ran his hand over the roan's neck. "Poney, Barlow says you know this part of the country."

Poney's thin legs looked like two bed slats when he stood in his stirrups and studied the barren chaparral prairie around them. "Best I can remember, there's a rundown village about a day from here by the name of Papagallos. East side of them mountains yonder," he added, pointing to the serrated blue line on the horizon. "In the foothills."

Nathan stiffened. "Foothills? Ridges?"

"Yep." Poney nodded. "Best I recollect, hogback ridges on both sides."

A grin played over Nathan's lips. He winked at Barney. "Sounds like the kind of country for a little ambush."

The older man grinned. "Sounds that way to me."

To the west, the sun was dropping low. Nathan looked over his small patrol. The hair on the back of his neck bristled. He had the feeling he was being watched. He studied the tangles of chaparral that spread as far as the eye could see, but saw no evidence of any living creature. "Let's us boil some coffee and then move on a couple miles for a cold camp. Out here, a jasper can spot a fire at night for miles." He glanced around once again, unable to shake the feeling someone was spying on them.

After a couple cups of six-shooter coffee and strip of jerky each, the patrol rode for another few miles before pulling into a motte of chaparral where they rolled out their bedrolls. There was no moon, but the bright stars lit the prairie with an eerie bluish silver glow.

After the small band had unsaddled and picketed their ponies, Nathan informed them that he was going to take a look around. "All day I had the feeling someone was watching. Tonight, we'll see if it was only my imagination."

After assigning Barney to guard the camp and Barlow the horses, Nathan slipped into the night, ghosting through the chaparral like a wraith, despite the thorns and briars.

From experience in the Rockies and the vast forests of East Texas, Nathan knew well how the night could play tricks with shadows. What appeared substantial from one perspective suddenly became nothing more than spectral limbs rattling in the breeze.

He lay motionless at the edge of the chaparral, studying the night about him. The next patch of chaparral was about a hundred yards. After several moments, he moved out in a crouch with his bowie in hand.

On his mocassined feet, he moved quickly with the silence of a black widow racing down her web. Upon reaching the shadows of the motte of chaparral, he remained silent and listened. All he heard were the sounds of the night. He wondered if maybe the spying notion was only in his head.

Moving cautiously, staying to the low ground, he finally reached the shadows of another patch, this one much larger than the others. From where he sat, he heard the sound of teeth gnashing, bellies growling, and horns clicking against the hard bark of mesquite.

Longhorns!

Nathan quickly made for the next patch of chaparral, not wanting to have any stock with those cantankerous, ill-tempered bovines with eight-foot horn spans and a disposition so unpredictable it would put a grizzly to shame.

Halfway across to the next patch of chaparral, he found himself in a long unused buffalo wallow, the bottom of which was thick with sedge grass and briars.

A sudden grunt froze him. Peering over the rim of the wallow, he studied the prairie around him, seeing nothing. Then he turned the focus of his attention on the dark mass of chaparral before him.

A shadow moved. The big man remained motionless.

Another grunt, and the shadow moved again.

Nathan relaxed. A wild hog, one of the

thousands roaming the prairie. Another shadow appeared from the chaparral several yards from the hog, startling the animal and sending it squealing across the prairie. The second shadow remained motionless.

Nathan's legs began to cramp from remaining in a crouch, but he dared not move. After what seemed like hours, the second shadow moved, heading in the direction of the ranger's camp.

The dark apparition glided from the darkness into the stark relief of the starlight, revealing a slight figure in the dress of an Indian.

Dropping lower, the big mountain man waited until the stalker had merged to the shadows of the patch from which Nathan had just come. Then he followed, knowing the cautious Indian would seldom look over his shoulder. All of his focus would be on the route to either side and before him.

The lithe Indian moved with the grace of a mountain lion. The dim light reflected off the Indian's dark face. He wore the gaudy headband of the Mexican Kickapoo, a band of outcasts that immigrated to Mexico a few years after the Texas Revolution.

Nathan pulled back in the shadows of the patch of scrub oak as the man slipped closer to the ranger camp.

Then the Indian froze. He peered directly at Nathan, but the big man was swallowed up by the shadows. After several moments, he continued his sinuous journey toward the chaparral.

Without warning, one of the horses nickered. The shadow on the ground froze. Another horse nickered. Voices erupted from the camp, causing the Indian to leap to his feet and like a wraith, dart through the night to the patch of scrub oak from which Nathan was watching.

Breathing harshly, the Indian dropped to the ground in the gloom of the chaparral. Drawing a deep breath, he peered back in the direction of the ranger camp.

That's when he felt the needlepoint of the bowie in his back.

CHAPTER
TWENTY-ONE

In his cobbled-together Spanish, Nathan muttered, *"No mueva ni usted muere."* Do not move or you die.

The Kickapoo froze.

Five minutes later, the small patrol of Texas Rangers stared down at the diminutive Kickapoo squatting in the starlight. Their eyes glittered with malice.

The Indian's black eyes continued shifting from the angry faces back to the iron T on Nathan's arm. Nathan tried to read this diminutive man's eyes, but the shadows cast by the stars were too thick.

In broken Spanish, they learned the Kickapoo's name was Mecina, who, with a half dozen of his tribe, served as a scout for Jarauta's guerillas and Canales' troops.

Barlow narrowed his eyes. "I say we cut his throat right now."

Mecina looked up at Nathan in fear.

Nathan shook his head. "Not until we get the information we came for." He squatted in front of the slight Kickapoo. "Jarauta? Canales? Where are they?"

Mecina frowned.

"¿*Donde* Jarauta? ¿*Donde* Canales?"

The Indian's eyes lit up. He pointed west. "Monterrey. Me," — he jabbed his finger in his chest — "me, I am to learn how many follow and report to the padre."

Nodding thoughtfully, Nathan searched for the correct words. "¿*Cuan largo adelante?*"

Screwing up his thin face in concentration, Mecina looked hard into Nathan's rugged face. Then a smile broke the frown on his lips. "Ah, '*Cuan lejos. Lejos.*'"

Nathan knit his brows then nodded. "*Si. Lejos. Cuan lejos.*"

The small dark man shrugged and held up two fingers. "*Dos.*"

With a satisfied grin, Nathan looked up at the rangers. "Two days ahead."

Barney frowned. "What was that other stuff? That gibberish?"

Laughing, Nathan explained. "Blame my Mexican. I asked how long ahead, not how far." The laughter faded from his face. He pointed his iron T at the squatting Indian. "You know Selman, Sims?"

Mecina thought a moment, then shook his head.

"What about a Mexican called Luis Salado? You know him?"

Again the slight Kickapoo shook his head.

Though he was well-experienced interpreting body language, Nathan couldn't tell if the Indian was lying or not, for the shifting starlight played tricks with facial expressions.

Poney Hall spoke up. "Now can we cut his throat?"

Panic in his voice, the slight Indian blubbered. "But, senors. The Federales, they force my people to go with them. They threaten our families back in the mountains if we not do as they say."

Poney Hall snorted. "Bull!" The lanky ranger looked at Barlow. "What do you say, partner?"

His eyes fixed on Mecina, Nathan spoke up, his voice low, but crusted with ice. "I don't know if he's lying or not, but we don't kill him" — the Kickapoo's shoulders sagged in relief, until Nathan added — "unless he refuses to take us to Jarauta."

A murmur of consent came from the patrol of rangers.

Poney nodded. "I can go along with that. Then what?"

"Then, if he doesn't try to do us dirty, we'll send him back to his people."

The dark-skinned Kickapoo stared up at Nathan in disbelief, then quickly said, "Me, I do as you ask. Mecina never lie." He made the sign of the cross.

Nathan arched a skeptical eyebrow. He held out his hand to Mecina. "The parfleche bag over your shoulder. Give it to me."

The diminutive Indian stiffened. He hesitated.

Poney shucked his Colt.

Reluctantly, Mecina handed Nathan the parfleche bag.

The others looked on curiously as Nathan rummaged through the beaded bag. He retrieved a small bundle wrapped in deerskin. He held it up and spoke to the Kickapoo. "Lie to us, and I will destroy your *mis-aami*. Be true to us, and I shall return it." He tossed the parfleche bag to Mecina. "Understand?"

Mecina gulped, his eyes fixed on the leather bundle in Nathan's hands. He nodded jerkily. "Mecina not lie."

Nathan nodded. "Good. Where's your horse?"

The Kickapoo pointed to the east.

"Go. We wait."

Joe Barlow exclaimed. "You're letting him

go? He'll run off."

With a faint grin, Nathan held up the bundle. "No he won't. This is his *misaami,* his sacred bundle containing the *manitooaki* he worships. Without this, if he is killed, he will wander the darkness forever." He shook his head. "He won't run off."

Ten minutes later, Mecina returned, and the small band of rangers traveled the remainder of the moonless night. As the sun rose over the chaparral prairie behind them, they entered the foothills of the Sierra Madres.

Nathan, as every single ranger behind him, rode with every sense alert, expecting ambush at any moment, but as the morning passed into noon, and — several hours later — night covered the rocky slopes of the mountain range without incident, they reined up by a small spring among a jumble of boulders that would hide a small fire.

While a fire was being laid, the small Kickapoo gestured to a hogback ridge a mile to the west. "There Padre Jarauta camp."

Nathan looked at him in surprise. "You are certain?"

Nodding emphatically, the Kickapoo replied. "*Si.* Much water. He has big camp there. Many times." He pointed to Nathan.

"You wish I take you?"

Barlow grunted, "I'd be careful here, Nathan."

Barney agreed.

Lifting an eyebrow, Nathan grinned. "Don't worry. You're going with me." He nodded to Mecina. "If it's a trap, shoot him."

The little Kickapoo shook his head emphatically. "No trap, senor. No trap."

An hour later, Nathan and Barney lay beside the Kickapoo on the ridge overlooking a small encampment of a half-dozen fires. Although the distance was too great to discern individuals, Nathan could tell many of them were what was called *el pistolero empleado,* the hired gunman. Without taking his eyes off the encampment below, he muttered, "Stay here. I want to slip in closer."

"Watch yourself," Barney warned.

The big mountain man shifted his glance to the Kickapoo. "You watch yourself. And him. He crosses us — well, you know what to do."

Barney pulled his Paterson Colt and cocked it. "Don't you worry none."

The upheaval of the Sierra Madres millennia previous had left the slopes strewn with jagged boulders of all sizes, so Nathan made his way closer to the camp easily.

Soon he was able to make out their words, but they were the words common to most fighting men around the fire at night, words imagining the future and the lustful dreams of what the two hundred dollars a month would buy for them.

Nathan guessed the camp held about fifty to sixty pistoleros, half white, half Mexican, many of the former dressed as he, in buckskins. His gray eyes scanned the rugged band of hired guns, pausing to study any jasper wearing a beard.

He remembered the description Torres had given them. Sims was tall and skinny with a scar across one eye. And Selman, he had already seen.

Peering through a tiny space between two boulders, he studied the men squatting around the nearest fire. Most were bearded, but none were Selman. Muttering to himself, Nathan eased back, then like a phantom shadow, darted through the boulders to a vantage point near the next fire.

His gaze swept over the campfire. Three vaqueros sat huddled together, laughing and gesticulating. Several feet beyond the fires sat a lone figure smoking a pipe and staring into the night.

Nathan froze, peering into a face as familiar to him as his own, One-Toe Ned, a grizzled mountain man with whom Nathan had wintered a few times back up in the Rockies in the late twenties and early thirties. "Damn," he muttered. "I figured that worthless old beaver killer was dead."

Before the last word rolled off the mountain man's lips, Ned rose and sauntered into the darkness outside the camp. The three Mexicans watched him, and when he disappeared, they pointed at him and laughed.

Without hesitation, Nathan ghosted through the boulders in the direction Ned had taken. Moments later, he halted abruptly when, beyond a boulder, came the sound of a man relieving himself.

Easing forward, Nathan peered around the boulder.

Ned kept his eyes forward. When he finished, he straightened his buckskins. Then he muttered in a guttural voice, "Reckon you got your eyeful, son?"

Nathan grinned to himself. He was a superior tracker. Among the Indians in the mountains, word was spoken that Nathan Cooper could track a spider over rocks. But as far as he was concerned, there was one man his superior, and that was

One-Toe Ned.

In a soft voice, Nathan whispered. "Ain't all that much to look at, Ned."

Ned spun in surprise.

Nathan hurriedly said, "Don't say nothing, Ned. Not yet."

Tall as Nathan, but fifty pounds lighter, Ned studied the darkness where Nathan crouched. "Say when."

Glancing toward the camp, Nathan whispered, "I'm looking for help, Ned."

The wiry mountain man cut his eyes in the direction of his fire. "Stay put. I'll be back."

Breathing softly, Nathan watched Ned return to camp, pick up his soogan, and head off in a different direction. Five minutes later, the scrape of gravel sounded from behind.

Ned squatted in the shadows. "It's been a hell of a long time, Nathan. I figured you was dead." He spotted the iron T on Nathan's left arm. "Looks like you almost was."

With a sarcastic grunt, Nathan replied, "Almost was, but if that bunch here catches me, you might be figuring right. You working for Jarauta?"

"Money like that's hard to pass up, a boogered-up old codger like me. Hell, I figure what I make here will set me up with a cabin in the high lonesome where I can live out my days in peace. But, what do you mean, that bunch?"

"You and me, we spent a heap of time trapping together, Ned. You wasn't the easiest old bastard to winter with, but you never done me wrong, and I never done you wrong. I'm counting on that one more time."

The shadows filled in Ned's face so Nathan could not read his expression, but the shifting of the wiry man's feet in the gravel told Nathan his words were understood. "I'll lay it out for you, Ned. You don't agree, fine. All I'll want is time to get out of here."

"Hell, Nathan. I don't understand a damned word you're saying."

"I'm a Texas Ranger, Ned, one of them chasing you boys."

For several seconds, Ned remained silent. "A ranger, huh?"

"Yep, but not for the reason you might figure." In the next couple of minutes, Nathan told his story, then concluded. "So, like I said, it turned out they sold out to Jarauta, and the only way I could run them down was by joining up. And soon as I have their scalps, me and my father-in-law is heading back to East Texas. I don't care about this war, I just want their scalps." He paused and added. "You'd be welcome to join us up in East Texas — that is, if you've stopped snoring like a damned old bear."

Ned blew softly through his lips. "Damn. I'm mighty sorry, Nathan. Mighty sorry." He paused. "I know them fellers you mentioned, Selman, Sims, and that Mexican, Luis Salado. Why, they're down in camp now."

Nathan caught his breath. "Now? Where? Point them out to me." He fought the excitement building in him.

Quickly Ned spoke up. "The fire on the west side. At the edge of a small patch of chaparral. Next to the padre's."

Surprised, Nathan blurted out. "The padre? You mean Jarauta? He's here too?"

"Yep, heading for Monterrey, but don't go doing nothing crazy tonight. I could use the money Jarauta pays, but you and me, we go way back. Hold off tonight, and I'll hand them three over to you tomorrow."

The hair on the back of Nathan's neck tingled. "Tomorrow? How do you figure that?" He studied Ned warily.

His voice dropping lower, Ned replied. "We're pulling out tomorrow around noon. There's a pass in the mountains due west of us. You know it?"

"No."

"How many guns do you have?"

Nathan hesitated to reveal his lack of strength, but he and Ned had fought together and saved each other's bacon more than once. "Ten."

"More'n enough. Me, I've spent a heap of time down here the last several years. That pass is mighty ticklish, too spooky to try at night, but if you get there at first light, then the ten of you can jump this bunch. Jarauta rides at the head of the column with them three right behind him." He paused, then chuckled. "I'll make it a point to ride at the tail end of the column. Just look for a coonskin cap and don't shoot at it."

For a moment, Nathan considered his old friend's plan. "I just want to get those three."

Nodding slowly, Ned replied. "I don't blame you." He rose. "I'm going back to the fire. I'll tell 'em I got lonesome for their company." He paused, noting Nathan's gaze kept going back to the distant fire. "If you're bound to slip around and eyeball those three, be mighty careful. If you get caught, you're on your own."

CHAPTER
TWENTY-TWO

As Ned disappeared into the night, Nathan drew several deep breaths in an effort to still the excitement pounding in his chest. The torment of the last weeks and months, the miles of tracking, the days of hating, the nights filled with paralyzing dreams were coming to end.

He knew he was taking a desperate chance, but as fickle as war was, this could be his last opportunity to exact his revenge for the murder and desecration of his wife. Who's to say? He could catch a slug tomorrow.

Silently, he slipped around the camp. Sliding beneath a tangle of mountain briars overlooking the dying fire below, he peered down at a half-dozen slumbering men. In the flickering firelight, he spotted Frank Selman and the scarred face of Otis Sims. Two of the other sleeping jaspers were white and two Mexican. Of the two Mexicans, one wore a mustache — Salado.

He studied the white gringos, burning their faces into his brain. Salado was different. He looked like a hundred, a thousand other Mexicans. The only difference was the mustache drooping below his fat lips.

Here was his chance, Nathan told himself. He eased his Paterson Colt from the holster. Three well-placed slugs, and his promise would be fulfilled. His heart thudded in his chest. At that moment, two vaqueros came up to the fire and squatted beside Selman. With a curse, Nathan backed away. He had no choice now but to go with Ned's plan.

Back in camp, Nathan gathered the other rangers and quickly laid out his plan. "If we pull out now, we can skirt the guerilla camp and reach the pass by morning. That'll give us time to set up for that bunch."

Poney grimaced. "I been a heap of places in Mexico, but never around the mountains in this part of the country."

Barlow pursed his lips. "Can you trust that jasper, Nathan?"

The big mountain man nodded. "We wintered together several years. He never did me wrong."

Walker frowned. "But none of us knows the lay of land up there, Nathan."

The big mountain man turned to the diminutive Kickapoo in their midst. "No, but he does."

Mecina remained expressionless.

"You understand of what we speak. You will guide us around the camp." He glanced back at Walker. "If we can get Jarauta, that'll put a kink in Canales' tail."

The small Indian nodded. "I do as you say."

"You know the place of which we speak?"

"*Si.*" He nodded west.

"How far?"

He shrugged. "Not far. Maybe two hours."

For a few moments, the rangers discussed the idea. Then Joe Barlow spoke up. "Look, boys. Each of us carries two Colts in our belts, another couple in our saddlebags, and a carbine. We got the firepower to handle that bunch, especially from ambush. Poney and me say let's go."

The others agreed.

Nathan nodded. "We'll pull out around three or so. That'll put us there a little before daylight."

Later, Nathan lay staring at the starry heavens above. Barney whispered, "I reckon it's about over."

Nathan muttered, "I hope so. Just remember how I described them. Sims and Selman. They'll be at the head of the column. They're the ones we want. We'll worry about Salado later."

The night was clear and crisp. Mecina led the small patrol in a wide circle around the guerilla camp, pulling up some time later as a dark wall arose from the prairie.

Mecina gestured to it. "There is where we go."

Back to the east, the first traces of false dawn stretched its fingers into the darkness overhead. Nathan grunted, "Let's go."

Barlow pulled up beside Nathan. "Looks like we'll hit it just about sunrise the way we figured."

Behind them, the sky grew lighter. The rock-and-sand prairie gave way to the rocky plates of the Sierra Madres. The towering ramparts of the gray mountains rose high overhead. Mecina pointed to a break in the forbidding walls staring down at them. "There is pass."

Nathan clicked his tongue, sending his roan up the trail and into the pass. "Let's get situated, boys. We got a few hours to kill."

Poney Hall grunted, "Unless they come early."

Barlow chuckled. "Wouldn't bother me none."

The other rangers nodded their agreement.

As soon as they entered the pass, Nathan's experienced eyes recognized it as an ideal spot for an ambush. The steep slopes were dotted with boulders behind which an army could hide. The hair on the back of his neck bristled.

They rode deeper into the pass, and the deeper they pushed, the more the hair on the back of his neck tingled. He studied the pass ahead warily, suddenly realizing there was nothing treacherous about the pass to prevent a night passage as Ned had cautioned.

The truth hit him between the eyes like a singletree. "Damn," he exclaimed, jerking his pony around.

Before his roan's front hooves struck ground, the canyon walls erupted in gunfire, reverberating off the granite walls. Slugs whizzed past, ricocheting off the limestone walls and humming past his ears.

"Trap! Trap!" he shouted, digging his heels into his roan and leaning low over the frightened horse's neck. A slug burned his arm. Another slammed into the iron T and splintered, sending shards of lead stinging into his thigh.

Black-powder smoke and frantic shouts punctuated by gunfire filled the narrow pass. The rangers shucked their Colts and fired blindly while driving their ponies from the narrow defile.

As the small patrol bolted toward the entrance of the pass, another barrage exploded. Ahead, a half-dozen vaqueros and Anglo gunmen crouched behind boulders at the mouth of the pass, pouring slug after slug into the small patrol.

Nathan cursed. Ned had suckered him and the others. He looped his reins over the iron T and shucked his Colt. Standing in the stirrups, he gave out with a bloodcurdling Comanche war cry and drove his straining pony toward the blazing rifles ahead of him.

And then his blood ran cold.

Peering over the top of a gray boulder was One-Toe Ned, a leering sneer on his face as he thumbed lead at Nathan.

A slug stung Nathan's arm, but the hot blood coursing through his veins paid no attention. He clenched his teeth, swearing to kill the man who had betrayed him.

At the last moment, the small group of guerillas broke and ran as the larger-than-life specter of a giant with bared teeth and blood in his eyes bore down on them.

Three of them fell from the devastating fire of the Texas Rangers.

Ned ducked behind a boulder, then scurried up a narrow trail ascending the slope.

Nathan jerked the roan around and leaped to the ground.

Behind him, Barney and Joe Barlow yanked their ponies to a halt. "Nathan," shouted Barney. "Dammit, not by yourself. Get the hell back here."

By now, the remaining rangers had wheeled around and raced back. Within moments, they set up a perimeter behind boulders and began returning fire to protect Nathan.

The trail twisted up through narrow fissures in the gray granite walls of the Sierras. Protected from millennia of weather, many of the protruding shards of granite created when the walls split apart to form the narrow trail remained defined and sharp, while those exposed to the weather had been smoothed, so that fingers could not acquire a secure grasp.

Like a mountain lion, Nathan bounded up the steep slope, hearing the frantic grunts above as One-Toe Ned scrambled to escape.

Despite the urgency pounding in his chest, Nathan moved cautiously, pausing at each bend, at each fork in the trail. He was too close now to Selman and Sims to get himself shot up.

Cursing to himself, Ned scuttled up the slope to the summit of the pass. He paused, frantically scanning the rocky plateau for a place to hide.

A crooked grin split his bearded face when he spotted a jumble of boulders less than twenty yards from the trail. Quickly, he slipped in among them and recharged his carbine and belt pistols.

Then he waited.

Moments later, the crown of a black floppy hat appeared just over the rim of the trail, then quickly vanished.

Ned chuckled to himself, then called out, "It's a Mexican standoff, Nathan. Stick your head over the edge, and I'll blow it off. And you know, I don't miss when I got time, and I got time now."

Crouched below the rim, Nathan cursed. Given time, Ned was an unerring shot, and if he remembered right, that old mountain man was armed with a carbine and one, maybe two belt pistols. And Ned was patient. He could afford to be for he had more time to spare than Nathan.

From below, the sound of gunfire had slackened off. Periodic bursts echoed through the pass.

Without warning, footsteps slipping on rock sounded from down below the first bend in the trail. Quickly, Nathan eased several yards back down the trail just as Barney stuck his head around the bend and growled, "Did you get him?"

Shaking his head, Nathan explained that Ned had him pinned down.

Barney grimaced. "Some of our boys is hit bad. We got to get them back where we can tend them." He glanced at Nathan's leg. "You're bleeding!"

"It isn't bad." Nathan glanced over his shoulder at the summit of the trail. He turned back to his father-in-law. A shrewd grin cracked his rugged face. "Give me your shirt and hat," he muttered, quickly slipping his buckskin shirt over his head. "Then ride out on my pony. Leave yours behind. I'll catch up."

A frown wrinkled Barney's forehead, but he did as Nathan said. Moments later, clad in the mountain man's garb, he clambered back down the trail. Nathan followed to the first fork in the trail, then eased up that fork to the first bend.

There he crouched, and waited.

Several minutes later, the sound of retreating hoofbeats echoed from below. From high on the mountain trail, the rangers were too distant to discern features, but Nathan's floppy hat and buckskin shirt were easy to make out.

Behind the boulder, Nathan remained motionless, his ears straining for the sound of Ned descending the trail.

He hoped his onetime trapping partner would take the bait.

Moments later, a victorious whoop sounded from above, followed by the crack of a carbine and then the clattering of boots on the rocky trail. Nathan pressed against the wall of the fork, peering around the bend at the main trail.

The footsteps grew louder, and then One-Toe Ned came into view at the fork less than ten yards distant. In a cold voice, Nathan growled menacingly, "I plan to kill you, Ned."

CHAPTER
TWENTY-THREE

Without a moment's hesitation, Ned grabbed a belt pistol and fired at Nathan, who jerked back instantly. The slug hit the granite wall behind the mountain man and shattered, peppering him with shards of granite.

Dropping to a crouch, Nathan shot a glance around the bend, catching Ned squinting at where Nathan had been. He fired again, but Nathan pulled back just before the slug hummed past inches from him.

The clink of metal against metal echoed down the trail. Nathan glanced out to see Ned frantically reloading a belt pistol. "Too late, Ned," he said, stepping from behind the bend and aiming the muzzle of his Colt at his old friend's belly.

Ned's grime-covered face blanched. His black eyes narrowed shrewdly. "You ain't the kind to shoot me down in cold blood,

Nathan. I know you better than that."

His finger tightened on the Colt's trigger, then slacked off. He went closer and glared at his old friend. "It was a damn bad thing to do, Ned, turning traitor on a friend."

Ned shrugged. "It was the money. I told you. And rangers is an extra fifty dollars."

With a disgusted grunt, Nathan growled, "Money won't be doing you no good now."

A frown wrinkled One-Toe Ned's forehead. "You ain't going to give me a chance?" He nodded to the bowie on Nathan's hip. "You used to be a fair knife fighter with the Piekann Injuns up above the Muscleshell."

In one swift move, Nathan holstered his Colt and shucked his bowie. Every muscle tense, he replied, "Why not? You'll be deader than a beaver hat one way or another."

Ned grinned. He started to reach for his knife, but his hand darted inside his coat and jerked out a small hideout pistol and swung the muzzle toward Nathan.

Faster than the eye could follow, Nathan hurled the bowie.

Ned felt the impact against his chest. He clenched his teeth, trying to squeeze the trigger of his small pistol, but his fingers refused the commands his frantic brain was sending.

A great lassitude swept over him, and he felt himself falling into an ever-darkening abyss.

As wary of One-Toe Ned as a rattlesnake, Nathan approached the sprawled man with caution. The small pistol had fallen from Ned's limp fingers. Nathan kicked it away, then with his toe, rolled Ned over.

The bloodstain over Ned's heart continued spreading. Nathan knelt and with a sharp jerk, yanked the fifteen-inch blade from his old friend's heart. He stared into the closed eyes as Ned's breathing became more shallow.

Ned managed to open his eyes. He tried to grin. "Wasn't nothing personal, Nathan. Nothing at —" His voice died away.

Nathan pushed to his feet. "The hell there wasn't, Ned. The hell there wasn't."

From below came the sound of footsteps.

Quickly, Nathan backtracked up the fork, following the trail until it forked again. At the juncture was a large fissure in the granite wall. He paused. He had no idea where the trails led, so for the moment, he was content to remain where he was.

A few minutes later, excited voices

sounded down the trail. Nathan slipped into the dark fissure and crouched. The voices grew closer.

Nathan froze when two vaqueros paused at the juncture of the narrow trails, staring at Ned's body.

The vaquero in the lead pointed to the right fork, instructing his partner to investigate it while he searched the left fork. Reluctantly, the second vaquero agreed. Cautiously, he crept up the trail.

Nathan held his breath as the vaquero halted, staring up the trail. He could hear the small man's ragged breathing. If he turned around, he would be staring directly at Nathan. No sense in waiting for that, Nathan told himself. Easing to his feet, he shucked the bowie, grabbed the blade by the spine, and using the handle as a club, slammed it into the unsuspecting vaquero's skull.

Moving silently, Nathan stepped over the prone figure and disappeared up the right fork of the trail.

After several minutes winding and twisting through the maze of trails that spread like a spiderweb through the mountain, Nathan emerged onto a trail that led to the desert below. He paused and searched the countryside in an effort to orient himself, to get the lay of the land.

He spotted Barney's pony in a patch of mesquite and catclaws. Beyond stretched several miles of Tobosa grasslands, their two-foot stems swaying gently in the footsteps of the wind passing over them.

Moving cautiously, he made his way to the desert and into the motte of mesquite where the pony grazed.

Midafternoon, he ran across the ranger's trail. An hour later as he approached a thicket of catclaws, wiry trees filled with thorns and stunted by drought, a familiar figure stepped out.

"Wondered when you was getting here," Barney drawled.

"Made it as soon as I could." He looked around. "Where are the others?"

Barney hooked a thumb over his shoulder. "Heading back for a doctor. Turned out, three of our boys was shot up mighty bad." He paused, arched an eyebrow, and shrugged. "The Kickapoo's dead. Died in here," he said, nodding to the thicket from which he had appeared. "Didn't have no shovel, so I covered him with rocks."

Nathan grimaced. "Well, I got to say in his favor, that one, he did all right by us."

"Reckon so." He turned and headed back into the thicket. "Come on in. Got some jerky and sweet water."

"First, show me his grave." He pulled the Kickapoo's *misaami* from his possibles bag. "This needs to be buried with him. It'll help him find his way home."

Squatting in what little shade the scrawny canopy of thin leaves cast, Nathan related what had taken place up on the mountain, while he plucked the shards of lead from his thigh.

"So he's dead, huh?"

"Yep."

"Serves him right. That was a foul trick he played. Deserves what he got." Barney paused, staring at the canteen in his hand. "And you and him was once friends?"

Nathan harked back to those days. "Yep, but old Ned, I reckon he was a different body then. I don't know if I can blame him much or not. Different folks give in to different things."

Barney studied his son-in-law closely, sensing a tenuous premonition in Nathan's words. "Maybe so, but backstabbing an old friend ain't nothing to be proud of."

With a chuckle, Nathan changed the subject. "Well, I reckon we've lazed about and palavered long enough. You ready to ride?"

Brushing the dust from his worn trousers, Barney replied, "Where to?"

Frowning, Nathan nodded to the east. "Catch up with our boys, I reckon."

That night they camped in the foothills of the Sierra Madres. The nightmare came back to haunt Nathan. He sat up abruptly, cold sweat beading his forehead. He glanced at Barney, who slumbered peacefully. Slowly, he lay back, staring at the stars overhead, wondering just what the dream meant.

Hours dragged. As false dawn grayed the sky, Nathan arose, his eyes burning from lack of sleep. Moments later, Barney climbed from his blankets and stretched. He frowned. "What's that?"

To the east, a cloud of dust boiled from the horizon, a cloud so large, it had to be churned up by several hundred riders.

The two Texians remained hidden back among the boulders until they could determine the identity of the approaching detachment.

Slowly, the dark figures drew closer.

Barney grinned at Nathan. "Them's American troops."

"Well, I'll be — looks like Taylor finally got off his lazy tail." Nathan studied the half-dozen or so point riders, finally recognizing Ben McCullough and some of his rangers.

The big mountain man's assumption was correct. Taylor and his troops were marching on Monterrey, and McCullough's patrol was the general's point guard.

Nathan and Barney fell in with the rangers. Later that day, they joined their old regiment under Jack Hays, which had been ordered to scout for the battalion led by General G. L. Worth. "Tomorrow, we ought to reach San Francisco del Ora," Hays said. "Well in sight of the Saddle Back and Miter Mountains surrounding Monterrey."

Barney grinned at Nathan. "Maybe we'll run them yahoos down in Monterrey."

Drawing a deep breath, Nathan grunted, "Maybe."

Two nights later, Nathan stood on a sawtooth ridge staring down at the lights of Monterrey in the valley below. Unconsciously, his large hand drifted down to the handle of his bowie. The ominous words uttered before a battle by Chief Tatsicki-Stomick of the Piekanns fifteen years earlier flashed into his mind. "My blade is thirsty for Crow blood," the old chief had muttered prior to battle.

Imperceptibly, Nathan nodded. He laid his hand on his bowie. He knew how the old chief felt.

Next morning, Hays' regiment of rangers rode out early, assigned to skirt Monterrey and cut off the road to Saltillo to the southwest while Taylor attempted to take the city of Monterrey, which was defended by Santa Anna's hand-picked general, Pedro de Ampudia.

Barney cursed at the delay of entering Monterrey, but Nathan pointed out that cutting off all escape routes would force the three murderers to remain in the city.

By nightfall, a detail of 150 Texas Rangers camped on the Saltillo Road.

Next morning, an excited ranger burst into camp, shouting, "Colonel Hays, Colonel Hays! Mexicans! A whole army, coming up the road from Saltillo."

Hurling his coffee aside, Hays leaped to his feet. "How far?"

"Six, maybe seven miles back. We spotted them from the top of the pass."

Hays grinned at Nathan and Barney. "You boys ready for a good fight?"

Nathan's reply was to grab his saddle and

head for the rope corral.

Ten minutes later, the detail moved out west along the narrow road winding through the mountains. Having idled about in the few months since Palo Alto and Resaca de la Palma, the rangers were ready for a fight.

At the top of the pass, Hays reined up beside a half-dozen rangers who were peering toward Saltillo. Joe Barlow nodded to Hays. "There they be, Colonel."

Barney whistled softly and glanced up at Nathan. "There's a heap of them fancy-dressed jaspers."

Nathan narrowed his eyes. The Mexican troops wore gaudy coats of green and scarlet and black leather shakos. "I'd guess three or four regiments, maybe six, seven hundred," he muttered.

Ben McCullough pulled up beside Hays. Keeping his cold eyes fixed on the Mexican army, he muttered, "What you got in mind, Jack?"

Devil Jack Hays glanced at Nathan, who was staring at the oncoming army. With a crooked grin, he replied, "I don't know about you, Ben, but I'm looking forward to a little excitement."

McCullough grinned. "I reckon we all are." He glanced at Nathan.

The big mountain man nodded. "Like Laredo, I reckon."

Hays and McCullough laughed.

"Like Laredo," Hays replied.

With Hays leading the way, Nathan and McCullough at his side, the detail of rangers trotted down the road toward the approaching army. Over his shoulder, Hays ordered, "Pass the word. Keep your sidearms holstered, but keep them ready, boys. When I say jump, you best be right with me, or you'll get left behind."

The rangers rode easy, but their eyes quickly took in every movement of the approaching army. As one, they flipped the leather thongs off the hammers of their Colts, ready to fill their hands at their colonel's command.

As the rangers grew near the Mexican army, Hays raised a hand in peace.

Astride a silver-embossed saddle on a coal-black horse, the Mexican officer held up his hand in reply. He was dressed in black pantaloons and a bright red tunic criss-crossed by a decorative John Brown belt. He held himself stiffly, looking in pained condescension at the slovenly-dressed rangers.

Hays nodded. "Howdy, Colonel."

Arching an eyebrow, the hatchet-faced colonel sneered. "I am Lieutenant Colonel Elizondo Najerea. You will step aside. I am bound for Monterrey."

Hays didn't move a muscle. A faint grin spread over his face, making him look even younger. "Sorry, Colonel Najerea, sir. This is as far as you go."

Anger knit the colonel's face. His black eyes shifted to gaze at the rangers behind Hays. A smug smirk curled his thin lips. "A gringo boast. Even you can see you are badly outnumbered. Now, move aside, or I will give the command to crush you."

Nathan shot an amused glance at Devil Jack Hays. All a jasper needed to get on Hays' wrong side was to issue such an arrogant challenge. "I think the feller means business, Jack," Nathan muttered.

Hays laughed. "I reckon he does, so I suppose we best do something about it." With a wild scream, Hays shucked his Colt and dug his heels into his pony's flanks.

As one, the rangers leaped forward in the midst of wild shouts and bellowing six-guns.

Hays' first blast knocked Colonel Najerea from his silver-embossed saddle, dead before he hit the ground.

CHAPTER
TWENTY-FOUR

The ferocity of the sudden attack stunned the elite Zapadores Battalion, sending it reeling back in a frantic attempt to fight off the savage Texas Ranger regiment that swept through the ranks, sending panicking soldiers scattering in every direction and lancers racing back to Saltillo.

Ten minutes later, Hays reined his rangers in. "Let 'im go, boys. We done our job."

Nathan pulled up beside him. "Nary a scratch on any of our boys, Jack."

Hays chuckled. "I'd be damned put out if there was."

As if by magic, peasants appeared from the rocky mountainside. Hays quickly elicited their aid to bury the dead soldiers for whatever they found on the bodies.

The peasants cooperated eagerly.

Over the next few weeks, while Taylor's soldiers and marines battered at the city, small bands of rangers took it upon themselves to make lightning attacks on the strung-out battlements of Monterrey.

More than one battery of Mexican artillerymen or riflemen looked up to see a dozen savage rangers astride wide-eyed horses come slashing through their positions with pistols blazing. Before the blink of an eye, the rangers vanished into the night, leaving dead Mexicans behind. *Los diablos sangrientos,* they began calling the rangers — bloody devils.

Hays knew what his regiment was doing: the same thing that the other ranger regiments were doing. He knew their little sojourns into Monterrey were against orders, but he also was well aware there was no way to keep a thousand rangers squatting around a fire for weeks on end. So, he judiciously looked the other way.

On four other occasions, Mexican forces tried unsuccessfully to break through from Saltillo, but the rangers sent them packing.

Slowly Monterrey crumbled.

As the weeks dragged past, Nathan grew impatient.

One morning, Hays strode up to their fire. "All right, boys. Looks like we're getting out of here. Word just came in that Taylor wants us to take terms of surrender down to the general in Monterrey. Barney, you stay with here with Ford. He's going to be busy getting things put together for us to move out. Nathan, you ride down with me and Ben."

Thirty minutes later under a white flag, Nathan, Jack, and Ben rode into Monterrey. They halted on the outskirts of town upon the order of an officer, Colonel Moreno.

Moreno rode out to meet them, accompanied by a dozen brightly garbed lancers.

Hays handed him the terms of surrender. "General Taylor requests these terms be delivered to General Ampudia." Moreno hesitated, glancing around at the Mexican force behind him. With a grin, Hays added, "Anything happens to us, Colonel, a thousand Texas Rangers will come charging in here, and you'll think old Satan himself has done took over your town."

The colonel hesitated, then nodded briefly. "I will see the general."

Within ten minutes, Moreno returned with General Ampudia's capitulation.

Two days later, the enlistments for the Texas Rangers were over, and General Taylor, seeing the opportunity to rid himself of a major headache, gleefully sent them back to Texas, keeping only a handful.

"We got to stay, Barney. That's the only way we can keep looking for those three," Nathan muttered.

Barney Wills dragged his shirtsleeve over his sweaty forehead. "I reckon you're right, Nathan, but I sure am getting mighty tired of the soldier-boy games we got to play."

Nathan shrugged his shoulders and turned to Hays. "The general's making a big mistake, Jack. One ranger is the same as a dozen of those soldier boys."

Jack lifted an eyebrow. "You ain't getting no argument from me, Nathan. Old Zack says he doesn't want to have to put up with a thousand rangers that got nothing to do."

Barney and Nathan exchanged puzzled frowns. "Nothing to do," Barney exclaimed. "We got Monterrey. We ain't stopping here, are we?"

Hays shrugged. "It don't make sense if we do. From what I hear, there's army politics involved." He squatted by the fire and lowered his voice. "I was waiting outside Old Zack's tent when I heard him cussing some general by the name of Scott. Winfield Scott. You boys ever heard of him?"

Both rangers shook their head. Hays continued. "Seems like Scott's on the way to Mexico, and he don't want Zack getting no more publicity."

Puzzled, Barney frowned. "So? What does that have to do with this here war?"

Nathan grunted. "It's been my experience that most wars last a heap longer than they need be just because one jasper wants to look better than someone else."

"Well," Barney growled, "that sure don't make no sense."

Hays chuckled. "Most wars don't."

Over the next few weeks, the few remaining rangers were sent out on patrols in an effort to locate Canales' or Jarauta's guerillas. They found little sign, but the guerillas were growing bolder. Munitions turned up missing; horses were stolen; staples vanished from the mess halls; and from time to time, snipers directed fire at small patrols.

The city of Monterrey was under tight U.S. control, and between patrols, Barney and Nathan frequented the cantinas, searching for the remaining three scavengers. The big mountain man knew that despite U.S. occupation, the narrow *calles* and dark *callejones* hid angry eyes and sharp knives. He and Barney searched warily, never taking their eyes off their backs.

Despite the frustration of a futile search,

Nathan's nightmares did not return to haunt him. For the first time in months, he slept the night through without awakening in a cold sweat.

The morning after a dozen kegs of black powder and two hundred pounds of lead disappeared from the armory, Taylor exploded in frustration. He demanded permission to reenlist two hundred rangers, but his request was denied. In its place came Major William Polk, brother of the president. Enrico Villamez, who wore a well-coiffed goatee, and José Hernandez, both Mexican loyalists opposed to Santa Anna, accompanied him.

"He is here to tighten security," Taylor's aide explained when Hays asked of the major's mission.

Nathan remembered the pompous man. He expected repercussions as a result of his encounter with Polk several months earlier.

Only once during the initial meeting did Major Polk glance at Nathan, but it was enough for the big mountain man to read the hate still burning in Polk's eyes, although nothing in his tone or manner suggested he held any grudges. "We have a job to do," he told the few dozen men facing him. "The security measures we plan to implement are nothing new to you regular officers." He nodded to Hays and McCullough. "Irregular officers might find some of the measures, ah . . . confining, but rest assured, we can make our situation here much more tenable."

Under his breath, Barney whispered to Nathan, "What'd he say?"

Nathan whispered back. "I'm not sure, but I don't trust him."

"I don't either," Hays muttered later that day. "But we're saddled with him. Just watch your back. Last time he was here, we embarrassed him. He isn't the kind of hombre to forget that."

The next few weeks passed slowly.

The search for the three scavengers proved fruitless, and more than once, Nathan and Barney wondered aloud if they'd made a mistake by reenlisting. But each time, the burning desire for revenge told them they had made the right decision. Still, the cantinas of Monterrey offered nothing; the mountains around the city seemed to have swallowed Canales' and Jarauta's guerillas.

A few weeks later, having returned from a patrol just before dawn, Nathan was sleeping in his tent when a young private awakened him with the news that Major Polk wanted to speak with him.

The major gave no hint of their previous confrontation. Very cool and professional, he said, "Hays is on patrol, Cooper. I just received word of a possible guerilla encampment to the southeast in the mountains near a small village called Marin, about three hour's ride. Take a dozen men and see if there is anything to it."

Nathan studied Polk for several moments, trying unsuccessfully to read behind the impassive expression on the man's face. Finally, he nodded. "Right away, Major."

Upon spotting the small village of Marin just before noon, Nathan led his small patrol into the mountains, away from the eyes of the village.

From behind a jumble of boulders where they crouched, Joe Barlow whistled softly. "There must be at least four hundred of them old boys down there."

"At least," Poney Hall muttered.

"Well," drawled Nathan, "we've done what the major wanted. Let's get back with the news."

The patrol moved silently, wending its way down the narrow trail to the desert floor.

No sooner had the rangers left the protection of the boulders than the afternoon exploded in a barrage of gunfire, as two waves of guerillas hit the small patrol, one from either side.

Instinctively looping the reins about his iron T, Nathan shucked his Paterson Colt and, in a move reminiscent of Laredo and the Saltillo Road, jerked his roan to the left and, standing in the stirrups and firing his Colt, charged into the maw of the fire-belching pistols and muskets.

The other rangers followed, screaming and firing. The move caught the guerillas by surprise. They broke and scattered. Immediately, Nathan wheeled about and charged the other wave as it barreled toward them. His eyes swept the oncoming faces, searching for Selman or Sims.

Slugs hummed past, tugging at Nathan's shirtsleeves. One scorched his cheek, his roan shied as a slug burned a leg, and another slug tore off a chunk of his saddle horn.

Their charge carried them through the second wave. As they swept past, Nathan spotted a familiar face, the hatchet face of Enrico Villamez, Major William Polk's aide.

The unexpected and savage charges by the Texas Rangers completely demoralized the guerillas, and as one, they wheeled about and — being cut off from the village by the rangers — scattered into the foothills, leaving their dead and wounded behind on the desert floor.

The rangers reined up. Joe Barlow grinned. "Reckon they was the ones what got surprised, huh, Nathan?"

At that moment, Nathan spotted Villamez heading up into the mountains. With a savage snarl, he started to rein around.

Barlow shouted, "Let the greaser go, Nathan. We got to get back with the information Polk wanted."

Nathan's eyes blazed in rage. "You get back." He drove his roan up the mountain trail after Villamez.

With a curse, Barlow growled, "Why in the hell is he running off by hisself like that?"

Barney pursed his lips. He said nothing, but he had noticed a change in his son-in-law, and not one for the better.

CHAPTER
TWENTY-FIVE

The well-worn road undulated through the foothills, forking frequently, forcing Nathan to rein up and listen for the clatter of hooves on rock. Nathan drove the game roan hard. The surefooted animal glided over the rocky road, and the sounds Nathan pursued seemed to be growing louder, which meant he was gaining on Villamez.

The road led higher into the mountains, in places clinging precipitously to the steep slopes that dropped hundreds of feet to jagged boulders below.

When Nathan spotted the aide, his first thought was that Major William Polk had deliberately planned an ambush. Polk hated him. Nathan had embarrassed the man in front of his subordinates. On the other hand, the major was the president's brother.

For all Nathan knew, Villamez might be a spy for Canales or Jarauta. A burst of excitement coursed through his veins. He might even know the whereabouts of Selman and the other two. If Nathan could just capture him.

Suddenly, the squeal of a frightened horse and a man's scream sounded around a bend in the narrow road. Nathan urged his pony faster.

Around the bend, the big mountain man reined up, seeing nothing. Movement on the road before him caught his eye. The chilling buzz of rattles cut through the still mountain air.

"Whoa, boy, whoa," muttered Nathan, pulling the roan to a halt several feet from the rattler. "Let's don't crowd that feller. It appears he's spoiling for a fight."

Nathan backed the roan away. The rattler remained coiled, its spade-shaped head swaying from side to side. After a few moments, the rattlesnake uncoiled and slithered rapidly across the road to disappear into a fissure in the side of the mountain.

With a click of his tongue, Nathan urged his pony near the edge of the road. He grimaced when he spotted horse and rider a hundred feet below on the rocks. Villamez lay sprawled on his back on a boulder, a bloody smear running out fanlike from his crushed head.

■ ■ ■ ■

During the ride back to camp, Nathan decided that his second theory concerning Villamez was closer to the truth. The idea of the president's brother turning traitor was too big of a bite to swallow. The logical answer was that the aide was a spy who had wormed his way into the employ of the major by means of some conniving scheme.

That idea made sense. Now all Nathan had to do was convince himself.

Back in Monterrey that night, Nathan, with his father-in-law and Jack Hays, sat in front of a small *chiminea* sipping pulque and staring at the flames. Barney, who had had a couple drinks too many, snarled, "It wouldn't surprise me none at all if Polk was behind it. He don't like you, Nathan. Jack there can testify to that."

Hays nodded. "In spades."

Barney continued, "I don't care if he is the president's brother. Besides, I never voted for Polk nohow."

Nathan chuckled. "Who are you kidding, Barney? You probably didn't even vote."

The older man bristled. "That don't make no mind. I wouldn't have voted for him even if I had voted."

Jack cleared his throat. "I reckon it does look mighty suspicious, but looks aren't always what they seem. Now, I don't care for the major, and I know he hates you for that little incident in the tent. You not only scared the hell out of him, you embarrassed him in front of others. But he sure doesn't strike me as one so cold-blooded to get a dozen rangers killed off just to get back at you."

Nathan remembered the surprised look on Polk's face when he reported in. "Maybe so. Maybe not. I'm not as trusting as you, Jack, but I don't want to kill someone just on suspicion." He paused, and his deep voice dropped into a threatening growl that sent chills down his two friends' spines. "But if I ever find out he did send me out to get bushwhacked, he'll never live to see the next sunrise."

Days turned into weeks, weeks into months.

Nathan and Barney were counting the hours until their enlistment was up. After countless days of wrangling, the two had decided to chance Mexico on their own. "After all," Nathan had explained to Jack one night as they sat around the small fire in the *chiminea,* "someone reins us up, we'll just tell them we're looking to join up with Jarauta. They're like us. We can't tell one Mexican from the other; they can't tell one gringo from the other."

Jack paused rolling a cigarette and nodded to Nathan's iron T. "With that stuck on the end of your arm? Hell, Nathan. I reckon every greaser in Monterrey knows you and has spread word to every guerilla in the state of Nuevo Leon." He paused and shook his head in sympathy for his friend. "Look, I know you're getting impatient. I don't blame you, but the truth is —" He nodded to Barney. "And you know it too, Barney. The truth is, your only chance of finding those scavengers is here with old Zach. You might not like it, but them are the facts."

Nathan's face darkened as he looked hard at the smaller man. After a few moments, he grimaced and shook his head. Jack was right. Taylor was his only chance. But he was tired of meaningless patrols through the mountains surrounding the sprawling city.

Abruptly, the door burst open and Joe Barlow rushed in, his face dark with rage. "Jack. Come quick. It's Poney. He's carved up something fierce."

Outside the room in which the rail-thin

ranger lay, a crowd of grumbling rangers had assembled. Hays, followed by Nathan and Barney, shouldered through. "Let us by, boys," Hays said in his soft voice. "I'll let you know what's going on."

"Hell, Colonel," said a voice from the crowd. "We know what's going on. It's them greasers. They cut old Poney to pieces."

From the corner of his eye, Nathan saw Barney jerk to a halt and take an inadvertent step back when he spotted the lean ranger on the bunk. His belly had been split open, his throat slashed, and one eye cut out. Nathan tightened his throat, a measure he had learned years back up in the Rockies when witnessing some of the savage leavings of various Indian tribes.

His eyes quickly assessing the hopelessness of the young ranger's condition, Nathan watched as Hays knelt by the boy's side and took his hand. "We'll get word to your folks up in Liberty, Poney. Don't you fret none about that."

The butchered ranger gave no indication he had heard Hay's promise, but his fingers clutched Hay's hand.

His eyes hard and cold, Hays looked up at Joe Barlow. Barlow read the question in his colonel's eyes. He nodded sheepishly. "Him and a couple other old boys went down to the *pueblo de chicos*."

Hays' lips curled in a snarl. "Boys' Town, huh?" He turned accusing eyes on the two rangers at Barlow's side. "Hank, George. You boys go with him?"

Shuffling their feet, the two rangers burned holes through the floor with their eyes. "Yessir," Hank muttered.

"You knew my orders. These people here hate us, and I can't blame them."

George jerked his gaze from the floor and glowered at Hays. He gestured to Poney. "That don't give them no call to cut one of us up like that."

His voice as cold as his eyes, Hays growled. "Why not? We come here and take over their homes. We kill their husbands and brothers and sons. Some jasper did that to you back home, would you just stand there and let'em get away with it?"

George bristled. "That's different. That —"

"No, it ain't," Jack barked, cutting off the ranger's retort, "and you know it." He shot a blistering look at the second ranger. "You both put Poney here just as much as them greasers did."

Barlow interrupted, "Poney was going anyway, Colonel. We all tried to stop him, but he was mule-headed stubborn. George and Hank here rode along with him just in case." He paused and added with a hint of resentment in his voice. "He was looking for something to do besides shine the seat of his pants sitting around here."

The intimation in Barlow's tone was not lost on Hays. For a moment, the slender colonel's eyes narrowed, and then his shoulders slumped with understanding. He glanced at Nathan who was staring at him with a knowing grin on his grizzled face. "We're all tired of sitting around, Joe." He drew a deep breath and turned back to Poney just as the young ranger released his grip on Hay's hand.

Outside, Hays faced the rangers clustered around the door. "Poney's dead. We all know what happened. I'm telling you now. There ain't many of us left since the others went back to Texas. We got to look after each other, and one of the best ways is to stay away from the *putas* down in Boys' Town. They get you into a room all by your lonesome like they did Poney, and you'll end up like him."

A voice called out from the rear of the crowd, "When are we going to do something besides sit, Colonel Hays?"

Hays stretched his neck to peer over the

rawhide tough rangers facing him. He took in their cold eyes, their hard faces grizzled with several days of whiskers. They were fighting men, not prone to lazing about. Their kind either cleaned up trouble, and if there were none to clean up, then they made their own. "Who is that back there?"

The rangers parted and a lanky ranger nodded. "It's me, Colonel, Bill Lindsey from San Patricio."

A faint smile played over Hays' lips. "We been together a long time, Bill."

"Yes, sir, Colonel. All the way back to Laredo."

Hays sighed. "Well, Bill, I wish I could tell you what you asked, but I can't because I don't know." He looked around at the hard men staring at him. "Something might break in five minutes, or five days, or five weeks. We just got to be patient. Something will break."

Nathan studied his slight friend, piqued by the tone of his voice, which suggested that perhaps Hays suspected more than he was letting on.

Bill grunted. "No disrespect intended, Colonel, but, patience ain't one of my strong suits."

Several assenting mutters rolled from the crowd of rangers.

Hays chuckled. "Mine neither, Bill. Mine neither."

That night, a faint noise awakened Nathan. He lay motionless, his fingers wrapped around the handle of his bowie. After a few moments, he recognized the muffled sound as the saddling of ponies.

A grin flickered over his lips, and he closed his eyes.

He wasn't certain just what was on the fire, but one thing was likely. The next morning should prove mighty entertaining.

During the night, a storm broke. Lightning lanced the dark mountains looking down on the sprawling city. Rain lashed the narrow *calles,* forcing citizens to dash from door to door in a futile effort not to be soaked by the downpour.

The rain slacked off to a steady drizzle as a half-dozen rangers sat in the mess hall next morning, putting themselves around steaming coffee and hot biscuits and beans.

Without warning, the door burst open, and General Zachary Taylor stood glaring at the rangers. He wore his usual faded green coat over gray trousers two sizes too large.

He paused in the open doorway, his cold, impersonal eyes scanning the room. When their gaze landed on Jack Hays, the general strode to him, mud falling from his boots in great chunks. "Colonel Hays!"

Casually, Jack stood. "Morning, General. Care for some breakfast?"

Taylor's eyes narrowed as they scanned the curious rangers looking on. "No, thank you," he replied sharply. "I have just had a visit from the *alcalde* of Monterrey, and he informed me that this morning, six of his citizens were found hanging by the neck in the plaza down in the slum they call Boys' Town."

Hays nodded. "Anything me and my boys can do to help?"

The general's gaze grew more intense. "Did any of your men leave the encampment last night?"

"No, sir. Not to my knowledge."

Nathan arched an eyebrow.

Taylor continued, "Your rangers have always had trouble with the Mexican populace."

"That's true, General. But like I said, all of my rangers were here last night. Is the *alcalde* saying we were involved?"

"No, but it is known that one of your men was killed down in that section of town

253

yesterday."

Hays nodded. "Poney Hall. Good man, but he went against orders."

Suspiciously, Taylor eyed the onlooking rangers. "You don't think your men would have sought retribution?"

With a chuckle, Hays replied, "Human nature, general, but like I said, my boys were here last night."

Bill Lindsay pushed to his feet from behind one of the tables and drawled, "Excuse me, General Taylor, sir, but this morning, one of the Mexican boys who delivers supplies told me that a bunch of grea — I mean Mexicans in town had been stealing horses and supplies from us. They went to confession down at the church, and the priest made them feel downright guilty about it. So guilty that they hung theirselves."

Taylor's craggy face froze. He glared at Lindsay who looked back with childlike innocence on his face.

Suppressing a grin, Hays spoke up. "I heard that story too, general, but I didn't put no stock in it. Still, you know those Mexicans. They're said to be hot-blooded, and it's mighty hard to figure out what someone like that will do."

CHAPTER
TWENTY-SIX

Old Zack eyed the rangers several moments, his craggy face revealing no emotion. Finally he turned back to Hays. "Colonel, send half your men to scout the Saltillo Road. We have orders to take the city."

A roar of approval erupted from the contingent of Texas Rangers. Nathan eyed Jack who, seeing the question in the big mountain man's eyes, shot him a smug grin. So, Jack had been holding back.

Leading six rangers, Devil Jack Hays rode out the Saltillo Road an hour later with Nathan and Barney at his side. Nathan arched an eyebrow. "You knew something was coming up, didn't you, Jack?"

The youthful colonel grinned. "I've been around long enough, Nathan, to know that politics shape much of the strategy of a war. Last week, Old Zack got word that Winfield Scott and ten thousand soldiers were coming into Vera Cruz, and that Scott would take command of the army, Taylor's included. Now, word is Old Zack wants to be president of the United States. Scott has the same ambition."

Nathan grinned. "So that's it, huh? Taylor wants to put a few more victories under his belt before he turns over the reins to Scott."

Hays winked at him. "Exactly."

Shaking his head, the big mountain man growled, "Hell of a way to run a war."

To Nathan's surprise, they encountered no guerilla harassment along the road to Saltillo. An hour before sundown, they rode into a small village a few miles from Saltillo where they were met by an undemonstrative, but surly populace.

Joe Barlow accompanied Hays into a market while Nathan and the other rangers sat astride their ponies outside. Minutes later, Hays and Barlow returned, the latter lugging a bulging tow sack, which he tied to his saddlehorn.

Barlow swung into his saddle. "We eat good tonight, boys." He patted the sack. "Goat."

A couple of miles out of town, they pulled into a tangled motte of chaparral and built a small fire. Squatting around the fire smoking cigarettes and drinking thick coffee while the goat haunch broiled, the rangers engaged in hushed conversations.

Jack plopped down by Nathan and pulled out the makings. While he built his cigarette, he muttered, "Got some news back there, Nathan. I figure you'll be glad to hear it. Jarauta and his men are in Saltillo. He has a new lieutenant, a big gringo with a large black beard." He tapped his teeth. "And missing some front teeth. Always with him, like his own shadow, is a skinny cowpoke with a knife cut across his right eye."

Nathan looked around at Jack in surprise. "You certain?"

Hays nodded. "The storekeeper I bought this grub from told me. Several of the guerillas rode in last week and hurrahed the town. Raped several of the young women. His daughter was one."

Blood pounded in the big mountain man's ears. His pulse raced. He glanced to the southwest in the direction of Saltillo.

"In the morning," Jack said, "I'll send two boys back and tell Taylor the road is clear. The rest of us will scout the outskirts of town. Keep an eye on anything unusual."

Nathan slept but little that night, remembering the months and the miles he had pursued the killers. Almost nine months and a thousand miles. And now, two of them were within five miles. He flexed his fingers, trying to imagine just how they would feel around Frank Selman's neck.

For the next three days, the five rangers watched the city of Saltillo, seeing very little activity. Nathan and Barney had insisted on taking the south road that twisted through the mountains to Ciudad Victoria. On the morning of the fourth day, the sun had not even washed away the shadows of the night from the narrow alleys when the sleepy village became alive with commotion. Nathan grimaced against a sinking feeling in the pit of his stomach as the narrow streets filled with armed riders, all packing gear on their ponies.

Jarauta's troops were moving out.

"Damn!" Nathan exclaimed, pounding the side of his fist against the rocky boulder behind which he was watching. He glanced to the northeast. "Damn, damn, damn!"

"Where in the hell is Old Zack and his boys," growled Barney, feeling as helpless as a newborn kitten. "There ain't no way we can slow that bunch down in time for Taylor to get here."

Staring down at the troops preparing to

move out, Nathan considered his father-in-law's words. He studied the road winding its way out of Saltillo. His eyes narrowed in triumph when they focused on a limestone ridge overlooking the road a quarter of a mile distant.

"Maybe not, but a jasper over yonder would have a bird's-eye view when they rode past," he said, pointing to the rocky shelf above the road. He nodded to the Hawken roundballer on his pony. "Well within the range of my saddle rifle."

Barney frowned. "If you're thinking what I think you're thinking, you got no more brains that a turtle has feathers. That close up, they'll run you down for certain."

Ignoring the older man's remark, Nathan studied the slope. From where he sat, it appeared there was enough cover on the slopes for a single jasper to lose himself from any pursuit. He rose from where he crouched behind the boulder and swung into the saddle. "Stay here, Barney. Makes me feel better knowing someone is watching my back."

The older man shook his head in frustration. "At that distance, I ain't going to be no help. Stop and think about it, son. So you get one of them. If they get you, there's still two of them jaspers left."

With a crooked grin, Nathan replied, "Then it'd be up to you, partner." With a click of his tongue, he wheeled the roan about and headed for the distant mountain slope.

Barney let loose with a string of oaths as Nathan disappeared amongst the chaparral and boulders.

Glancing back toward town, Nathan clenched his teeth when he spotted the guerillas swinging up into their saddles. His keen eyes swept forward, picking out his trail to the selected ledge that was about two hundred feet above the road. He urged his pony to move faster.

The roan's hooves clattered over the rocky talus as he scrambled up the steep slope to the ledge. A thick growth of chaparral grew on the ledge, and Nathan broke a few branches to provide a narrow view of the road below. He studied his position and grinned. It was perfect.

At the rear of the ledge, Nathan discovered a trail leading higher up the slope before forking into a half-dozen different directions. He tied the roan at the junction of the forks. He paused momentarily to study the slope on which he and Barney had maintained surveillance of the village.

He spotted Barney and raised his hand. Barney responded.

Moving quickly, Nathan tugged a couple of dead logs near the rim of the ledge. Kneeling behind the fortification of logs, he checked his .50 Hawken and seated a new cap. He rechecked the loads in his two belt pistols and his Colt.

Then he turned his attention to the road below, where centuries of travel had cut ruts into the rock. The cool morning was filled with the gay songs of the black-faced thrushes and the tawny-winged woodcreepers.

From where he lay, Nathan's view of the road covered about fifty or sixty feet. He guessed he would have about twenty seconds from the time a rider first came into view and until he disappeared. He patted the dark forearm of the Hawken. With this rifle, that was more than enough time.

Within minutes, the distant clatter of hooves echoed up the rocky road. The song birds fell silent. The only sound other than the hoof beats was the beat of wings as the birds flew away.

Nathan slid the muzzle of the Hawken over the top log and cocked the hammer. Now he could hear a few voices mixed with the clatter of hooves and the rattling of *carretas.*

Nathan realized his fingers were cramping. He flexed them, touching the forefinger lightly to the trigger.

Suddenly, the first riders appeared, three vaqueros, studying the road ahead. Moments later, two more riders came into view, one in huaraches and wearing baggy white blouse and *pantalones.* He rode stiffly, with the carriage of royalty — shoulders back, head high. On his head, he wore a flat-crowned sombrero with a flat brim.

The other wore the trim uniform of a Mexican officer.

Suddenly, voices from behind caused the first rider to rein up. He turned his pony and looked back. Instinctively, Nathan knew he was looking at Padre Celedonia de Jarauta. Now, who was the officer?

Jarauta gestured to the rear of the column and shouted. "Ah, General Parades. Here comes one of my men from General Antonio Canales."

At that moment, a rider pulled up.

Nathan caught his breath.

The newcomer had shoulders the width of a double-bitted axe and a thick black beard down to his chest. The face was the one he had seen months earlier.

Selman!

Wasting no time, Nathan laid his cheek on the butt of the Hawken and lined the sights up on Frank Selman. He drew a deep breath and held it.

Slowly, he squeezed the trigger.

And just as he did, a vaquero rode into the line of fire.

Dense white smoke billowed from the muzzle of the Hawken, obliterating Nathan's sight for a moment. When the smoke cleared, Selman and Jarauta were pointing in his direction.

The vaquero lay on the ground, a bloody hole in his back.

Jarauta shouted. *"¡Amigos! ¡Allí! ¡En el saliente! ¡Mátelo!"* There! On the ledge! Kill him!

Muttering a curse at his bad luck, Nathan pulled his Paterson and jumped to his feet, even though he knew the distance was too great for a pistol. Despite the gunfire aimed in his direction, he brought the pistol up to bear on Frank Selman, but two other riders were milling about in front of the bearded scavenger.

Nathan hesitated, then fired.

CHAPTER
TWENTY-SEVEN

The big mountain man cursed as soon as he squeezed the trigger, knowing the lead ball was going wide. He spun and raced for his roan.

Moments later, he was urging his horse along a narrow trail twisting up the steep mountain slope covered with chaparral and boulders.

Within minutes, the sounds of pursuit faded away.

Taylor's army marched into Saltillo the next morning, meeting little resistance before taking over the city.

That night, Hays gathered his rangers to inform them that they were moving out the next morning for Ciudad Victoria in the state of Tamaulipas. They were on Jarauta's trail.

Later, Nathan grinned across the campfire at Hays. "Old Zack has sure got his eye set on the president's job, huh?"

Hays laughed and touched a match to a cigarette.

"I told you, didn't I? He wants to gobble up as much of this country as he can before Scott reins him in."

Nathan grinned at Barney. The older man nodded. They were moving ever deeper into Mexico, pushing Selman and Sims ahead of them. Nathan's smile grew grim. It was just a matter of time before they caught the two.

Within a month, Taylor had occupied Ciudad Victoria.

And then, to Nathan's chagrin, Winfield Scott ordered Taylor back to Monterrey 150 miles to the north.

Two days after Taylor retreated to the sprawling city, intelligence arrived that Santa Anna was approaching from the south with a large army, obviously to retake Monterrey.

The news assuaged Nathan and Barney's frustration at being forced to draw away from those they pursued. Now, Selman,

265

Sims, and Salado were coming to them.

Around the fires that night, as a cool February wind swept down from the mountains, fifteen somber rangers discussed the current state of affairs in hushed tones.

Joe Barlow took a deep drag off his cigarette and let the smoke drift up from his lips as he commented, "Yep, I remember Santa Anna. I had a cousin at the Alamo and friends at Goliad."

Barney spoke up. "Nathan here met some of those old boys from Goliad."

The rangers turned to him, and Joe asked, "You was there?"

Frowning over unpleasant memories, Nathan grunted, "I was just passing through. I was there when word come about the Alamo."

Bill Lindsay asked in disbelief, "You didn't stay?"

Nathan shot a murderous look at the lanky ranger, who recoiled in surprise.

Barney broke in. "He was after his little niece. The Kronks had stole her."

Lindsay nodded. "Oh. Hell, that being the case, I sure don't blame you none at all, Nathan. Did you get her okay?"

The big man just stared at the fire, saying nothing.

Lindsay frowned at Barney. "I say something wrong?"

The older man laid his hand on Nathan's shoulder. "That's why we're here now. Last year, she was kilt by scavengers, and them bastards are with this Jarauta jasper."

The rangers grew silent. One by one, they muttered their good-nights and slipped away to their bedrolls. When only Nathan and Barney remained, Barney whispered. "They didn't mean nothing by it, Nathan."

Almost inaudibly, he replied. "I know."

That night, the nightmare returned to haunt Nathan.

The next afternoon, Nathan was in the stable tending his roan when Ben McCullough stopped by. "The old man wants us to scout out Santa Anna's troops. You and me and four others."

In the next stall, Barney paused grooming his own pony. "When?"

McCullough halted him. "Not you, Barney. Sorry. Rip made a point of saying he needed you here."

Nathan could hear Barney bellowing and cussing until they rode out of camp.

Just before dark, the small patrol of rangers spotted the army less than ten miles from

Monterrey, but the light was too poor to determine Santa Anna's strength.

They looked on as the army camped on either side of the road. Later, the rangers gathered in a tangle of chaparral. "I say we wait until morning so we can get a fair count," said Joe Barlow.

Nathan disagreed. "Wouldn't be smart to wait. Santa Anna's sneaky. He sent his army at the Alamo at five o'clock in the morning. By the time the sun came up, all those boys was dead. Who's to say he won't drive this army into Monterrey tonight?" He paused and added, "I got personal reasons here. If we can whip Santa Anna, resistance in Mexico will stop, and I can get on with what I come to do. We need to get those numbers for Old Zack tonight, no matter what."

Bill Lindsay leaned forward. "And how do you reckon we can do that?"

McCullough broke in. "I'll tell you how. We'll just ride in down there amongst them. Hell, look at those rannies. Must be a five hundred fires down there, all burning greasewood and kicking up smoke so thick you can catch it with your fingers. Throw your blanket over your head and slump in the saddle. They'll figure you're one of them gringo gunnies." He looked at Nathan and, though the nighttime filled their faces with shadows, each man knew the other's thoughts.

Barlow chuckled. "Hell, why not? I ain't done nothing stupid in the last hour or so."

"Go in pairs," McCullough said. "Shouldn't draw as much attention as a single rider."

Nathan paused outside the camp and threw his rope over a dead mesquite. When Bill Lindsay frowned, he explained, "They spot us, they'll figure we're hauling wood back to our fire."

Lindsay laughed. "They ain't that dumb."

"Nope, you're right. They're not dumb, just a little too full of theirselves tonight."

When the younger ranger frowned, Nathan explained, "They figure they got Taylor outmanned and outgunned. Hell, he's already retreated a hundred and fifty miles. Santa Anna figures he's got the general on the run, so what have they got to worry about?"

Pulling the dead tree behind them, Nathan and Lindsay rode through the Mexican camp filled with wives, camp followers, and merchants hawking tequila, tamales, and *cabra*. Smoke from greasewood and sage hung heavy in the air, choking the lungs and stinging the eyes.

The pair of rangers drew a few curious stares, but, dragging the dead mesquite, they traversed the length of the encampment and back without incident.

Bill Lindsay whistled softly as they disappeared into the darkness outside the camp. "That there is a heap of Mexicans."

"I'm guessing fifteen thousand, General," Nathan said next morning when the small patrol reached Monterrey.

"That's four to one," McCullough added, eyeing the general's officers who were looking on.

Taylor studied the rawhide tough ranger. His eyes glittered with a youthful excitement that somehow seemed out of place in his craggy face. "Ten miles, you say?"

"And coming fast, General," Nathan said.

Taylor pondered his situation.

Nathan continued, "You don't have the troops to stop fifteen thousand Mexicans, not here."

Old Zack eyed the big mountain man curiously. "My thoughts exactly, Mister Cooper. That's why we're falling back to Angostura Pass near the hacienda of Buena Vista." He turned to his officers. "Gentlemen, we move out immediately."

■ ■ ■ ■

Riding with the point patrol Taylor had sent out, Nathan nodded appreciatively when he spotted Angostura Pass. He grunted and said aloud, "I got to hand it to the general. If I was outnumbered like him, here's where I'd sit my tail."

"Yep," drawled Devil Jack Hays, "Santa Anna has got to come head-on."

By evening, Taylor's battle lines were formed, including a company of the crack First Mississippi Regiment of Riflemen commanded by Colonel Jefferson Davis, Taylor's son-in-law, on the left flank. "The way I see it, Jeff," Taylor said, "he'll try the left flank. I'm sending the Texas Rangers over there with you. Use them however you see fit."

Davis nodded. "Don't worry, General, we'll hold." He nodded to Taylor's heavy cannons. "The way you have your artillery placed, we'll hold."

Taylor kept Nathan and Ben McCullough to carry dispatches.

The next morning, three Mexican officers wearing black service hats, red jackets with epaulets, and black pantaloons tucked into shiny black boots rode in under a white flag. Nathan and McCullough were squatting at the fire outside Taylor's tent when they approached. They rose to meet the riders.

Reining their warhorses to a halt, the Mexican officers stared down at the ill-dressed rangers with disdain. One urged his pony forward a few steps, then, straightening his shoulders, spoke in precise English. "Captain Mendoza, gentlemen. With permission, we would speak with General Taylor."

Before Nathan could reply, Taylor pushed open the tent flap and stepped out, wearing his usual disheveled uniform. "I'm Taylor. Who are you?"

The Mexican captain hesitated, then covering his surprise at the untidy man before him, nodded. "General Taylor, we carry a request from Generalissimo Santa Anna who calls for the immediate surrender of your troops. You will —"

Taylor's face turned livid with anger. He barked out, "Captain, you go back and tell Santa Anna that I said for him to go to hell."

CHAPTER
TWENTY-EIGHT

As soon as the Mexican couriers departed, Nathan grinned at Taylor. "Well, I can say one thing in your favor, General. You know how to start a war."

Taylor turned to the rangers. For the first time since Nathan had known the general, the old man smiled. "Boys, I hope you're ready for a fight. I got a feeling, it won't be long in coming."

Nathan chuckled. "I reckon you got a knack for understatement, General."

Taylor laughed, then grew serious. "Cooper, hightail it to Davis. Tell him the fight is coming. McCullough, you tell Wilson on the right flank the same thing."

"Good to see you, Nathan," drawled Hays after the big mountain man had reported to Colonel Davis. He nodded to the Mexican army assembling before them. "Looks like we'll catch the brunt of their lancer charge. Davis figures our rangers can cut through the lancer charge. I figure it that way too."

Nathan eyed the rangers surrounding them. Anxious for a fight, they grinned at him. Barney winked and patted the butt of his Colt. Hays nodded to the Mexican lancers. "Them old boys are pure army. The way I hear it, their papas and grandpapas was military. Word is that's the Tulancingo Cuirassiers, the best Mexico has. They know one way, but if that's taken from them, they're likely to be as discombobulated as a crib girl at a church Bible class. That's our job."

"Besides," Barney said. "We heard Jarauta and Canales is with Santa Anna."

Nathan's eyes grew wide. He looked questioningly at Hays. The youthful captain nodded. "A prisoner was brought in last night. Jarauta and Canales are out there."

"And that means Selman and Sims are there too," Barney said. "We'll —" He jerked to a halt at the sudden roar of cannon fire.

"Mount up, boys," Hays ordered.

Suddenly the approaching battle took on a different meaning for the big mountain man. Once he fought his way through the lancers, then somewhere out there were

Sims and Selman. Somewhere.

He swung into his saddle. He could feel the concussion from the roaring cannons, hear the whistling of the canister and balls. "How do we play it, Jack?" He looped the reins over the iron T and palmed his Colt.

Hays gave him a crooked, devil-may-care grin. "Just don't get in front of me if you don't want to be run over."

The rangers laughed and shucked their Colts.

"Here they come," Joe Barlow said, nodding to the four waves of lancers, each with twenty Mexican lancers resplendent in scarlet and green uniforms, charging across the valley toward them.

Devil Jack Hays' face grew somber, his eyes cold, his jaw set. Nathan and Barney pulled up beside him, and the remainder of the ranger company fell into a skirmish line beside them.

Nathan's roan jitter-stepped nervously. "Easy, boy, easy," Nathan muttered.

The first wave grew closer.

The Mississippi riflemen held their fire.

When the first wave of lancers was sixty feet away, Hays gave a wild yell and spurred his horse forward. As one, the line of fifteen rangers leaped forward. Teeth bared, they rose in their stirrups and pumped off slug after slug as they drove into the attacking force.

They slammed through the line.

Nathan holstered his empty Colt and shucked one of his belt pistols. Instead of wheeling about, he continued his headlong charge into the second wave. Fourteen rangers thundered at his side, their piercing war cries a chilling prelude to the second barrage of gunfire.

All about Nathan, the air thundered and roared with the cacophony of squealing war horses, murderous shouting, cracking gunfire, and piteous cries of pain.

He emptied his third Colt as he crashed through the fourth wave of lancers. Shoving it back in his belt, he grabbed his bowie and wheeled about. All he could see was a milling melee of red and green jackets and dusty cowpokes.

Clenching his teeth, he drove his roan into the midst of the fighting. Using the bowie like a tomahawk, he hacked left and right.

Suddenly his roan reared, pawing at the sky. Moments later, the triple-pointed head of a lance slammed into his saddle horn.

Instinctively, Nathan slashed backward with the fifteen-inch blade, feeling an impact and hearing a grunt. Without looking, he jerked the roan away from the lancer and spun around in time to see the red-jacketed lancer tumble off the rear of his war pony, his partially severed head bouncing off of his left shoulder.

Blood fury pounded in his ears as the big mountain man charged back into the fight, slashing left and right as the old Kronk war cries ripped from his throat.

And then suddenly, there were no colorful jackets around. A whoop and holler sounded behind him. Hays shouted at the top of his lungs, "We did it, boys, we did it. They're running back to their mamas."

Santa Anna launched another charge, and another, but the U.S. Marines, the First Mississippi Regiment of Riflemen, and a handful of Texas Rangers beat them back. Santa Anna finally retreated, and Taylor moved back to Monterrey.

Six of the rangers were killed in the battle, but the small company had littered the battlefield with over two hundred lancers and soldiers.

Colonel Jefferson Davis came to their barracks that night to pay his respects, despite the severe wound to his foot he received during the day's fight. "Back home in Mississippi, I heard word of you Texas Rangers. I never knew just how true it was until today." He saluted them sharply. "Any of you Texans decide you'd like a taste of Mississippi army life, just let me know. I'd be mighty proud to serve with you."

As Davis limped away, Nathan nodded to his retreating back. "Now, there's a man I wouldn't mind taking orders from."

Hays nodded. "He is a man of much integrity. Someday, Jefferson Davis will be a great man. Mark my words."

With news that Santa Anna was running back to Mexico City, Nathan's hopes soared. Around the fire that cool February night, he figured with the Mexican dictator's defeat, he and Barney could pursue the scavengers deeper into Mexico without having to worry about Mexican troops.

Barney agreed, but reminded his son-in-law, "Don't forget, we still got a couple weeks of enlistment left, Nathan."

McCullough rushed up to their fire, his leathery face contorted in anger. "Jack. Just got word. Scott is ordering us all to Vera Cruz."

Hays' eyes narrowed. "All?"

"Taylor's army. And that includes us."

Nathan's eyes met Barney's. The older man shook his head. "Let's us just wait until we get the straight of it," he muttered.

■ ■ ■ ■

The next morning, Sam Walker rode in, confirming the news. General Winfield Scott had indeed ordered Taylor's army to Vera Cruz. "From there," Walker said, "He plans to cut across the country to Mexico City, taking on Santa Anna in his own backyard."

After a fretful night, concerned that his pursuit of the scavengers might be delayed, Nathan was in a testy mood, touchier than a teased snake. His frustration was tying knots in his belly. He looked up from the fire. "What about here, Monterrey? What about those that have died so we can be here? Does Scott figure it isn't important enough to keep?"

Walker and Hays exchanged confused looks. Sam shrugged. "It don't make sense to me, neither, but them is the orders."

Nathan clenched his fist and made an effort to keep a tight rein on his temper. He looked at Jack, and in a soft voice that trembled with anger, said, "I'm getting mighty fed up with the soldiering business, Jack."

Walker cleared his throat. "You might not think so when I tell you what I just learned, Nathan." He glanced at Barney and continued, "Ain't you been looking for a greaser with the handle of Luis Salado?"

The frustration twisting Nathan's guts vanished as a burst of adrenaline coursed through his veins. "Salado? You damned right." He was almost afraid to ask the next question. "Why?"

"Ever chance I got after you told me about" — he hesitated and stuttered — "I mean, well, you know. What happened up there in East Texas."

Nathan nodded. "Go on."

"Well, I always asked questions about the three you're hunting. This morning I was talking to a couple soldier boys who had been guarding some of the prisoners we took yesterday. Right next door to us. Seems like a greaser looking for special treatment put them on to one named Luis Salado, who had bragged and laughed about ra— I mean about doing some bad things up in East Texas."

Eyes turning to ice, Nathan pushed to his feet. "Barney."

The older man rose quickly. "I'm right beside you."

"Take me to that soldier boy," Nathan said coldly.

Walker nodded. "Glad to."

The U.S. Marine private had no compunction in turning the Mexican named Luis Salado over to Sam Walker.

Salado looked up at Walker in alarm. "Please, senor. I have done nothing. Do not kill me."

Walker sneered, "Then you best do what I say."

Outside the compound, Walker pointed to a swaybacked sorrel. "Up there, amigo."

The puzzled man did as he was told.

Around the first corner, he saw Nathan and jerked his pony to a halt. His black eyes spotted the iron T on Nathan's left arm. While he had never come face-to-face with Nathan Cooper, he recognized the man from the stories spread through Texas and Mexico.

He panicked and yanked his sorrel around.

CHAPTER
TWENTY-NINE

Sam Walker drove his horse into Salado's and slammed the muzzle of his Colt across the Mexican's back. "Just you be quiet, and you won't get hurt. Try to run again, and I'll put a hole in you big enough to drive a stagecoach through."

On the outskirts of the city, they rode into an empty adobe that had supported the spring and summer vegetable bazaars. The large, dark structure smelled of wet mold and rotted vegetables.

When Walker forced Salado to ride into the shadowy building behind Nathan and Barney, the frightened Mexican wet his pants.

Nathan swung down from his roan and eyed the trembling man. He couldn't resist a faint smile at the man's urine dripping from the belly of his horse onto the dusty floor.

Studying the quivering man, Nathan struggled to control his rage, vaguely aware that the veneer of civilization in which he, with the help of his wife, Marie, had managed to cloak himself, was slowly peeling away, much as the current of a stream washes sand from the shore.

The hot blood of revenge surged through his veins.

He yanked Salado from the swayed back of his sorrel and slung him to the ground. "Now, you talk, Mex, or I swear to God, I'll gut you like a hog."

Salado blubbered, "I know nothing, senor. By all that is holy, I am innocent of what you think."

Nathan waved the blade of his bowie menacingly. "Frank Selman and Otis Sims. Where are they?"

The frantic Mexican climbed to his knees, his hands grasped in prayer beneath his chin. "By the grace of the Virgin Mary, I do not know those of whom you speak, senor. I am a simple *gachupine* from the Iberian Peninsula. They force me to fight to save my family."

Sam Walker sneered and kicked the kneeling Mexican in the back. Salado spun to the ground, moaning. Walker stomped on his hand, spreading his fingers on the ground. He fired a shot that tore a chunk from the ground inches from Salado's outstretched fingers. "Next time, I'll blow your whole damned hand off, you stinking greaser. You understand?"

Clutching his head, Salado knew he would be killed if he refused to admit he was a member of Selman's band. He nodded jerkily. "I tell, senor, I tell you."

Half-truths rolled from his lips as he struggled to his knees. "I was there, but I do no harm to the senora or her children." He thought of the scar on his forehead from the time he ran into a limb. "I try to stop them, but Senor Selman, he give me this," he blubbered, pointing to the scar.

The words exploded in Nathan's brain. He lunged at the crying Mexican, but Barney grabbed him, digging his clawed fingers into the big man's shoulder. "Hold it, partner. Hold it. Let's hear him out."

Nathan made to throw off his father-in-law's hand, but hesitated.

Salado continued, relating the details of that day, details that drove Nathan ever closer to exploding. "It was Selman and Sims and Davis" — he paused and added — "and Alfredo Torres. I knew what they did was wrong." He crossed his breast. "I knew the Holy Virgin was looking down."

284

He shook his head. "I did not want to displease Her. I never go in house, but stay in my saddle."

Stepping forward and extending his bowie, Nathan hissed through clenched teeth, "You lying little bastard. I'm going to spill your worthless guts all over the ground."

Walker stopped him. "Hold on, Nathan. Just a minute now. Hold on."

The big mountain man turned his icy gray eyes on the wiry Texas Ranger. "What for?"

Sam drew a deep breath and looked up into the big man's face. His black eyes met Cooper's gray ones. "I ain't no Mexican lover. Given a reason, I could kill one an hour and it wouldn't bother me not a whit." He paused and gestured to Salado with the muzzle of his Colt. "I ain't a religious jasper, but I never killed an hombre what didn't deserve it. Now maybe this one deserves killing for something, but just being there ain't no reason."

Nathan seethed with rage. "You believe that story he told?"

Walker studied Salado for several moments.

His forehead wrinkled in a frown, Barney spoke up. "I believe him, Nathan. God help me, but I believe him. I don't know why. I don't want to, but I do. We can't kill an in-

285

nocent man." He hesitated. "My daughter, your wife — she'd never like that. You know it, and I know it." He paused and added, "Hate is taking hold of you, Nathan. I been seeing it coming. You can't hate like you been doing. It'll tear you to pieces."

Muscles trembling as he strove to contain his fury at his father-in-law's words, Nathan looked down at Barney. He read the conviction, the earnestness in the older man's face, and muttered, "I don't give a damn, Barney. He was there. I'm going to kill him for that. I promised her on her grave that I would revenge her no matter how long it took."

Barney's lips quivered with emotion. "I want them that did it as much as you. More even, because Marie was part of me. I raised that child after her ma died. I loved her more than anyone. Sometimes, I think even more than her ma. You wasn't around for those first twenty-some-odd years when she was growing and becoming the woman you married." He paused, closing his eyes and drawing a deep breath. "You think I don't dream of revenge? That's all I think about, but revenge on those who done it. It ain't this poor greaser's fault if he just happened to be there. You can't kill a jasper for that."

The big mountain man clenched and unclenched his fingers about the bone handle of the bowie. He glanced at Sam Walker, who merely shrugged, but in the shrug, Nathan read the wiry ranger's agreement with Barney.

He turned his fiery eyes back on the huddled, trembling Mexican. He drew a deep breath and slowly lowered his knife. "I think you're both wrong. This one deserves to die. But —" He shook his head and, sheathing his knife, swung into the saddle. He looked down at them and shook his head slowly. "I know I got hate boiling in me like a devil's cauldron, and I figure that hate can twist my thoughts about a heap, but until the day I die, I can never get the picture out of my mind of Marie lying there on the floor all helpless."

He jerked the roan about. His jaw grew hard, and his cold eyes glared at the cowering Mexican. "I swore I'd kill those that done this. If I find out you're lying, then . . ." His words trailed off.

Luis Salado shivered and ducked his head to hide the sly smile on his lips.

Nathan rode from the bazaar. Walker prodded Salado onto his horse and muttered to Barney, "That old boy has got himself a bunch of hate inside."

Barney swung into the saddle. "He's turning hard, Sam. I've seen it coming the last several months. He was always hard, especially when I first met him ten years ago, but there was a side of him that — well, I guess you could say he sort of reined in. Marie, my little girl, his wife, helped him rein it in. But now —" He nodded at Salado. "He could have killed that greaser with no more feeling than squashing a cockroach."

Walker climbed on his pony and grabbed the reins of Salado's horse. "I heard he once lived with the Karankawa's."

"Yep. He was young then. Just off a couple years as a cabin boy with LaFitte."

"I'd heard that before. I think Jack told me."

"It's the gospel. Then he lived with the Kronks two or three years. Was blood brothers with José Maria, the chief. When the chief's boy got rattlesnake bit, he blamed Nathan. Sent a couple braves out to kill him, but they knew better. Turned him loose."

The two rangers leading the Mexican pulled onto the narrow *calle* and headed back to camp. Walker grunted. "I never heard that."

Barney chuckled. "There's a heap you ain't heard about Nathan. After he got away from the Kronks, he went into the Rockies, trapping. When he come back years later, his family was all kilt, and his niece, Ruthie, was took by the Kronks. That's how we met up with him. He was chasing them, and them damned Injuns near kilt him dead. He lost his arm, but he kept going. He chased them all through Texas, and finally got the little girl back. Had to kill his blood brother, José Maria, but he done it."

Walker groaned. "Hell. After all that, then these damned scum come through and ki —" He caught himself and, embarrassed, glanced at Barney. "Well, I don't blame him for the blood in his eyes. I just don't know how you manage to handle it yourself."

The older man turned a knowing eye at Sam Walker. "It ain't easy, Sam. It ain't easy. But there's got to be a line somewhere. Otherwise, we ain't no better than the animals." He shrugged and hooked his thumb over his shoulder at Salado. "Who knows? Maybe Nathan's right, and I'm wrong."

That night, the prisoners escaped.

Always a light sleeper, Nathan jerked awake at the first shout. Moments later, the night erupted with gunfire. He dashed to the

289

window as several prisoners scattered into the night.

He muttered a curse, and then in the glare of a barn lamp, spotted Luis Salado, musket in hand, darting around the corner of an adobe and disappearing up a narrow street that led into the foothills surrounding the city.

Nathan grabbed his bowie and vaulted through the window.

Within moments, the prisoners vanished into the cold darkness of the foothills, pursued by random shouts and occasional curses; but Nathan, like bark on a tree, clung to the trail of the prisoner he believed to be Luis Salado.

Salado's breathing grew ragged; his lungs burned from exertion as he climbed higher into the foothills of the Miter Mountains.

The slender Mexican paused beside a twisted mesquite on the side of the trail, gasping for breath and listening hard for any pursuit. His heart jumped when he heard the rattle of rocks on the trail below, and then a sneer twisted his thin lips. He was in the mountains of his youth, and he knew every inch of the foothills and peaks.

Silently, he moved upward.

Nathan followed, his eyes narrowed in cold rage, filled with iron determination that could only be satisfied when he killed Luis Salado.

Placing his huarache-clad feet carefully, Salado moved quietly, higher and higher along the rocky trail. Desperation and fear, fueled by anger at the treatment he had suffered earlier in the day, drove him. Below, pursuit continued. He listened hard, and after a few moments, he was convinced only one American followed. He grinned evilly. He knew of a bend in the trail above from which he could surprise his pursuer.

Another hundred feet higher, Salado found the fissure that he sought in the granite bluff. The niche opened onto the narrow trail.

Someone bursting from the fissure and catching his victim unaware could indeed hurl him from the trail, down the steep slope, and over a precipitous drop-off that fell a thousand feet.

Salado slipped back into the shadows of the fissure. The faint shuffle of feet on gravel came from below. The wiry Mexican crouched in the darkness and waited.

The sound of feet grew closer.

Suddenly, all sound ceased. After a moment, the chirruping of crickets cut though the pregnant silence of the night. A few seconds later, night birds chirped.

Salado felt sweat gathering on his forehead and stinging his eyes despite the cool February weather. He tried to slow his breathing.

And then the footsteps on gravel drew closer.

CHAPTER THIRTY

Nathan paused at the bend in the trail, straining for any sound. He heard nothing other than the chirruping of crickets. The hair on the back of his neck bristled.

Peering around a slab of granite, Salado froze when he spotted the silhouette of the iron T at the end the big man's arm. His eyes narrowed in anticipation of slaying the gringo who had so abused him earlier. He clenched his teeth and crept forward silently.

Drawing a deep breath, Salado lowered his shoulder and charged the hulking shadow before him. He slammed into the shadow's back, knocking him forward over the edge of the trail.

Nathan heard the footsteps, but before he could spin, a force slammed into him, driving him into space.

Instinctively, he tightened his grip on his

knife, and like a cat, fought for balance in the darkness, well aware from his years with the Karankawa of the necessity of landing as upright as possible so the great muscles in his legs could absorb the brunt of the shock.

He struck on his feet, but his backward motion sent him tumbling head-over-heels down the steep slope. Jagged shards of granite slashed at him, and his head slammed into a boulder, stunning the big man. He rolled to a halt, arms spread, staring unseeing at the starry heavens above.

Luis Salado peered into the darkness, muttering a curse when the bluish silver light from the stars fell on the mountain man lying motionless near the rim of the drop-off.

He jerked his musket to his shoulder, then hesitated. He cast a furtive glance back down the trail, wondering if any more of the devil rangers were coming. Certainly, he told himself, if they heard a shot, they would come to investigate. Silence was his ally. He must not break the silence.

He gingerly picked his way down the slope to the motionless figure below. He'd crush the ranger's skull with his musket, then push the body over the edge.

Somewhere in the fuzzy recesses of his head, Nathan heard the rattling of rocks. He opened his eyes. The stars blurred together. He blinked, trying to focus on the tiny white diamonds above.

The rattling sounded again. Without moving his head, he shifted his gaze to the slope above as the starlight reflected off baggy white clothes on a small figure picking its way down the talus.

Instinctively, Nathan knew the identity of the man. He remained motionless except for his fingers flexing around the handle of his bowie.

Salado stepped onto the ledge and stopped at Nathan's feet. He peered down at the motionless figure. A smug sneer twisted his cruel lips. "So, gringo, it is I who will drink pulque and remember the pleasures of your woman tonight while the buzzards feed on your carcass."

He swept the musket over his head, ready to club the figure on the ground.

Before Salado could swing the musket, Nathan slammed his heel into the swarthy man's knee, knocking his leg from under him. With a startled scream, Salado fell forward, onto the point of Nathan's bowie, driving the blade through his heart.

He died instantly.

Nathan stared down at the dead Mexican for several seconds, then expertly scalped him and rolled him off the precipice. "That's three," he muttered.

The next day, to Nathan's chagrin, he and a handful of rangers, leaving Hays and Taylor behind, pushed out for Vera Cruz. Their job was to deliver two thousand of Taylor's troops for support to General Winfield Scott's army of U.S. soldiers and marines. That Scott had no use for Texas Rangers was widely known, and the idea of working for him left an unpleasant taste in Nathan's mouth.

"Cheer up," Barney said with a crooked grin. "Look at the bright side. Sims and Selman has done dropped out of sight. Maybe we can pick up word of them over there."

Nathan grunted.

After reporting in at Vera Cruz, Nathan and his ten rangers were called to General Scott's quarters and ordered to find a route to Mexico City.

Three weeks later, Nathan and Barney

reported back to Scott. "We found several routes, General, but we don't have enough rangers to protect the troops along the way. There is a heap of guerillas out there."

Barney grunted. "He's right, General. Once you get deep into the country, there ain't no way you can protect your supply lines."

Scott lifted an eyebrow. "That's the job for my Corps of Engineers. They will put down any trouble we face along the route as well as keep the supply lines open. We run into problems, they can handle them."

Nathan's eyes grew hard. "With all due respect, General Scott, but your engineers can't handle what's out there. You need more rangers. Jack Hays is back with Taylor. He can be here a few days with a couple hundred more rangers. Then I reckon we've got a chance to make it through."

Scott narrowed his eyes. "Cooper. I've made it clear that I have no love for your rangers. The last thing I need around here is more of you damned wild savages. I've got ten of you now. That's all I want." He paused and added, "Every city we've occupied with you heathens, we've had complaints from the citizenry. Our war is not with the citizens, but Santa Anna's army."

A sneer curled one side of Nathan's lips.

"General, you haven't faced that army yet. When you do, you'll learn mighty fast the damned citizens in this country is the army. Yeah, there've been complaints, but if you read the reports, you'll see that the guerilla attacks on our troops come from those citizens you want so hard to coddle."

Scott's face grew livid. He clenched his teeth. He trembled with suppressed anger. When he finally spoke, the emotion in his voice was tightly controlled. "Cooper, I don't argue with subordinates. I give orders, and I expect them to be carried out. If not, I'll have you up before a court martial and then a firing squad."

Nathan eyed the general coolly. In a soft, almost gentle voice, he replied, "You give the orders, General Scott. If you want the rangers to follow them, make sure you give the right ones."

The two men eyed each other, one with hate, the other with disgust.

Three days later, led by the handful of Texas Rangers, a two-thousand-man detachment of U.S. Marines under Major William Polk moved out on the road to Cordoba, planning from there to spearhead a movement up to Puebla. According to Scott's engineers, the road was secure.

The morning of the second day, Nathan and Sam Walker rode up to Major Polk as the commander climbed into his saddle. Nathan gestured up the road to Cordoba. "Major, a few miles ahead the road runs between two ridges." He nodded to Sam. "Me and Sam here figure we need to take another look at those ridges."

Sam cleared his throat. "I know the general's engineers said the road was secure, but them ridges is a mighty inviting place for an ambush. Jarauta's guerillas could slip in there real easy."

Polk studied the two rangers warily, well aware of their dislike for him. A career soldier, Polk had no intention of making any decision that might antagonize his superior, thus costing a promotion.

"I'm quite satisfied with the scouting reports, gentlemen."

Sam started to retort, but Nathan laid his prosthesis on the ranger's arm, staying him. Brow furrowed, Sam looked around at Nathan.

"You heard the major, Sam. Let's us move out."

As they rode back to their assignments at point, Sam muttered, "That dumb bastard couldn't drive a nail in a snowbank."

The big mountain man chuckled. "That

means we got to do the driving for him. Truth is, I didn't figure he'd pay us no mind."

Sam frowned. "Because of Scott?"

The grin on Nathan's lips grew wider. "Because he wants a promotion."

On the peak of a ridge, Frank Selman peered around a jagged uplift of granite at the column of soldiers riding toward him. He cast a glance to his left and to his right, grinning cruelly at the three hundred men sprawled on their bellies or kneeling behind boulders ready to loose a terrible barrage on the approaching army.

Across the road on top of the far ridge, Otis Sims held his carbine over his head. Selman nodded. Their plan was both simple and devious. As soon as the contingent of soldiers filled the valley between the ridges, Selman would open fire. Sims' men would hold their fire, giving the startled soldiers below time to scurry from the road and take protection behind the boulders against Selman's attack. As soon as the U.S. Marines had their backs to Sims' contingent, he would open fire.

The ten rangers rode with Polk's column at point, swing, flank, and drag, with Sam and

Nathan at point. As they approached the rugged ridges of black granite towering over the road a hundred feet, Nathan dragged the tip of his tongue over his dry lips. The ridges looked to be about a half mile in length.

Inside his head, a warning bell sounded. While birds flittered from tree to tree and rock to rock, Nathan couldn't help feeling that not all was as it should be. More than once, he had experienced the nagging feeling up in the Rockies and down on the coastal prairies. The few times he had ignored the nagging feeling had ended in serious trouble.

Sam glanced at Nathan nervously, then turned his keen eyes back to the slopes above. "I don't like it."

Muttering softly, Nathan replied, "Me neither."

Sweat rolled down Nathan's back as he sat stiffly in the saddle, his gray eyes scanning every boulder, every twisted mesquite, every rugged granite uplift on the ridge.

Time dragged. Beyond the ridges, the safety of the chaparral-dotted prairie beckoned.

Sam and Nathan rode a hundred yards ahead of Major Polk and his staff. Sam glanced at Nathan and nodded to the prairie. "We're almost out, Nathan."

"Not yet, Sam, not yet." His words were grim.

Without warning, the north ridge exploded with gunfire, raking the column below.

CHAPTER
THIRTY-ONE

The murderous barrage slammed soldiers and horses to the ground like so many sticks of straw. Startled officers shouted commands above the roar of gunfire, sending soldiers scrambling for protection under the south ridge.

Nathan spun, his keen eyes sweeping the north ridge. His blood ran cold when he spotted a large man wearing a heavy beard. Selman!

Moments later, sporadic gunfire from the U.S. forces answered the barrage from above.

And without warning, a salvo of racketing guns ripped down from the south ridge into the soldiers' unprotected backs. Soldiers screamed and fell. Horses squealed and broke away from their dismounted riders. Shouted orders went unheeded.

Nathan fought to bring his frightened roan under control.

Sam shouted. "Nathan! What do we do?"

Quickly sizing up their position as untenable, Nathan wrapped the reins around his iron T and shucked his Colt. He charged into the melee. "Back, back," he shouted, waving the six-gun.

As he swept by Major Polk, he saw the fear in the older man's eyes. He shouted again, "Retreat, Major, retreat!" Suddenly, ahead of him rose a wall of Mexican guerillas, cutting off retreat.

Sam Walker reined up beside Nathan. "Where in the hell did they come from?"

Clinging to the back of his frightened roan, Nathan growled, "From out of the ground as far as I know, but they ain't stopping me."

Polk reined his remount to a sliding halt. He squinted through the smoke and shouted above the roar of musket fire, "Fall back! Fall back!"

The guerillas were moving in, trying to cut off the army's retreat, but with the rangers leading the way, Polk's troops burst through and regrouped beyond range of the guerillas.

Camp was subdued that night. Polk sent Sam Walker back to Vera Cruz with a report to General Scott of the deadly surprise. At

Nathan's insistence, he included the observation that, with the guerillas' capability of
moving in behind any troop, army supply
lines would be in great danger. The only
solution was more rangers, rangers strung
out from Vera Cruz to Mexico City, if neces-
sary.

Polk's lips curled in anger at Nathan's
blunt observation, but his failure on this
day had left him no choice but to endorse
the mountain man's recommendation.

Word spread quickly through the camp
that the major had refused Walker and
Cooper's request to scout ahead. As he lay
in his bedroll that night, Barney asked
Nathan if the gossip spreading through the
camp was true.

"Between you and me, yes. Don't let no
one else know. Polk's got his hands full, and
he can't handle no more problems." He
sneered. "I'm not taking up for him. He's
another one of those fancy soldiers who got
where they are because of who they know. I
just don't want no more problems keeping
me from finding those other two. Selman
was up there today."

"What? You saw him?"

"Glimpsed him. Then things got too busy.
But it was him."

Barney grunted. "Then Sims was around

somewhere too."

Next morning, Polk led his army back to Vera Cruz. As much as he hated to admit it, the rangers were right. His troops had been manhandled by the guerillas. Drawing a deep breath and releasing it in a drawn-out sigh, he knew he had to convince the general to send for more rangers.

Polk grimaced as General Scott ranted and raved. Finally, his blustering choked off. Red-faced, he glared at Polk and his staff of cowed officers. As much as he wanted to prove the mission had failed because of incompetent leadership, he had prudently resisted the urge to lead the troops himself.

On the one hand, a successful march and ultimate victory would enhance his political ambitions. On the other, if Polk were right in his assessment of the value of the Texas Rangers and Scott were to meet the same fate, his dream of the presidency would be shattered beyond repair.

Steely-eyed, Scott barked at his adjutant to cut orders for Colonel Jack Hays to report to Vera Cruz within two weeks with as many Texas Rangers as he could recruit.

Exactly two weeks later, Hays rode in with

580 rangers.

As Hays and Nathan squatted around a campfire that night, Sam Walker and thirty rangers rode back into camp after patrolling to the north around Perote on Scott's orders. Hays and Nathan looked up as the grinning ranger strode up to their fire. "Find anything up at Perote Prison?" Hays drawled, his eyes twinkling in amusement.

Walker grunted. He held up a dime between his thumb and forefinger. "I said I'd get it, and here it is."

Hays chuckled. "What about the Texas flag?"

Walker nodded. "When those greasers made us raise that flagpole at Perote, I swore one day I'd fly a Texas flag from it. By damn, I did it, then tore the pole down and got my dime back."

Nathan laughed. "Sounds like a good day's work."

Walker chuckled. "You got no idea, Nathan. You got no idea."

Three days later, eight thousand troops under the watchful eyes of six hundred rangers moved out on the road to Cordoba, Puebla, and ultimately, Mexico City.

Guerillas made attempt after attempt from

the rugged heights of the Sierra Madres and the chaparral of the prairies to harass the troops.

But the rangers held them off and kept the supply line open back to Vera Cruz by dropping off patrols of rangers every few miles. These well-armed patrols of rangers, who never hesitated to jump neck deep in a fight, guarded every soldier, every horse, every wagon traveling between Vera Cruz and Scott's army.

All along the supply line, Jarauta's guerillas who attempted to break the American channel of supplies would look up and find a passel of wild-eyed, bloodthirsty Texas Rangers bearing down on them, their Colts belching death.

At Puebla, Scott split his troops, taking four thousand on toward Mexico City, despite dire warnings from Nathan and Jack Hays. "There's a hotbed of guerillas ahead, General," Nathan explained. "We reckon its Jarauta and Canales. They're sitting there on those ledges and just waiting for you to show up."

Scott clenched his teeth and glared at Hays, who nodded his agreement with Nathan's assessment of the situation. Growling, Scott replied, "I have four thousand U.S. soldiers and marines, the elite of the U.S. Expeditionary Force. A handful of ragged beggars won't stand in my way."

"It ain't a handful, General Scott," Hays retorted. "Nathan and me, we figure that Jarauta and Canales has six or seven thousand soldiers up there."

"Jack's right. They're thicker than chicken splatter."

Scott sneered. "Soldiers! They're not soldiers; they're just dirty little Mexicans."

Nathan had no reason to hold Scott in much esteem, but what little respect he had for the man completely vanished. "They might be dirty little Mexicans, General, but a dirty little man fighting for his home can be mighty dangerous and one to keep an eye on."

Despite the warning, with a hundred rangers, Scott moved out on the Cordoba road the next morning at the head of a column of U.S. Marines in blue uniforms and garrison caps and mounted on well-fed mounts.

Sam and Nathan rode point. Sam nodded across the prairie to clouds of dust rising on the horizon. "Looks like we got company."

Nathan chuckled, but there was no smile on his rugged face. He nodded to the foreboding black ramparts of the Sierra Madres looming ahead. "And I reckon we'll be having us a heap more before long."

His face grim, Sam nodded. "I figure you're right on that guess, partner."

Suddenly from behind came the pop of a musket followed by a scream of pain. A marine grabbed his leg in anguish. At the same time, with Joe Barlow in the lead, a half-dozen wild-riding Texas Rangers charged the motte of chaparral from which the shot had come.

Several more shots came from the tangle of scrub oak to the north, but the rangers rode pell-mell into the thicket, firing at any moving object.

No sooner had they returned to the column than gunshots sounded from the south. Two horses went down.

The rangers bolted, cutting down a handful of guerillas in the chaparral.

The narrow road dropped down through ridges, over rolling hills, all the while drawing closer to the mountains. Jarauta and Canales' guerillas maintained a sporadic, but harassing fire throughout the morning until just before noon, when the Expeditionary Force entered the foothills of the Sierras.

Two patrols of twenty rangers each, one led by Nathan, the other by Sam Walker, vanished into the foothills, combing the rocky ridges for the guerillas.

For the next two hours, as the column of marines rode along the winding road, gunfire echoed from deep in the foothills on either side, but none of the fire was directed at the column.

Colonel William Rains, Scott's adjutant, turned to the general after another hour passed without any guerilla attacks on the column. "Well, General Scott, it appears those rangers are doing their job damned good."

Scott glared at his staff officer, then nodded tersely. "That's what they're paid for, Colonel."

Rains shivered at the chill in the general's voice.

Despite the rangers' efforts to persuade him that the position was too vulnerable even after patrols reported no enemy within sight, General Scott bivouacked his force on a meandering stream in the middle of a large valley. He put out sentries around the camp.

Sitting on a stool beside his fire that night, he listened intently as Sam Walker reported the results of ranger engagement with the guerillas. Nathan stood a couple steps behind Walker. "Killed several, General.

Heap more managed to sneak away."

Scott grunted. "At least you put an end to the sniping."

Sam hesitated. He glanced over his shoulder at Nathan and cleared his throat. "Well, reckon we did, General. But somehow it seemed a mite too easy."

"Too easy?" Scott frowned. "What do you mean by that?"

With a shrug, Sam replied, "Hard to say. A jasper would figure they'd want to fight more than they did, but when they spotted us, they skedaddled like a covey of quail."

General Scott smiled smugly at his adjutant, then spoke to Walker. "Simple, Captain. They don't have the stomach for a fight. That's obvious." He gestured to the valley in which they bivouacked. "That's why I have no reservations whatsoever about spending the night here."

Nathan had witnessed such subtlety of behavior many times among the Indians. They had the stomach for a fight, but usually when they ran, they had their own reasons. But he remained silent, knowing there was nothing he could say that would influence the general.

After the two rangers left, Scott reached for a cup of coffee. He held the cup while an orderly filled it. He glanced across the fire at his adjutant. "Well, Colonel Rains. Maybe now we're rid of the guerilla problem."

At that moment, the frightened squealing of horses jerked him around. He looked up, his eyes wide in disbelief as a great ball of fire arced through the black sky and crashed down upon the camp.

CHAPTER
THIRTY-TWO

The fiery ball slammed into the ground, splattering and hurling out smaller balls of fire, lighting the bivouac for a quarter of a mile around. Gunfire erupted from darkness covering the surrounding ridges.

Men shouted; horses squealed; a steady barrage of gunfire issued from the night.

Moments later, another fiery ball from a second ridge lit the heavens and smashed into the ground, followed almost immediately by a third ball of fire from yet a third ridge.

Nathan and Sam were halfway back to their fire when the first ball lit the sky. "What the hell is that?" Sam shouted. "You see that?"

"Catapults!" Nathan shouted above the cacophony of the confusion enveloping the camp.

Sam looked at him, bewildered. "What?"

"You heard me, catapults. They must have

moved them in after we scouted the area." He grabbed Sam's arm. "Follow me," he shouted, yanking the lanky ranger after him and disappearing into the night.

Ten minutes later, Nathan and Sam crouched behind a boulder at the base of the ridge from behind which the balls of fire had come. Along the crest of the ridge, the yellow bursts of muzzle blasts punched tiny holes in the darkness, providing Nathan a clear map of how to skirt the guerillas.

He whispered over his shoulder. "Stay with me and be quiet."

Sam nodded, dragging his sleeve across the sweat rolling down his forehead.

Ghosting from one boulder to the next, Nathan led the way to the crest from where they could see the catapult that had been constructed from heavy timbers. The draft horses that pulled the catapult were picketed a hundred yards away, so the fire wouldn't spook them.

Three soldiers of Santa Anna's army operated the weapon. Not far from the fire were two wagons, each loaded with balls about three feet in diameter. As the two rangers looked on, two of the men rolled a ball down a ramp off the wagon and onto a cup at the end of the catapult arm. One quickly touched a torch to the ball, which erupted in fire. They stepped back and the third man jerked the lever, sending the fiery sphere into the dark sky.

The levered cup remained upright, bits of fire burning at the cup. Quickly, the three soldiers cranked it down and expertly extinguished the flames with sackcloth.

Nathan glanced at Sam. "Ready?" he whispered.

With a crooked grin, Sam nodded. "Any time."

Nathan led the way through the boulders to within twenty yards of the catapult. The guerillas were laughing and joking while they rolled another ball onto the catapult. Nathan pointed to the slight Mexican operating the lever. "Slip over behind him. I'll take care of these two. And do it quiet."

Sam unsheathed his knife and disappeared into the darkness. Nathan eased forward, like the Karankawa, using the sage and cactus to break his shadow. Moments later, he slipped into the shadows cast by the wagon.

He stiffened as the shuffling of feet approached. The slight Mexican never looked around. He rolled the missile off the wagon. Like a wraith, Nathan rose and slipped up behind the slight man. Grasping the blade of the bowie, he slammed the handle into the guerilla's temple. He dropped soundlessly.

At that moment, the second Mexican looked around and froze, as Nathan touched the point of the blade to the frightened man's neck. He motioned the man to the ground.

While he could be merciless and cold, Nathan could see no reason to kill these men. They were protecting their homes, their country, just as he would do. The big mountain man quickly bound and gagged the man, then he and Sam set the catapult on fire. "Two more to go, Sam," Nathan whispered as he glided into the night.

Within two hours, the other two catapults were in flames.

Stone-faced, Scott listened to Walker's report. The crusty general's eyes shifted back and forth between Walker and Cooper. Each time Scott locked eyes with the big mountain man, he sensed Cooper's unspoken reproach at his decision to bivouac in the valley. And he couldn't help wondering just what effect tonight would have on his presidential ambitions.

The next few weeks and months were

measured in inches. Peon guerillas under the leadership of Padre Jarauta and General Canales swept down from the jagged ramparts of the Sierras, striking and running. And when the marines pursued, they ran into Santa Anna's lancers. The Mexican dictator countered every move of the U.S. Expeditionary Force.

The weather grew cool as autumn pushed in. The Texas Rangers worked without sleep for days, intercepting and then pursuing the ragged bands of loyal Mexicans.

The days blurred for Nathan and Barney, keeping them so busy, they had little time to think of Frank Selman and Otis Sims, except when a new batch of prisoners were brought in for interrogation.

The Texas Ranger battalion was stretched thin, unable to maintain complete security of the supply lines back to Vera Cruz. Walker and Cooper pleaded for reinforcements, but General Scott paid little attention.

Santa Anna sent more troops, laying siege to the city of Puebla. Days turned into weeks.

Nathan grew restless with the incessant patrols that seemed to go nowhere. He peered to the north in the direction of Mexico City. Somewhere out beyond the

Mexican forces were two men, the last two. Unconsciously, he laid his hand on the parfleche bag tucked under his belt, the one that held the two scalps of those who murdered his family.

In his mind, he had no doubt Sims and Selman were still out there. He cut his eyes toward his father-in-law, reading the same impatience on the older man's face. Soon, he told himself, or I'll be forced to take it in my own hands.

One morning, squatting by his fire sipping six-shooter coffee, Nathan's keen eyes noted several staff officers reporting to General Scott's tent. His mind raced, wondering what plans the general had in mind.

Army gossip spread through the camp.

At noon, Jack Hays rode in with General Joe Lane and three hundred more rangers escorting a thousand of the new Walker Colts, a heavy piece of iron designed by Sam Walker and built by Sam Colt.

The massive revolver mounted a six-shot cylinder chambered for a .44 caliber conical bullet; the revolver weighed an unprecedented four pounds, nine ounces. Powered by sixty grains of black powder, the Walker Colt, claimed Texas Ranger adjutant Rip Ford, was as powerful as the U. S. Model

1841 "Mississippi" rifle.

Admiring one of the new revolvers, Walker looked at the rangers around him and held the revolver over his head. "Boys," he proclaimed, "this piece of hardware is as effective as a common rifle at a hundred yards and superior to a musket at two hundred."

General Lane looked on, with a degree of trepidation, as the Colts were issued to almost nine hundred Texas Rangers, nine hundred tall, broad-shouldered, rawboned gunnies with thick beards and cold eyes, whose gnarled hands handled the Colt like a newborn baby and whose skill could make it sing like a mockingbird.

He shook his head slowly, wondering if General Scott had any idea of what he was unleashing on the Mexican people.

A week later, the troops had not budged.

Nathan glared at Jack Hays. "Why isn't the general moving out? We got enough rangers and firepower now to take over the whole damned country by ourselves."

Jack shrugged. "He will, Nathan. He's making plans."

The response was a weak excuse. Hays knew it and Nathan knew it. "That ain't it, Jack. I'm beginning to wonder just how much the general wants to get to Mexico City."

At that moment, Rip Ford sauntered up, squatted, and reached for the coffee pot. He sipped the thick black liquid, then arched an eyebrow at Hays. He pointed his cup at Sam Walker. "You're moving out tomorrow. Word come in that Canales is up northeast at Huamantia. General Lane's taking a patrol of rangers out. General Scott wants you to ride along with them."

Sam grinned, his slender face wreathed in a broad grin. "It's about time," he muttered. "The seat of my pants is growing slick sitting around here."

Nathan spoke up. "I'll go with you, Sam."

Barney volunteered, "Me too."

Rip shook his head. With a broad, satisfied grin, he announced. "Nope. General wants you to take a patrol up the road to Mexico City. See what we got ahead of us."

The big mountain man's pulse raced. He stared at Ford in disbelief. "We're moving up?"

The wiry man grinned at Nathan. "Sure looks that way."

The two patrols moved out before sunrise the next morning.

Nathan patted the new Colt on his hip.

"You got us a mighty nice piece of work here, Sam. This could turn this war around."

Sam's grin faded into a sad frown. "I just hope it helps you find them what did such a terrible thing to you, Nathan. I surely do."

Their eyes met. Nathan extended his big hand, and Sam Walker clasped it.

That was the last time they would speak.

CHAPTER
THIRTY-THREE

The narrow road to Mexico City wound across lush plains watered by streams of cool water flowing from the rugged mountains. The only sign of human life was the occasional peon standing beside the road, watching dispassionately as the rangers rode past.

Leaving the valley and moving into the foothills, the hair on the back of Nathan's neck bristled. It was unusual not to see more peons along the road. He glanced at the ridges ahead, and the reflection of sunlight flashed brilliantly.

Barney glanced at his son-in-law. "What's bothering you, Nathan?"

Pursing his lips, Nathan kept his eyes on the rugged mountains surrounding them. "Up there. They're watching. I don't know if they plan on jumping us or just keeping an eye on us."

Barney squinted into the jagged ridges rising from the road. "I ain't seen nothing."

Sunlight flashed off metal high on the ridge. "There," said Nathan. "You can see the reflection."

Every eye in the patrol watched the rugged slopes surrounding them. There was an undercurrent of sharp exclamations and muttered curses when one of the rangers spotted a flash of light.

Nathan looked over his shoulder. "Spread out, boys. Those old boys might be bad shots, but clustered up like we are, one of them might get lucky."

His gray eyes studied the terrain ahead. The valley through which they rode narrowed. Thick patches of chaparral dotted the ground, offering ideal concealment for snipers. A tiny bell sounded in his head when he spotted the narrow road disappearing behind a hogback ridge of slab granite a quarter of a mile ahead. He reined up and glanced around. Spotting Mabrey Gray, he said, "Mabrey, how about you and me riding up the road apiece and see what's around that bend?"

The wiry ranger grinned. "Let's go."

"The rest of you wait here. Keep your eyes open. I got a bad feeling about this place."

Even before they reached the ridge, Mabrey glanced at Nathan. "You hear that?"

Nathan shook his head. "No."

The wiry man cupped his hand to his ear. "There it is again. A horse whinnying."

Nathan reined up.

The day was still, the air unmoving. He and the smaller man stared at each other. After a few tense moments, Mabrey nodded. "There it was again."

With a crooked grin, Nathan muttered, "You got the ears of a bobcat. Let's take it slow."

Leaving the road, they angled to the tip of the granite ridge.

Without warning, several Mexican lancers barreled around the ridge, and lowering their pikes, charged the two rangers.

Though puzzled over the sudden appearance of the Mexican soldiers, Nathan shucked his Colt and charged the lancers with Mabrey right at his side. Nathan knocked two from their saddles as they raced through the lancers.

Wheeling about to reengage, Nathan glanced to his left, and his blood ran cold. At least five companies of lancers were mounted in formation behind the hogback ridge.

Suddenly, he realized Santa Anna was planning on attacking Puebla, and he and his rangers had upset the dictator's plans by the chance discovery. That's why the lancers had charged them — an attempt to keep the sneak attack a secret until Santa Anna was ready to spring his surprise on Winfield Scott's force.

On the next pass through the remaining lancers, Nathan and Mabrey knocked two more from their saddles. Mabrey reined up for another charge, but Nathan signaled him to follow as he raced back to the waiting rangers.

Their job now was to make it back to Puebla with news of the impending invasion by the Mexican forces.

Just outside of Huamantia, Sam Walker reined up, waiting for General Lane. "Huamantia is over that ridge, General," Walker drawled. "Hold up here while I ride ahead and see what's facing us." He waved to a handful of his rangers to accompany him.

Ten minutes later, he returned, his face flushed with excitement. "About two hundred of them, General." He nodded to the forty rangers around them. "With these new Colts, we can make short work of them."

Lane, caught up in the excitement, nodded. "Lead out, Mister Walker."

Word spread quickly through the column. The rangers' eyes glittered with anticipation as they shucked their big Colts and fit their boot heels snug against the stirrups.

Walker sat stiffly in his saddle, every sense alive, every muscle tight as a clock spring. At the top of the ridge, they halted, peering down the road at a company of Mexican lancers with carrot plumes on their black leather shakos and arrayed in single-breasted blue jackets with white trousers.

Without taking his eyes off the opposing force, Walker chuckled. "There's your reception committee, General."

Lane grinned. Over the last few weeks, he had come to admire the grit of these Texas Rangers. All of the derogatory terms addressed to them might be true. They might be profane, immoral, and whiskey-guzzling, but they were one hell of a fighting unit.

For several moments, the two forces stared at each other. The lancer company lowered its pikes and began a slow walk up the road.

Behind Walker, Joe Barlow growled, "Hell, Sam, looks like them old boys is going to give us a welcome."

Several rangers chuckled.

"Looks that way," Sam replied. "So, what do you think, boys? Let's meet them halfway."

Even before his words left his lips, he dug his spurs into his pony and lunged forward.

Half a second later, forty warhorses, nostrils flaring and eyes rolling with excitement, thundered down the road toward the on-coming company of lancers.

For a moment, the lancers hesitated. When the rangers cut loose with their Colts, the lancers broke and raced back toward the small village beyond the next ridge.

Adrenaline coursing through his veins, Sam Walker stood in the stirrups firing at the retreating lancers. They disappeared over a second ridge, and the Texas Rangers pounded after them.

As Walker topped the ridge, he jerked his pony to a sliding halt. "Dammit to hell," he muttered, staring down the slope at what appeared to be reinforcements five times the size of the lancer company.

Rangers cursed and fired as their horses wheeled about.

A devastating volley of musket fire raked the ranger company, wounding several including Sam Walker.

General Lane waved the rangers back. "Fall back, boys. Get out of here."

Seeing Sam Walker slumped over his pony's neck, Joe Barlow grabbed the reins. "Hold on, Sam. Hold on."

The lancers pounded after the rangers. From time to time, a handful of rangers reined up, and with their Colts, poured a rain of lead plums into the lancers, forcing them to pull up.

After a few miles, the lancers gave up pursuit. "Looks like they quit, General," a ranger commented.

Lane nodded. "Just keep moving, boys." He pulled up beside Walker. Joe Barlow shook his head. "He's dead, General. A damned shame. He was good man."

Nathan stared at Hays in disbelief as the slight colonel gave him the word on Sam Walker, but he didn't have time to mourn the loss of his friend, for Rip Ford rushed in with word that Santa Anna was massing his army outside Puebla for an all-out attack.

With the troops from Huamantia joining up with those from Mexico City, General Scott guessed he was facing twenty-five hundred to three thousand enemy forces.

"If we let Santa Anna enter Puebla, it's going to be hell of a fight, General," Hays exclaimed. "It'll be door-to-door."

General Scott frowned at the younger man. "Do you have a better suggestion, Colonel Hays?"

Jack grinned at Nathan. "Give me five hundred rangers, and I'll settle the problem for you, General. With five hundred, I'll keep Santa Anna out of Puebla."

A faint sneer curled Scott's lips as he pondered Hays' request. "Daring, isn't it?"

"Look, General Scott. Hit the Mexicans with what they don't expect, they'll break and run." He nodded to Nathan. "We've done it before; we can do it again."

Scott glanced at General Joe Lane, who nodded his agreement. Nodding slowly, Scott agreed.

Hays and Nathan gathered their rangers, splitting them into two groups — each made up of six companies of forty rangers — just as the sun dropped behind the mountains.

"Santa Anna is camped at the junction of the roads to Mexico City and Huamantia." Hays paused, his eyes narrowing. "We'll give him a dose of his own medicine," he said, eyeing the company commanders before him. "Like he did at the Alamo, we'll hit him before sunrise. We'll catch those bean eaters with their pants down. Nathan here will hit the camp on the Mexico City Road. I'll take the Huamantia road." He paused. "If we break Santa Anna's back here, the war's over."

After the company commanders returned to their men, Nathan muttered, "Moving five hundred men is mighty noisy, Jack. They'll hear us before we're halfway there."

Hays grimaced. "If we stay off the hard-pan, we can get closer, but even if they hear us coming, we're going to clean their plows."

That night, Rip Ford ducked into Nathan's adobe. Nathan was sitting on his bunk, sharpening his bowie. Ford grinned, eyeing the knife. "Ready for the morning, huh?" He paused. "Well, I just learned something that'll put a spring in your step." Nathan frowned up at the older man. Ford continued. "In that bunch from Huamantia, there's three guerilla companies."

Nathan paused, the question filling his eyes.

"Yep. Frank Selman is leading one of them companies."

His ice-cold eyes riveted Ford. "I want the Huamantia road, Rip."

Ford grinned. "I figured you would. I done set it up with Devil Jack."

Barney grinned and slapped Nathan on the shoulder. "Tomorrow could the day, Nathan."

Nodding slowly, Nathan returned to sharpening his bowie. "Yep," he softly replied. "It could be that."

CHAPTER THIRTY-FOUR

Each Texas Ranger carried a .52 Hall-North smoothbore in his saddle boot, a Colt .44 in his holster, double-shotted pistols and Paterson Colts under his belt, and either a bowie or an Arkansas toothpick in a sheath on his hip.

A front blew in during the night, bringing with it a cold rain. Nathan awakened and listened to the patter of rain against the wood-slab door. He grimaced. The change in weather was a mixed blessing. While the rain might drive the cold into the bones, it would silence the movement of the rangers and keep the Mexican soldiers in their tents. At the same time, it would make it much more difficult to spot Frank Selman.

He lay awake staring into the darkness over his head. Finally, he rolled over and fell into a dreamless slumber.

■ ■ ■ ■

On Hays' orders, an hour before the troops moved out, several rangers rode out for the Mexican camp, planning on slipping in and taking out any sentries who could spoil the surprise attack.

At three a.m., the rangers moved out, bundled in heavy mackinaws with collars pulled up about the ears and slickers to ward off the cold rain.

Nathan pulled his companies up in a ravine between two ridges a quarter mile from the slumbering Mexican camp. He couldn't resist a smug grin. In just a few minutes, there was going to be a heap of surprised Mexicans down below, especially Frank Selman.

Rain continued to fall in a steady, chilling drizzle.

The hard men ignored it, their blood heated with the anticipation of the coming fight. As one, they sat in their saddles, eyes narrowed, iron jaws set, every muscle tense, every nerve on edge, and every thought focused on the impending battle. Suddenly, a gunshot echoed through the steady pattering of rain. With a wild yell, Nathan spurred his roan and the game animal lunged forward into the night, headed for the few flickering fires below.

Behind him, 240 horses, mounted by screaming rangers, pounded through the mud.

Standing in his stirrups, Nathan fired at the ill-clad guerillas tumbling from their tents. Panicking, they scattered like quail in every direction, leaving clothing, weapons, and horses behind, in an effort to escape the savagery of the rangers sweeping down on them.

Faces were a blur. Once Nathan thought he spotted Selman dash from a tent. By the time he wheeled about, the face had vanished into the night.

From the west came echoing gunfire as Hays and his men smashed through the Mexican camp.

Within minutes, the battle was over. While a few bodies lay in the mud, the majority had vanished into the rainy night. Nathan stayed a few rangers who wanted to pursue the fleeing soldiers. "We done our job boys. Don't get carried away."

Later, Hays grinned like a schoolboy and slapped Nathan on the shoulder. "We pulled it off, Nathan. We damned well pulled it off."

Two weeks later in early December, eight hundred Texas Rangers with Hays and Cooper at point triumphantly led the U.S. Expeditionary Force into Mexico City.

Sitting stiffly in his saddle and eyeing the throngs of sullen faces staring up at him from both sides of the narrow streets, Hays muttered, "It don't appear these pepperbellies are tickled to see us, do it?"

Nathan suppressed a grin. "It ain't going to get no better, Jack. Mark my words."

At that moment, a snarling peon stepped from the crowd and hurled a rock at the column of rangers. George Buckalew, a short-tempered ranger from Columbia, instinctively shucked his sixgun and shot the Mexican. The crowd fell back in shock, shouting at the rangers, *"Los Tejanos Sangrientes!"* Bloody Texans.

Reluctantly, Hays put Buckalew on report, punishing him with stable duty for two days.

When General Scott questioned the soft punishment, Hays explained, "Hell, General. Someone chunks a rock at you big enough to tear off your head, what are you going to do, kiss his ass?"

Scott's craggy face darkened. He eyed the

slight colonel malevolently for several seconds. Behind Hays stood twenty Texas Rangers, rawboned and steely eyed with amused grins on their faces, as they awaited his response.

With a loud snort, Scott turned on his heel and strode away. A ranger started to snicker, but Hays shot him a look that froze the marrow in the ranger's bones.

The city offered a passive, but stubborn resistance to the U.S. occupation while diplomats from both countries hammered out a treaty both sides would accept. The city was a cauldron of unrest, of tension strained to the breaking point, and the name, *Los Tejanos Sangrientes,* became a common shout from the dark shadows behind open windows along the narrow *calles.*

But no more rocks were hurled.

Days passed slowly, dragged into weeks. Devil Jack Hays had his hands full keeping the intemperate rangers on a leash. "Dammit, Nathan," Jack had barked, "I can't get the general to see that these damned rangers don't care none about sitting on their butts. They want to fight, and this peace-making is getting on their nerves."

Nathan grinned crookedly. "Can you blame them, Jack? I don't cotton none to lazing about either." He paused and studied the slight captain seriously. "Their tempers are on edge, Jack. It ain't going to take much to set them off."

The detonator of the ranger explosion came early one morning, when a young ranger by the name of Adam Allsens came in draped over his saddle, his wrists tied to his ankles under the belly of his horse, his intestines looped over his saddle horn like a rope.

Cooper and Hays expected a storm of incensed rangers, but the companies remained quiet. There was no outbreak of rage, of threats, of retribution. Young Allsens was gently taken down, dutifully cleaned up and dressed, and buried in a local cemetery.

Hays frowned at the lack of emotion shown by the rangers. "I don't understand it, Nathan. I figured every mother's son of these old boys would be charging out of here with blood in their eyes."

Nathan glanced at Barney who lifted an eyebrow as if to say he had no idea what was going on in the mind of the rangers. "Don't go reckoning it's all over, Jack. I've seen Kronks and Flatheads give no sign of how they felt, only to be dodging a knife blade the next second."

Jack eyed him curiously. "You reckon they're up to something?"

With a shrug, the big mountain man replied, "Wouldn't you be?"

Midmorning of the next day, a young private approached Nathan in the stable where he was grooming his roan. "General Scott wants to see you, Mister Cooper. You and Colonel Hays. I just told the colonel. He'll be waiting for you at the general's office."

Barney frowned over the back of his pony and grunted, "What kinda burr you reckon's under the general's saddle now?"

Nathan shrugged. "Who knows?"

General Scott was livid. "Eighty," he exclaimed, the veins in his neck bulging, "eighty damned Mexicans dead — laying all over the streets of Mexico City." His eyes blazed, and he jabbed a finger at Hays several times. "It was your damned rangers that committed such an atrocity, Colonel."

Nathan interrupted, "Well now, General Scott. It might look that way, but just how do you know the rangers were the ones behind it?"

Scott sputtered, "Who else? Yesterday, one

of your men comes in all carved up. Today, looks like a damned buffalo hunt out there. Besides, General Taylor informed me of the incident in Monterrey the day after a ranger got himself killed."

Hays started to protest, but Scott held up his hand. "I know, I know. The Mexicans hung themselves out of remorse for stealing horses. That's bull-crap, and you know it."

Clearing his throat, Hays replied, "No disrespect intended, General Scott, but whoever informed you that rangers done it is lying. None of my rangers was out last night except on patrol, and those old boys I trust with my life." The expression of pure innocence radiated from the slender ranger's face. He held his hand up, palm forward. "As the good Lord is my witness."

Scott sputtered for words.

At that moment, a knock at the door interrupted, and Rip Ford stuck his head in. "Excuse me, General Scott, but you said you want to be kept informed about Jarauta or Parades. Just got word that Jarauta is heading for Otumba." He glanced at Nathan and winked.

Hays and Nathan looked back at the general, their eyes asking the question. Finally General Scott drew a deep breath and released it in a long sigh. "Hays, I want that padre."

Jack glanced at Nathan then nodded. "You'll have him, General."

Thirty minutes later, with Nathan leading, a sixty-five man company of Texas Rangers rode out, heading northwest to the small, sixteenth-century village of Otumba.

At the head of the column, Nathan rode warily, his keen gray eyes quartering the rugged landscape into which they ventured. Gnarled mesquite and stunted oak dotted the foothills. The road and steep slopes were deserted except for the occasional *pastores* tending sheep.

On a ridge above the small village of Otumba, Nathan reined up, peering down into the silent town. As they watched, one or two children dashed across the narrow streets, casting frantic glances over their shoulders at the rangers on the sawtooth ridge.

George Buckalew and Joe Barlow pulled up beside Nathan. Buckalew grunted, "Looks deserted, Cooper."

With a wry chuckle, Nathan replied, "Looks can kill you, George. Tell you what. Pick a few men and circle west around the town. I'll go east. Let's us see what we can

340

find out before we go riding in."

Thirty minutes later, the two patrols met on the far side of the village. "Ain't seen a thing, Nathan. A couple old women and kids. That's about it," said Barlow.

Studying the road, Nathan chuckled and dismounted. With the tip of his boot, he kicked a horse biscuit. "That don't surprise me." He glanced at the village, then over his shoulder. "Them we're after are gone. Headed back this way." He glanced around. "Any idea where this road goes?"

"San Juan Teotihuacan," said Joe Barlow.

George Buckalew spoke up. "Maybe it was the Mexican army."

Arching an eyebrow, Nathan replied, "I figure guerillas — Jaruata's men. No grain in the droppings. Mostly grass."

"So now what?"

Nathan glanced at the setting sun and hooked his thumb toward the village. "Too late to trail after them tonight. Let's pay the good folks down in the village a visit. Pass the word. I don't want none of them mistreated unless they cause problems. And leave the women alone."

A ranger grinned. "Hell, Nathan. You saying we can't have no fun?"

Nathan smiled. "Reckon that's just what

I'm saying. If these folks don't give us no cause for trouble, we don't give them none. Clear enough?"

A handful of citizens, the local *alcalde* among them, were waiting at the town plaza when the rangers rode in. The *alcalde* nodded obsequiously. "Senors. Welcome to our village. We are poor peons, but what we have, we will gladly share with you."

Nathan assigned sentries on the outskirts of the small town. "I don't expect trouble, but if comes, I don't want it to surprise me." The remainder of the ranger company camped on the main plaza.

As darkness crept over Otumba and dancing lights from the campfires cast eerie shadows on the adobe and rock buildings surrounding the square, curious eyes looked on. And when the aroma of boiling stew from the ranger camp curled through the village, three or four children ventured forth.

The rangers, rugged, cold-blooded, and violent, invited the wary children to join them. Soon, a dozen laughing boys and girls played around the fires in the rangers' camp.

Later, as the fires burned low, a furtive figure ghosted through the night, evading the sentries, and scurrying up the road to San Juan Teotihuacan.

At the top of a ridge, he paused and peered back down at the slumbering rangers. "Enjoy your rest, gringos. You will need it tomorrow."

CHAPTER THIRTY-FIVE

During the night, a cold front blew in, bringing with it a chilling rain.

Nathan shivered next morning as they rode out.

The road to San Juan Teotihuacan wound through the Sierra Madres like a snake, around towering peaks, beneath jagged ridges, and between gigantic volcanic uplifts twisted into grotesque shapes. Sixty-five sets of wary eyes searched the forbidding peaks staring down at them.

George Buckalew pulled up beside Nathan. "I reckon I should feel good that we ain't seen nobody spying on us, but I got a feeling they're up there anyways."

Nathan chuckled. "They're up there, George. Question is, when are they coming down?"

An hour later, the company rode into a small valley less than a half mile in length and breadth. In the middle sat the small village of San Juan Teotihuacan, its cheerless buildings blending in with the drab prairie.

On the outskirts of the small town lay the ruins of an ancient presidio, its adobe walls crumbling. In the middle stood three sides of an old mission with its roof caved in.

The deserted streets were suddenly filled with armed guerillas on horseback and afoot. One moment, the streets were empty, and the next, like floodwaters coursing down a dry streambed, they burst from the small village in a torrent of screaming, savage charge toward the Texas Rangers.

The company of rangers pulled up and shucked their Colts. Barney whistled softly. "Looks like we got us a welcoming committee, boys."

"Then let's don't let them regret it." Without hesitation, Nathan charged the village, followed by sixty-four howling rangers, all standing in the stirrups and coolly aiming the large Colts that belched death.

The sudden charge and the galling barrage of lead smashed the attacking guerillas. Their ranks wavered, then broke, scattering like quail as the hard-faced rangers bore down on them. Despite the heat of battle, Nathan had a nagging feeling something was wrong — the guerillas gave ground too easily.

The rangers charged through the small village. Nathan wheeled his roan about, and his blood ran cold.

From the foothills on either side, hordes of screaming guerillas charged them. The first wave of Mexicans once again filled the narrow *calles* of the village.

Barlow reined up beside Nathan, his face grim, his jaw set. "Looks like we bit off a bit more than we can chew."

Nathan guessed they were outnumbered ten to one, too many for even the elite of the Texas Rangers. Then he remembered the ruined presidio. "Maybe not," shouted, digging his heels into his roan. "Follow me!"

The small company of rangers charged the village.

The guerillas dropped to their knees and pulled their muskets into their shoulders, awaiting the charge of *Los Tejanos Sangrientes.*

At the last moment, just beyond range of the guerillas' weapons, Nathan cut sharply to his left, leading the thundering company of rangers around the village and into the welcome refuge of the crumbling presidio. They jumped the eroding ramparts and dismounted, leaving their remounts behind the walls for protection.

With their .52 Hall-North smoothbore

rifles, the rangers paired up, taking their positions around the perimeter of the ramparts with only seconds to spare before the first wave of guerillas attacked.

Before the guerillas came within the effective range of their shotguns, a merciless fusillade of gunfire from the rangers blasted the line of Mexicans like rag dolls. The line hesitated, wavered, then with a throaty scream, continued its charge.

The rangers pulled out their Walker Colts, and the small valley echoed with the steady thunder of .44s.

Just before the first charge reached the broken walls, it fell apart. Thick white smoke filled the air, tasting like sulfur and stinging the eyes. Two more times that afternoon, the Mexican guerillas charged, but each time they were beaten back with heavy losses.

Just before dark, a rider on a gray horse emerged from the village carrying a white flag. Barney glanced at Nathan. "Reckon they're giving up?" he chuckled.

With a shrug, Nathan replied, "Not likely." He rose slowly, watching warily as the rider drew near.

The grizzled vaquero stopped a few feet before the walls and nodded. "Senor. I bring word from Padre Jarauta. If you surrender, you will not be harmed. You and your men will be escorted to the border where you will be given your freedom. If not, he will not spare a man. The padre, a most generous man, expects your answer in the morning."

His eyes cold, Nathan nodded. "He'll have it."

Joe Barlow, who had ambled over, looked around at Nathan sharply. When the rider was out of earshot, Barlow exclaimed, "Dammit it to hell, Nathan. You ain't about to consider his offer are you?"

A wry grin played over his face. "Just buying time, Joe. Just buying time."

Barlow studied the larger man. "I say we mount and bust through them greasers out there." He glanced around at the other rangers who had gathered around. They nodded their agreement.

"What about the orders Scott gave us? He said he wanted that padre. And I say we get him, then go back."

George Buckalew stepped forward. He folded his long arms over his chest. "And just how do you reckon on doing that?"

Nathan shrugged. "Nothing to it, George. Tonight, you and me is just going to saunter into town and ask the good padre to take a ride with us."

Buckalew's eyes grew wide. "We're what?"

"You heard me. We'll ride in and invite him to take a ride with us. Simple." He nodded to the gray clouds overhead. "Tonight'll be dark. Mighty dark."

Barlow arched a skeptical eyebrow. "What if the clouds blow away?"

"They won't." Nathan cut his keen gray eyes at the scudding clouds. "They won't. Weather's turning worse. It'll be darker than the inside of a cow tonight. You can bet on it."

He was right. The thick clouds held. The night was like pitch, blacker than a raven's wing, and the wind blew cold and sharp.

"Any guards the padre has out will be huddled around a fire," Nathan whispered as he and Buckalew made ready to move out. "Just stay with me."

Buckalew had never seen a night so dark. All he could make out of Nathan was a blur just a few inches away as they eased over the crumbling walls and made their way to the village.

Suddenly Nathan stopped and whispered, "Stay here. There's a sentry ahead."

Buckalew wanted to ask how the big mountain man knew, but he had vanished like a ghost. Buckalew waited, huddling in his heavy coat and peering into the darkness. After what seemed hours, Nathan reappeared. "Jarauta's at the cantina. That's his headquarters. Two streets over. Let's go."

Before Buckalew could utter a word, Nathan had moved away. The lanky ranger followed, often more by sound than sight.

Nathan squinted into the darkness, his sharp eyes cataloging various shapes into definition. More times than he could count, his keen vision and finely honed perceptions had kept him from harm's way.

He paused at the corner of an adobe and peered into the inky darkness of a narrow street. From what the sentry had told him before he bound and gagged the frightened man, the cantina should be directly across the street. He squinted at the flat roof over the small building, but the shadows were too thick to discern any shapes.

The biting wind howled as it swept along the hardpan street. If any sentries were on the roof, they were probably huddled in a corner out of the wind. No one in his right mind, they would figure, would be out on a night like this.

He studied the darkness, picking out tiny lines of yellow light flickering through the cracks in the wooden shutters over the windows in the cantina. Nathan reached back and laid his hand on Buckalew's arm. "Right across the street. Move quiet. Now."

Seconds later, they crouched outside the cantina door. "Now what?" Buckalew whispered.

"Just wait."

Nathan rose silently and slipped along the wall to a shuttered window. He peered through the cracks, spotting three bundled figures on the floor in front of the *chiminea*. He scanned the rest of the cantina, which appeared to be a single large room.

Dropping into a crouch, Nathan eased back to the door. "Three in there."

"Jarauta?"

"Can't tell. They're sleeping." He reached for the door latch.

"How will we know?"

"I've seen him. I'll recognize him," Nathan spoke over his shoulder as he eased the latch up and opened the door. The figures on the floor continued to slumber.

Buckalew slipped in after Nathan and closed the door.

One of the sleeping men suddenly opened his eyes and stared up in disbelief at the two rangers. Nathan recognized him. Padre Celedonia de Jarauta. Before the padre could utter a word, Nathan slammed the muzzle of his Colt across the man's temple, then quickly threw the slight man over his shoulder.

When he turned for the door, a string of curses exploded behind him, and he spun just as Frank Selman, his teeth bared in a snarl, sat up in his blankets and swung the muzzle of his pistol toward Nathan.

Behind Nathan, Buckalew's Colt spewed fire.

Selman screamed, stabbed his hand to his head, and fell backward, arms outstretched. For a long, frozen moment, Nathan stared at the bearded figure.

Buckalew grabbed his arm. "Nathan! Get out of here."

Stunned by the sudden chain of events, Nathan quickly gathered his thoughts and hurried after the lanky ranger, disappearing into the night even as lights began popping on around the small village. Once or twice, the rangers and their burden backed into shadows as excited men raced toward them.

Ten minutes later, they were back in camp with their trophy, Padre Celedonia de Jarauta.

CHAPTER
THIRTY-SIX

When the sun rose next morning, Nathan and a handful of rangers stood at the crumbling wall with a white flag, ignoring the few flurries of snow whipping past them on the sharp winds.

Bundled against the chill, Barney stared up into the face of his son-in-law. "You sure it was Frank Selman?"

Nodding slowly, Nathan grunted in disappointment. "It was Selman." He paused, his jaw set, his eyes cold. "I wanted to be the one, Barney. I wanted to make that bastard suffer like he made . . ." His words faded out.

Barney gave his a wry grin. "I know, Nathan. Me too. I could have carved him to pieces without a second thought. But at least he got what he deserved. That only leaves one now, Otis Sims."

Moments later, riders appeared from the small village.

After they approached, Nathan signaled for two rangers to bring the padre out. The consternation on the guerillas' faces when they spotted him brought a grim smile to Nathan's lips. He quickly laid out his ultimatum.

"We're riding out of here with the padre. One shot, and he's dead. *¿Usted comprende?*"

The two vaqueros nodded. *"Si."*

Two days later, Nathan and his Texas Rangers handed Padre Celedonia de Jarauta over to General Winfield Scott, and the general informed them that the Treaty of Guadalupe Hidalgo had been signed, marking the end of the Mexican War.

That night, as the cold wind howled around the thick adobe walls, Nathan and Barney, with a handful of rawboned rangers, sat before the flames dancing in the terra cotta *chiminea* reflecting on their mission of the last couple years, a mission that had come to an end as abruptly as it had started.

Despite the death of Frank Selman, Nathan still felt he had been cheated. For almost two years, the searing fire of vengeance had driven him. He wanted to kill them all. He told Barney how he felt.

The older man nodded. "We both was cheated."

"We still got one left, Barney. Now that the war's over, I reckon we can go about our business down here without no interference with the Mexicans. And we don't have much time to waste, the way I figure it. With the war over, those guerillas will scatter like quail. I figure Sims will too."

Jack Hays spoke up. "I don't know about that, Nathan. There's still a heap of guerillas and soldiers out there that don't figure that treaty's worth the paper it's written on. And they're gathering under that rebel Parades, who doesn't recognize the treaty."

Joe Barlow worked a chaw of tobacco around in his cheeks and squirted a stream on the floor. "Parades! The one who was the Mexican president?"

"Yep. General Mariano Parades, the one-time president of Mexico. Him and that padre you old boys brought in are the leaders. Now, we got one of them. Now all we got to do is get the other one."

Barney frowned. "That don't make sense. The Mex government signed a treaty saying they give up. That ought to mean the whole shebang gives up, don't it?"

The old man among the Texas Rangers, "Rip" Ford chuckled. "That makes too

355

much sense, Barney — especially down here. Mexico has always been a hotbed of revolution. One batch of pepperbellies don't like what another batch is doing, they overthrow them with guns. And then in a few months, another bunch gets a wild hair, and they overthrow the first bunch. Why, it's near next to impossible to keep up with who's in power and who ain't. Ten, twelve years back, when old Sam Houston cleaned Santa Anna's plow at San Jacinto, you'd never have figured that little greaser would be president of Mexico again, but here he is."

Puzzled, Barney looked at Rip. "You're saying that we just signed a treaty saying we won the war, but we got to keep on fighting?"

Hays laughed. "Don't make no sense, does it?"

"It sure don't," Barney replied, shaking his head. "But then, I never seen no politician that made much sense."

The next morning at chow in the company mess hall, Nathan and Barney were putting themselves around fried beef and beans when Jack Hays rushed in, his eyes dancing with excitement, and a grin as wide as the Rio Grande on his face. He slipped across the table from Nathan and leaned forward. "You heard the news?"

"News? What news?" Nathan frowned.

"The padre. Jarauta. He's gone."

Nathan stared at the slight colonel in disbelief. "Gone? What are you talking about, gone?"

Jack chuckled. "Just walked out. A work party comes in every morning with supplies, and he just joined in with them and walked out. The general is swelled up like a poisoned pup, he's so mad. Done put a lieutenant and two guards on report. Threatened to shoot them, though he knows he can't do nothing like that."

Nathan muttered a curse, but he couldn't help grinning at the general's frustration over the missing padre. There was no love lost between him and Scott, but on the other hand, he and George Buckalew had taken a mighty risky chance in kidnapping the padre. Suddenly, a thought hit Nathan. Now that Jarauta was free, then maybe that's where he could find Otis Sims, the last of the five.

Barney leaned forward. "What happened? How did Jarauta get out?"

Jack shrugged. "Best we can piece together, this morning some of the little pepperbellies delivered some supplies into the building where they were keeping the padre. One of them must have slipped him some duds, because the guards insist all of the workers were dressed alike. He couldn't tell one from the other."

At that moment, Rip Ford entered, looked around, spotted Jack, and hurried over. "Jack. The general wants you. Now."

Jack arched an eyebrow at Nathan, then replied, "He say what about?"

"Major Polk with that damned smug look on his face was with him. I wouldn't be surprised at all if he sends you and Polk after Jarauta and General Parades. Word is, them two is at Tulancingo."

Nathan stiffened. He reached across the table and laid his large hand on Jack's arm. Hays looked around. "Barney and me want to go with you, Jack. Can you fix it?"

Hays studied Nathan and Barney a moment. "You heard Rip. Polk's going along. You know what he thinks about you. Remember your suspicions about Villamez? Now, I don't believe Polk run you into that ambush on purpose, but if he did, then you're asking for trouble. You'll be out front, and he'll be in the back." He paused and added somberly, "I've seen a heap of good men get it in the back by accident."

The big mountain man's eyes narrowed,

and he muttered, "To hell with him. I'll roll out my soogan right next to Satan himself to get Sims. This might be my last chance."

The slight colonel lifted an eyebrow. "Your funeral."

After Hays and Ford left, Barney turned to his son-in-law. "You really believe that, Nathan? About Sims, I mean?"

Nodding slowly, Nathan kept his eyes fixed on the closed door through which the two rangers had disappeared. "Maybe back in Texas we could run him down, but down here" — he paused and made a wide sweep with his arm — "finding him down here would be might near impossible."

Heading northwest out of Mexico City in the teeth of a chilling drizzle, Nathan glanced over his shoulder at the companies of rangers. "Looks like the general meant business about General Parades, huh?"

Rain dripping from the brim of his Stetson, Hays grinned. "Two hundred and fifty rangers, a hundred and thirty dragoons, six hundred lancers, and a dozen twelve-pounders? I'd say he meant real business."

Barney nodded to the back of Major Polk at the head of the column. "I'd feel a heap better with someone else up there."

Nathan and Jack grinned, but said nothing.

Two days later, Polk camped his force at the entrance to the nine-mile-long valley, at the far end of which sat the village of Tulancingo. The drizzle had abated, the temperature had dropped, and the icy blasts howling in from the north kept rangers and soldiers huddled in their heavy coats.

Despite the weather, an undercurrent of expectation, of excitement swept through the detachment of rangers, who knew that their objective was at the end of the valley.

That night just after dark, Hays called Nathan to his fire. George Buckalew looked up as Nathan approached. Hays cupped his hands and blew into them to warm his numb fingers. "We need more intelligence on the village than what we have." He glanced at the patchy cloud cover overhead. "They'll be a new moon tonight. Nathan, you and Buckalew find a spot to spy on the village. Get a feeling for the place. Polk plans to stay here another day. Let me know what we're facing before we move out." He handed the big mountain man a brass telescope. "This'll come in handy, I reckon."

Nodding, Nathan pushed to his feet. "What about Polk's intelligence?"

Hays drew a deep breath and shot a furtive glance in the direction of Polk's tent. "Let me put it this way: I'd feel better hearing about what's waiting there for us from my own kind."

Nathan studied his old friend for several moments, seeing in Jack's eyes that he didn't trust Polk anymore than Nathan did.

Three hours later, the two rangers found a secure niche among the jagged ridges above the village from where they could spy on the activities below without fear of discovery.

After picketing their ponies, Nathan and Buckalew crouched behind the wall of scrubby mountain cedar and, through the brass telescope, studied the dark village below.

Nothing moved.

Throwing blankets over their shoulders, the two rangers huddled deep into their mackinaws and awaited morning.

With the rising sun, the village came alive with a great deal of activity, as soldiers of Jarauta and Parades' ragtag army constructed battlements around the village, blocking all roads in and out. On the outskirts of the village sat a large hacienda on small hill surrounded by whitewashed walls. A small chapel was fit into one corner of the grounds. An outside door led into it.

Men were scurrying about fortifying the hacienda.

Behind the village grazed a herd of horses near a rambling stable. "Must be close to a thousand head," Buckalew muttered.

Nathan grunted. "At least that many men. And artillery." He nodded to the half dozen small cannons on the perimeter of the village. "What do they look like, six-pounders?"

Buckalew studied the artillery pieces through the telescope. "I reckon. Maybe eight."

Stretching his arms over his head, Nathan yawned. "You want to sleep first?"

"Naw. You go ahead. I'll keep watch."

The day remained overcast with thick, dark clouds pushed by a chilling wind.

Nathan jerked awake around noon, his deerskins soaked with cold sweat as the nightmare came back to haunt him. He threw off his blankets.

Buckalew glanced over his shoulder and frowned at the sweaty sheen on Nathan's face. "You all right?"

Nodding jerkily, the big mountain man sipped from his canteen. "Yeah."

Forcing a chuckle, the younger ranger drawled, "You was sleeping so hard, I figured you might of up and died on me."

"Not yet." He drew a deep breath and drew his sleeve across his damp forehead. "I still got me a chore to take care of."

The lean ranger nodded. More than once over the last year and a half, he heard whispered gossip about the tragedy that drove Nathan Cooper. "Nothing going on down there. They finished fortifying the city, and now they're working on the hacienda."

Peering through the telescope at the whitewashed walls surrounding the grounds of the hacienda, Nathan grunted as he adjusted the eyepiece, bringing more definition to the features of the men scurrying over the hacienda like so many busy little ants. "Reckon that's where Jarauta and Parades is holed up. Wouldn't at all be surprised to —"

He stiffened. "Yep." He handed Buckalew the scope. "Take a look. There's Jarauta now. On the second-floor balcony."

"Sure as hell is. Who's that with him, Parades?"

Squinting down the ridge, Nathan shook his head. "I don't know who that hombre is, but he ain't Parades."

Buckalew looked around. "You've seen Parades?"

"Once. I ran across him and Jarauta and Frank Selman outside of Saltillo. I would of killed Selman there, but some poor vaquero rode between us just as I fired."

Turning back to the eyeglass, the lanky ranger studied the two men on the balcony. After a few moments, he handed Nathan the brass telescope.

Pushing the nightmare from his mind, Nathan nodded to the blankets in which he had wrapped himself. "Grab some sleep. I'll take over here. It don't look much like anything else is going on."

Suddenly, the hair on the back of his neck bristled.

CHAPTER
THIRTY-SEVEN

The big mountain man glanced around, but saw nothing out of place on the ridge. At first, he thought someone might be approaching, but a careful survey of the steep slopes proved him wrong.

Still, the prickling on the back of his neck continued to nag at him long after George Buckalew dropped off into a deep slumber.

No hombre who had survived among savage and hostile Indians ignored the warning signs of danger, and as far as Nathan was concerned, that tickling feeling on the back of his neck meant danger.

He flipped the rawhide loop off the hammer of his big Walker Colt just in case.

Throughout the afternoon, Nathan studied the village below, searching for a weak spot in the defenses without success. General Parades obviously had not acquired that title through some honorary award. No,

Nathan told himself, that jasper knows what he's doing. Major William Polk might not realize it, but he was going to have his hands full in the upcoming engagement.

He noted several women with prayer shawls hurrying down the narrow streets and entering a heavy door in one corner of the hacienda grounds — the hacienda chapel.

Just before sundown, a troop of guerillas entered the valley from the north. Nathan counted almost five hundred, a hundred or so on horseback, the others afoot. From where he crouched behind the mountain cedar, he saw that many of them carried old *escopetas,* blunderbuss shotguns inaccurate beyond twenty feet. Some carried smooth-bore flintlocks or ball-and-caps. All carried gleaming machetes at their waists.

A soft voice at his shoulder startled him. "Reinforcements, huh?"

"You move quiet," he muttered.

"From you I figure that's a compliment."

"I counted about five hundred."

"Makes fifteen altogether." Buckalew nodded to the hacienda. "They finish down there?"

"About an hour ago."

Buckalew studied the hacienda. "Looks

like Polk will have to blow the gates down to get into the hacienda."

Nathan swung the scope back to the tall, timbered gates, one on each of the four walls. Chuckling, he muttered, "First, he's got to get through the town. Then —"

He froze, the telescope focused on a lanky cowpoke knocking on the gate to the hacienda. Quickly, Nathan adjusted the definition of the scope until he had a clear view of the man's face. Despite the fading light, he made out the pronounced scar that ran across the jasper's right eye and down his cheek.

Otis Sims! The last one!

Buckalew sensed the sudden urgency in the big mountain man's movements. "What?"

Nathan shook his head, continuing to adjust the clarity of the scope. The hacienda gate opened, and Sims disappeared inside. Nathan continued to scan the hacienda, but the rail-thin scavenger did not put in another appearance.

He lowered the scope.

"What was it, Nathan? What did you see?"

Closing the scope, Nathan handed it to Buckalew. "Go back and tell Jack what the situation is. Be sure to tell them the location of the artillery."

Buckalew stiffened. "Me? What about you? What are you going to do?"

Ignoring the question, Nathan continued, "They'll have to use the twelve-pounders to knock out Jarauta's artillery, then blow the walls down around the hacienda."

"But what are you going to do, Nathan?"

"I'll wait here in case they make any changes Jack needs to know about."

The lanky ranger nodded. "Makes sense." He rose and quickly tightened the cinch about his pony's belly and swung into the saddle. He glanced at the clouds overhead. "Looks like a clear day tomorrow. You take care. If I know Jack, he'll be here at first light."

By midnight, the village was asleep except for a few late night carousers. The fleeting clouds above were patchy, casting deep shadows over the village one moment, and lighting it brightly with starlight the next.

After Buckalew had ridden out, Nathan laid out his plan. The stable was the first step. Then, he had to make his way down a narrow street to the entrance to the chapel. From there, he could gain access to the hacienda grounds.

Moving silently, Nathan ghosted along the

ridge. He paused and threw a blanket over his broad shoulders. Using the shadows cast by the sage and chaparral, he slipped in among the grazing horses. Several lifted their heads and perked their ears forward curiously as he moved like a wraith through the night to the stable.

Easing through the shadows of the stable, he suddenly froze as a mumbling voice sounded in the darkness. Reaching out, he touched the adobe wall. Quickly, he squatted and drawing his knees up to his chest, pulled the blanket over his head, feigning sleep.

After a few minutes, the mumbling ceased.

Nathan waited. Finally he rose to his feet. He felt around the wall to a door and slipped outside. On the other side of the street, two figures were walking in his direction. Nathan pulled the blanket over his head and stumbled drunkenly along the side of the stable, all the while peering from under his eyebrows at the approaching two men.

As they drew near, Nathan laid his hand on the butt of his Colt while still continuing his charade. One of them called out, *"¡Amigo! ¿Qué está equivocado, también mucho pulque?"* What is wrong, too much pulque? They laughed as they passed.

Nathan breathed a sigh of relief.

Moments later, he reached the chapel and slipped inside.

Above the chancel was hung a great cross of the crucifixion. At the side of the chancel, flickering candles cast a dim light over the nave. Nathan slipped into the shadows in the rear of the chapel, planning his next move.

Without warning, a door near the chancel opened and three well-dressed hidalgos entered. Nathan recognized Padre Jarauta, General Marino Parades, and the Mexican noble he had earlier seen on the balcony with the padre. He pressed deeper into the shadows.

The three sat in a front pew, deep in conversation.

Finally, Padre Jarauta rose and departed, leaving Parades and the one from the balcony.

Outside, a rooster crowed.

Nathan cursed under his breath. Time was running out.

After what seemed like hours, the two hidalgos left through the same door they had entered. Quickly Nathan slipped from the shadows and followed after them. Halfway down the nave, he heard the rear door open.

Quickly, he knelt by a pew and bowed his head.

He heard footsteps coming toward him. Just before they reached him, they scraped to a halt.

Head bowed, the big mountain man remained kneeling, but under the blanket, his large fingers were folding around the bone handle of his bowie. The back of his neck burned. Whoever stood behind him was staring at him.

Several long moments passed. Nathan could hear the man's ragged breathing. After a few more seconds, Nathan slowly rose to a crouch and, keeping his back to whomever was behind him, made supplicating gestures to the cross behind the chancel while easing backward.

Suddenly, a guttural voice spoke. "You! Hombre! Who are you? What are you doing here?"

A hand spun Nathan around.

"Nobody's supposed to be here except them hildalgo —"

Nathan stared into the startled face of Otis Sims.

CHAPTER
THIRTY-EIGHT

"You!" Sims gasped, his eyes bulging in disbelief.

Lunging forward, Nathan swung a left uppercut, smashing the iron T into Sims' bony jaw, breaking it and driving the startled jasper back against the rear wall of the chapel. At the same time, he drove the fifteen-inch blade of his bowie into the man's abdomen and jerked up, opening the stunned scavenger's belly from groin to brisket.

Sims tried to scream, but Nathan's muscular arm was crushing the dying man's throat against the adobe wall. Bony fingers clawed frantically, helplessly at Nathan's straining muscles. A bloody froth gathered at the side of Sims' thin lips.

Teeth bared savagely, Nathan stuck his face almost nose to nose with the dying man. He growled. "Hell's waiting, you son of a bitch." He yanked the blade from the thin man's belly and felt the warm flush of blood pouring from the open cavity.

"Hey! What's going on here?"

Nathan spun at the strident voice from behind, instinctively dropping to a knee and hurling the bowie backhanded.

Before the roughly dressed cowpoke could utter another word, the bloody blade slammed into his chest, knocking him back against a pew. For a moment, he stood staring wide-eyed in stunned disbelief at the bone handle protruding from his chest, and then his knees buckled and he slumped to the floor.

Leaping across the floor like a mountain cougar, Nathan retrieved the bowie and quickly relieved Otis Sims of his scalp. He rose to his feet, and a startled exclamation jerked him around.

"What the —"

Staring into the eyes of a ghost, Nathan's animal instincts failed him for a fleeting moment as he gaped unbelievingly at the stunned face of Frank Selman, a fresh wound on his forehead.

Startled to see Nathan Cooper, the massively built killer hesitated a moment before slapping leather.

In one fluid motion, Nathan leaped aside and hurled his knife.

Without warning, cannon fire broke the early morning silence, throwing off the aim of both men. Selman's slug tore splintered chunks from the back of a pew, and Nathan's bowie thudded deep into one of the heavy timbers supporting the chapel.

Outside in the gray of false dawn, the cannonade continued, the concussion of its explosions shaking dust from the ceiling above. Nathan shucked his Colt as he hit the floor and scrambled to the end of the pew.

When he glanced up, Selman was gone.

Muttering a curse, he leaped to his feet and raced after the killer, pausing to tug the bowie from the timber.

Outside the chapel door, he spotted Selman disappear around the corner of the hacienda. He followed, ignoring the startled men pouring out of the surrounding buildings.

Overhead, cannonballs and canister rounds whistled as they arched through the air and smashed into walls and roofs with deafening roars.

Pausing before rounding the corner, Nathan crouched and peered around the corner. An open door beckoned him into a darkened room. Beyond the door was another set of doors, French doors. A grim smile played over his lips. "Two can play that game, Selman," he muttered, backing away into the fading darkness so he could swing unseen around the open doorway.

Several frightened guerillas were running helter-skelter in an effort to evade the falling cannonballs and exploding canister shot. Nathan blended in with them until he could reach the French doors. He figured on smashing through the doors, hoping to catch Selman watching the open door.

For once, the big mountain man caught a lucky break when a frightened guerilla with his sombrero bouncing against his back darted through the open door to avoid the falling cannon fire. A moment after the small man disappeared into the room, two booming reports echoed over the thunder of cannons. The man stumbled backward from the open door, clutching his chest.

Nathan saw his chance. He lowered his shoulder and hurled his large body through the glass doors, shattering them. He hit on his back and rolled to a sitting position, quickly pumping off three shots to give him time to find something that offered protection.

From the corner of his eye, he spotted a figure dart for the door and turn along the outside wall. Leaping to his feet, the big mountain man charged back through the glass doors hanging askew from the jambs in an effort to intercept the fleeing scavenger.

Just outside the door, he slammed into Selman, and the two men hit the ground in a tangle of arms and legs.

In the next moment, a half-dozen fleeing guerillas stumbled over the two adversaries, going down in a heap.

Selman leaped to his feet and shouted, *"¡Compañeros. Aquí está a un Tejano sangriento. Lo mata!"* Compadres. Here is a bloody Texan. Kill him!

The tangle of guerillas hesitated, giving Nathan time to leap to his feet and, in the midst of flying lead, scramble back into the room, which by now was filled with the dim light of early morning. His blood ran cold when he spotted the kegs of black powder stacked along the wall.

Behind him came the snap of a hammer, a moment of sizzling powder, and then the pop of a belt pistol. He grimaced and ducked his head, steeling himself for the explosion to come, but luckily the ball thudded harmlessly into the wall.

Nathan darted through a door and found himself in a hallway leading to another door several yards away. To his right was a flight of stairs. Without hesitation, he bounded up the stairs. At the top, he came face-to-face with two hatchet-faced vaqueros.

He jabbed a finger back down the stairs. "*¡Tejanos! ¡Tejanos!*"

The two looked at each other in alarm, then rushed by Nathan down the stairs. Quickly, he made his way to the end of the hall and slipped into a bedroom, which to his relief was deserted.

By now, the cannon fire had ceased, replaced by the thunder of muskets, the roar of smoothbores, and the pop of Colts.

Nathan glanced around the room. On one side was the second-floor gallery running the length of the building. Armoires sat on one side of the room with a vanity and other toilet items. Against another wall were settees and couches. A heavy four-poster bed rested against the third wall.

He jerked around at footsteps in the hall. Moving quickly, he slipped behind a couch next to the wall and held his breath.

The door squeaked open, then moments later, slammed shut.

Outside, the roar of battle grew closer.

Easing from behind the couch, Nathan made his way to the French doors opening onto the gallery.

The walls around the hacienda had suffered severe damage. Great holes gaped in the whitewashed walls, but as the Americans clambered through the holes, the sharpshooters within the hacienda kept them at bay. Beyond the heavy gates, Nathan spotted Devil Jack Hays urging his troop of rangers toward the hacienda. The big mountain man studied the heavy gates, realizing that if they were open, then the U.S. forces and the Texas Rangers could overrun the hacienda.

Suddenly, he spotted Frank Selman dash across the yard toward the stables. Spinning on his heel to follow, Nathan froze. He glanced back at the battle raging outside the walls. Marines, soldiers, and Texas Rangers were dropping on all sides. He glanced after Selman, who disappeared into the stable.

Above the cacophony of cannon fire, booming smoothbores, and the clang of saber against machete, came a shrill cry from Jack Hays. "Keeping going, boys! We're almost there."

Then Nathan remembered the kegs of black powder.

For a long agonizing moment, Nathan was torn between running down the last of the murderers or going to the aid of the rangers.

With an angry shake of his head, he gave the stable one last, reluctant glance, then yanked a heavy Saltillo blanket off of the bed. He threw it over his shoulders like a serape. Stooping to hide his height, he reached for the door.

Although the hallway was deserted, voices echoed from several rooms on the second floor. Taking a deep breath, he stepped into the hall and quickly descended the stairs, paying no attention to the voices around him.

The powder room was deserted. Nathan heaved a keg on his shoulder and turned to leave, when a voice stopped him. A grizzled cowpoke frowned at him. "Where you going with that?"

"Selman," he muttered.

The man shrugged. "Get hopping then."

With a short nod, Nathan headed for the rear door. The voice stopped him. "Where in the hell you going? Selman ain't out there. He's at the west gate."

Keeping his head down, Nathan muttered. "I thought he said the south gate."

"No, the west one, you tanglefoot. Come on. I'll take you."

Nathan remained silent, every muscle tense, every nerve ready to explode.

The guttural voice drew near. "You hear

what I said? Come with me." The bearded
cowpoke glanced at Nathan. His eyes slid
down to the iron T on Nathan's forearm.
He frowned, then his eyes grew wide in
recognition.

That was all he remembered, for the big
mountain man slammed the iron T into the
jasper's temple, dropping him like a pole-
axed steer.

Without hesitation, Nathan hurried from
the powder room with the keg of black
powder. Outside the walls, the battle raged.

Nathan angled across the hardpan for the
south gate, which as all the others was bar-
ricaded with rickety *carretas* and wagons.
The defenders of the gate paid him little attention, for they were desperately battling
the Americans outside the wall.

Looking neither left nor right, the big
mountain man elbowed through the guerillas defending the wall. Those who glanced
at him never guessed he was not one of
them.

He placed the keg at the base of the gate.

Steel fingers clasped his shoulder. "What
in the hell is that?" a guttural voice with a
Texas twang demanded.

Without looking into the man's eyes,
Nathan replied, "Selman's orders. If they
break through here, he wants to blow them

to pieces."

The voice screamed, "He's crazy as hell. Get that powder out of there."

Nathan spun, bowie in hand. The razor-edged blade slashed across the Texan's belly, knocking the stunned mercenary backward. Holstering the bowie, Nathan stumbled back several steps and, shucking his Colt, fired two lead plums into the keg of black powder. He fell forward on his belly, humping his back and covering his head.

CHAPTER
THIRTY-NINE

Clenching his teeth, Nathan expected a crushing blow at any second from the large chunks of adobe wall or the splintered timbers of the heavy gate, but all he received were a few minor bruises.

Moments later, a wild shriek of victory cut through the echoes of the explosion as fifty mounted Texas Rangers charged through the breach in the wall.

To avoid the trampling hooves of the bolting horses or being mistaken for one of Jarauta or Parade's guerillas, Nathan rolled quickly under a nearby *carreta* and huddled against the solid wheel.

Seconds later, he spotted Hays through the thick smoke. He shouted.

Hays looked about, frowning.

Nathan waved his hat from beneath the *carreta.*

Hammer cocked, Hays rode slowly over. A big grin creased his battle-grimy face when he saw Nathan peer out from beneath the battered cart. He shook his head and glanced at the splintered gate hanging on its hinges. "I should have figured only a crazy man like you would pull a stunt like that." He nodded in appreciation. "Obliged. They was cutting us to pieces out there."

With a wry grin, Nathan replied, "Buy me a whiskey, and we'll call it even."

Hays laughed. "Go to hell." Wheeling his pony about, the slight colonel spurred over to a riderless horse and led it back to Nathan. "Get up here where you belong or one of my boys might mistake you for a greaser."

Throwing off the Saltillo blanket, Nathan laughed and swung into the saddle on a rangy sorrel with a deep chest. "I ain't arguing with you on that, Jack."

By now, all four gates had been breached, and the blue-coated marines swarmed over the grounds of the hacienda.

His face flushed with excitement, Barney rode up, brandishing his Colt. "Good to see you in one piece, son."

Nathan's face grew hard. "He's here somewhere, Barney."

The older man frowned. "Sims?"

"Selman. Sims is dead."

Barney's eyes cut to the parfleche bag at

Nathan's waist, noting the fresh blood on the soft leather. He frowned. "I thought Selman was dead."

"So did I, but he's alive." Nathan nodded to the stables. "Last I saw, he ran in there."

Without a word, Barney broke open his Colt and reloaded. Nathan did the same.

With Hays at their side, they headed for the stable.

By now, only occasional gunfire broke the silence of the morning. The U.S. Marines were rounding up guerillas and herding them to one corner of the grounds. The Texas Rangers were still absorbed in hunting down and shooting any Mexican or gringo before they could surrender.

Wearing baggy white blouses and trousers, several Mexican guerillas emerged from the stable with hands over their heads, shouting, *"Rindo. Yo me rindo."* I give up. I surrender.

Nathan ignored them, focusing his whole being on the dark doors of the stable. Slowly, he drew closer, his big Walker Colt cocked, ready to fire. He didn't know what he would find. Perhaps Frank Selman was already dead, or wounded. He might have escaped in the confusion. Or he might be waiting in the shadows of the stable.

Without warning, a black stallion, nostrils

flaring, eyes wide, exploded from the darkness of the stable. Before the three rangers could aim and fire, the animal swept through them, causing Nathan's sorrel to rear and paw at the sky.

Struggling to stay in the saddle, Nathan swung his big .44 to bear on Selman's retreating back and squeezed. The heavy Colt bucked in his hands. In the next instant, two more Colts boomed.

Frank Selman's head popped back and his arms flew out to his side as he toppled backward off the galloping black.

With cold eyes and a steady hand, Nathan lifted Selman's scalp and stuffed it in the parfleche bag with the others.

At that moment, a marine hurried up to Hays. "Colonel, Major Polk wants you in the hacienda. He's captured one of those Mexican generals."

Hays nodded. "Nathan, Barney. Come with me."

Major William Polk, surrounded by members of his staff, stood behind a half-dozen marines holding their carbines on a well-dressed, stiffly erect Mexican, who was obviously a hildago — a man of noble rank.

Hays shot the man a glance, then spoke to Polk. "You wanted to see me, Major Polk?"

With a smug grin, Polk replied. "Colonel Hays, meet General Mariano Parades, the ex-president of Mexico."

Hays arched an eyebrow. "Quite a haul, Major," he replied. "What about Padre Jarauta?"

"Reports indicate he was killed in the attack. Once we get the general back to Scott, this insurrection will be over."

Nathan's eyes narrowed. He spoke up. "Excuse me, Major Polk. But that isn't General Parades. I don't know who he is, but he isn't the general."

Polk sniffed. "Oh? And just how do you know that?"

Nathan studied the prisoner. "I've seen the general, Major. And this isn't him."

Parades' eyes narrowed.

"When did you see him?"

"Just this morning in the chapel." He nodded to the hidalgo. "With this jasper and the padre. And then again some months back. He was with Jarauta and a Texian named Frank Selman. I was up in some rocks watching them when they was moving out of Saltillo."

Polk's face darkened. With his eyes fixed on Nathan, he spoke to one of his staff members. "Captain Philbin. What is the identity of our prisoner here?"

"Parades, sir."

His voice thick with conceit, he said, "And how was that determined, Captain?"

"He refused to tell us at first, sir, but when a bunch of the greasers we took as prisoners were questioned, they identified him. When we confronted him with their identification, he admitted that's who he was."

Polk lifted an eyebrow. "Well, Cooper? Can you argue with that?"

With a wry chuckle, Nathan shrugged. He'd done all he could to convince the major he had the wrong jasper. "It's your call, Major. It's no skin off my back. I don't know what this jasper's game is, but while we stand here palavering, the general is putting the miles between him and us. Like I said, I saw the two of them together this morning in the chapel. This one isn't Parades."

Polk snorted.

A week later, the day after his enlistment had expired, Nathan pulled his gear together for the long journey back to East Texas. Strangely, he felt empty inside. He puzzled over the feeling, thinking that somehow, he should have felt some elation, some jubilation in having carried out the promise he had made so long ago to his wife and niece.

But he just felt hollow inside.

He glanced at Barney who was busy rolling up his own gear. The older man was whistling a gay little tune, his face wreathed in smiles, happy that their grim job was now behind them.

Nathan jerked around as the door swung open and Jack Hays strode into the barracks laughing. "Well, you were right, Nathan. About Parades. That prisoner wasn't the general. He was the general's brother. Looks like he come in so his brother could escape." He grimaced. "No telling where Parades is now. General Scott climbed all over Major Polk like bark on a tree. One thing is certain, the major will never make lieutenant colonel, not if he stays in the army for fifty more years."

With a shake of his head, Nathan grunted. "I told him."

Still laughing, Jack replied, "Yep. Truth be known, I figure that galls him worse than the general's shouting." His grin broadened. "The general, he called Polk every name he could think of, and then made up some. You ought to feel right good."

He paused packing his saddlebags and looked up at Jack. "Why? Because a damn fool makes damn fool of himself over and over? Hell, Jack, William Polk will spend the rest of his life making a fool of himself. It wasn't me. It was him." He studied the slight colonel. "Thing I hate is that likely some other poor jasper will get himself killed while they're chasing after Parades."

"Still, it was a sight to see. Polk all red-faced. His lips clamped so tight they turned white. I still don't think he set up the ambush on you that day, but if he did, he's got his comeuppance now." He paused when he spotted their bedrolls on the bunks. "So you're really pulling out, huh?"

Nathan snugged down his bedroll. "Yep. It's over here. We done what we came for. Barney and me, we got our men, and you and the army got Mexico." He paused and looked around. "I figure I got the better end of the deal."

Ben McCullough came to stand beside Devil Jack Hays as Nathan and Barney disappeared up the road to Monterrey. "Going to seem kind of empty around here without them two. It was mighty comforting to know Cooper was by my side when we went into a fight."

Hays nodded. "With him at your side, you knew no one was going to get the best of you. Not ever."

CHAPTER
FORTY

The sky above was a brittle blue and the sun warmed the countryside with a portent of spring. A few miles from camp, Barney broke off his whistling, and for the next two hours, the two rode in silence, each with his own thoughts.

Finally, the older man turned to Nathan. "Well, we done it, Nathan. It's been a long time, but we done it."

The big mountain man lifted his eyebrows. "Yeah. It's done."

Nathan's flat tone made Barney frown. "You don't sound like you're any too happy over it. Something bothering you, Nathan?"

Forcing a grin, Nathan replied. "No. Maybe. Hell, I don't know what I expected to feel after we finished the job, but the empty feeling I got inside sure ain't it."

The older man pursed his lips and scratched thoughtfully at his floppy jowl. "It could be just the fact it's over and done.

For almost two years, we been thinking of nothing but them five. Now, them heathens is burning in hell. You and me, we got nothing pushing us no more. And we still got hurt to get over. That's why now we got to find something else to go after. Me, I figure maybe you and me might ought to set up a business down in Sabine Pass south of Aurora. Before we left home, word was the town was going to be a major shipping port. With all the timber up north, a sawmill would be a mighty sound investment." He paused. "What do you think?"

Nathan was a long time answering. Finally, he replied in a soft voice. "I don't hanker to be around folks right now. I reckon I'll put in a crop or two, raise some stock, do some hunting. Maybe after a spell, I'll have me a better idea of where I'm going."

Barney grimaced. He knew the source of the emptiness in Nathan's breast. He had lived through it years earlier when his wife had died, and now he felt it again with the loss of his daughter.

But there was a difference between a lifemate and a child. It was a different hurt, a different pain. Barney chewed on his lip. He had been fortunate when his wife died that he had a daughter on whom to pour his love. Nathan had nothing.

"All by yourself up there, it'll get mighty lonesome."

With a sad expression in his gray eyes, Nathan replied, "Marie's there. My whole family's there. Anytime I get lonesome, I'll just go out and have a talk with them."

The narrow trace from Liberty wound through the tangles of the ghostly Big Thicket that covered most of East Texas. At night, the woods echoed with the cry of a cougar or the bellow of a black bear.

Nights, Nathan slept peacefully, spared the terrifying nightmare.

Finally, after four weeks of travel from Mexico, they forded Turkey Creek. The farm was just beyond the next rise. In his mind, Nathan saw the log cabin with the dogtrot, the barn, and the springhouse. Not far from the cabin under a large white oak were seven grave markers, crude wooden timbers, four older ones marking the resting place of his brother and family and his Uncle Lige, and three newer ones for Marie, his wife, Ruthie, his niece, and Artis, her intended.

To his surprise, for the first time in two years, a warm feeling of satisfaction rolled over him, comforting him despite his earlier reservations. He was coming home. It would never be the same, but it was home. Here were his memories, his life.

As they turned off the trace onto the farm, Nathan jerked his pony to a halt and stared in disbelief. Barney muttered a curse.

The markers were missing and the seven graves were empty.

In front of them were the blackened remains of a large fire.

Barney exclaimed. "What the hell —"

An insane cackling came from the cabin.

Nathan looked up as Red Davis stepped onto the porch, a smoothbore rifle jammed into his shoulder. The right side of his face was horribly disfigured. The giggling man glared at them, one eye glittering with madness, the other an empty eye socket with a portion of an orbital bone missing back to the ear.

Nathan's mind flashed back to that night in San Antonio, remembering now how Davis had jerked his head just as Nathan fired.

The crazy man's babbling cut into Nathan's memories. "You took an eye from me. I swore I'd even things up with you. And I did. Lordy, Lordy, did I pay you back."

Barney growled, barely able to constrain himself, "You son of a bitch. Where's the bodies?"

Davis's laughter grew maniacal. "Gone. Gone to hell. Burned to ashes and fed to the hogs. Now, I'll do the same to you."

In that moment, Nathan realized the meaning of his nightmare as images of the horrifying premonition flashed through his head. The tenuous threads of civilized man to which Nathan had been clinging snapped. With a guttural roar of a mountain lion leaping on its prey, Nathan hurled himself from his saddle and sprinted across the hardpan for Davis.

The redheaded scavenger's eye went cold, and he squeezed the trigger.

The ball slammed into Nathan's side, knocking him back a step, but unable to halt the rage driving the big mountain man's legs.

Davis dropped the rifle and grabbed a belt pistol. He swung it up and fired just as Nathan leaped onto the porch. The second ball lamed Nathan's shoulder, but failed to stop his momentum. Teeth bared and a savage cry on his lips, he slammed into Davis, driving his bowie into the insane man's belly and ripping him open.

Davis screamed and grabbed his belly, trying to hold his intestines in.

Nathan stepped back, his gray eyes blazing like the pyres of hell. His great muscles bulging, he jammed the iron T under Davis's shoulder, grabbed his lapel with his hand, hoisted him off the porch, and slammed the struggling man into a set of deer horns hanging beside the door.

An anguished scream of pain ripped from Davis's lips. His whole frame began to quiver and spasm as the pain seared every nerve in his body.

Nathan stepped back, his lips drawn tightly over his bared teeth. "Now you bastard, I'm going to skin you."

Barney, who had gaped at the surreal scene in stunned disbelief, suddenly shook his head, clearing it of the numbing display of savagery he had just witnessed. He jumped from his horse and clambered up on the porch to grab the big mountain man's arm. "No, Nathan. You've done enough."

By now, Nathan was more savage than civilized. He threw Barney's hand off.

At that moment, the horns broke off the wall, and Davis fell to the floor, moaning piteously, the horns remaining in his back.

Uncertain as to Nathan's next move, Barney whispered, "Enough, Nathan. Enough."

Ignoring his father-in-law, Nathan

grabbed the horns and dragged Davis off the porch and through the forest to the shores of a backwater slough teeming with alligators.

Barney looked on in horror as Nathan methodically scalped the moaning man, then dragged him knee-deep into the black water.

Within moments, a half-dozen sets of eyes converged on the dying man.

Nathan watched impassively from the shore as great jaws ripped Red Davis apart. His demonic screams echoed through the forest.

Barney turned away in horror, fighting to keep his gorge from rising.

When the last scream had faded into the dark forest, Nathan, moving as if in a trance, opened the parfleche bag and retrieved the other four scalps. He tossed all five into the slough.

Back at the farm, Nathan knelt at the fire-blackened soil by the graves. He opened the parfleche bag, then gently scooped up a handful of soil and slowly poured it into the bag.

Without a word, he climbed into the saddle and looked down at Barney. The lines in his face aged him twenty years. In a soft, almost inaudible voice, he said, "There's nothing here for me anymore, Barney. Do what you want with this place."

Barney saw the blood staining his son-in-law's shoulder and side. "Wait a spell. At least until you heal up."

Overhead came the cry of a hawk.

He looked sadly at Marie's grave. "She was what held me here, Barney. She's gone now. There's nothing here. I don't belong no more." He paused, then added. "You're a good man, Barney Willis. I'm privileged to know you."

With a gentle nudge of his knee, he turned his pony and disappeared into the deep shadows of the great oaks and tall pines.

Barney continued to stare into the dark forest several minutes after Nathan disappeared. He blinked his eyes against the tears and stared at the gaping hole where his daughter had once rested.

Retrieving a small jar from the cabin, he filled it with the ashes, then fired the cabin and barn.

He swung into his saddle, and from somewhere deep in the wilderness, a cougar yowled.

Tears rolled down his leathery cheeks and a knot burned his throat. He glanced after

Nathan. "The privilege is mine, son. Good luck," he muttered, turning his pony south to Aurora.